Enlightened

Entangled Book 3

A Novel by Carlie Yates

Cardinal Moon

978-1733264938

To Zachary, Marcus, and Jacob. For all of your love and patience while I write these stories, while I figure out how to balance life between author and mom, I am forever grateful. Each of you bring immense joy into my life, and I am truly blessed to be your mother.

CONTENT WARNING!!

This book contains emotionally sensitive
subjects and situations.

PROLOGUE

Click

"She said yes!"

The crowd in the banquet room erupted in applause as Catherine Garner's cheeks turned pink. The diamond on her left hand sparkled beneath the lights as he held it out for all to see. Many women came forward to admire, and Catherine handled each with grace.

Phone cameras were shuttering, some silent, some heard above the murmurs and laughter, the claps of congratulations on the groom's back. Catherine's father was all smiles as he took the jokes of losing a daughter along with those of gaining a son.

Click click click

The sounds of pictures being snapped continued, each one capturing a different view of the bride to be.

The glow of her tanned skin.

The blonder highlights that the summer sun had brought to the surface.

The sparkle in her green eyes.

She was beautiful.

Radiant.

"Sir." A banquet worker came up, stopping a young man from taking another photograph with his camera. "This is a private party."

"That's alright," Brody Harris said as he placed his camera in his backpack. "I was just leaving."

CHAPTER 1

Deep In Thought

Catherine weaved around those who had followed the party back to the beautiful home in the hills her now-fiancé owned. Brad Montgomery came from old money, as her grandfather had, and he'd taken over his own father's company at a young age. The house was more modern than the house on the hill that Catherine had grown up in, and a far cry from the small home she'd moved to with her father.

This house had been what Catherine had dreamed about when growing up.

Until she'd grown past the need for material things to prove her worth.

"Excuse us."

Catherine heard her best friend Jen's voice above the others, and soon found herself being whisked into an empty office, its light coming on as the door clicked shut.

"Thank you for rescuing me." Catherine collapsed with a sigh into a chair.

"Rescuing? How am I supposed to rescue you when you say stupid shit like 'yes' to a guy you wanted to break up with?" Jen stood before Catherine with her arms crossed and a shock of teal hair falling across her forehead.

"If it helps, I didn't exactly say yes."

"Then what was that whole display about? And that ring on your finger?"

Catherine twisted the ring absentmindedly. "You know how I hate surprises. And in front of everyone, even."

"You're not answering my question."

"I just... well..." Catherine said as she looked at the ring. "I always thought that it would be Brody putting a ring on my finger. And it wouldn't look like this; it would be simple, elegant. It wouldn't be for show."

"I don't think Brad asked you to marry him for show. And seriously." Jen pulled up a chair and sat beside her. "You were supposed to break up with him last night."

"I ended up not talking to him last night." Catherine shrugged. "And I was going to do it today, but he sprung this surprise, and I didn't say anything. He just put the ring on my finger and declared that I said yes."

"Did anyone notice?"

"My dad." Her mouth twisted in a frown. "He knows I don't like surprises. Brad knows, too, he just... I guess he decided this would be an exception."

"So, what, are you moving in here now?"

Catherine shook her head. "I like my apartment. I like my job, for the most part. I like my life. It's lacking in some ways, but I still like it."

"Lacking how?"

"It's the strangest thing." Catherine turned her gaze to her best friend. "I thought I saw him there tonight."

Jen sighed, knowing exactly who Catherine was referring to. "I hardly think your engagement is something Brody would suddenly show up at."

Catherine scowled. "You said his name."

"And look! You didn't burst into tears or suddenly combust. Look, I don't know what happened or why, but he ghosted you, Cat."

"We broke up first."

"And then he changed his number, stopped answering emails, and deactivated his Facebook page. Not to mention it's been since just before high school graduation, one he should have been there for, but he never even returned to go to school."

"He had his reasons."

"So you say."

Catherine looked back down at the ring on her finger. "But that doesn't matter now."

"No, what matters is you said yes to a... okay, you're technically engaged whether you said yes or not," Jen corrected herself when Catherine shot her a look.

"I could marry him."

"And then what? Be miserable?"

Catherine shrugged. "Maybe settling down and having children would do me some good."

"Last we talked, you didn't want to do either."

"I don't want to settle."

And that's exactly what she'd be doing if she married Brad.

Settling.

The both of them deserved better.

"When are you going to tell him?"

"What do you expect me to do, walk out there in a room full of people and hand the ring back to him?"

"Is that why you let him put it there in the first place? Because it was expected of you?"

She'd done a lot of that as of late. She'd gotten her own apartment straight out of college, but other than that, everything else was falling in line with what others expected of her. She was expected with her fancy degree to move on from the dance studio, and she had, despite wanting so badly to return, to resume teaching beneath Maxine's guiding hand. She had started dating the hot exec who had introduced himself at the art gala because everyone thought she'd be crazy to say no.

And now, here she was.

"Catherine?"

"I don't know." Catherine sighed sadly. "I just don't know anything anymore."

"You're quiet."

It was past midnight when the last of the guests had left. Catherine remained behind to help clean up, and she sat alone on the plush white couch staring at the empty fireplace. She looked up at him with a slight smile. He was a gorgeous man, with light brown hair and eyes and an athlete's build.

He just wasn't Brody.

"Sorry." She shook her head. "Deep in thought."

He sat beside her and took her left hand in his, where the diamond ring remained. "You didn't take it off."

"No, I didn't."

"So, I was right."

"You were presumptuous."

"Would it be so bad, marrying me?"

Her heart ached at his question.

Brad had always been kind and gentle with her, even when he wasn't patient. "No," she finally said.

He just wasn't the one who'd walked away from her.

"How about I promise no more surprises."

"And I promise..." Her voice trailed off as she looked down for a brief moment before returning her eyes back to him. "I promise to think about it."

Because really, was it fair to Brad that she'd almost broken up with him because he wasn't her ex?

He kissed her forehead. "That's far better than a no."

"It's not a yes, either."

His smile would have sent any other girl straight into his arms. "It will be."

Catherine used a pillow to hit him in the gut. "Stop that."

His laughter was infections, and she found herself laughing along. "Our children will be beautiful, you know?"

And her laughter stopped. "I'm not ready to discuss children now." It was hard enough to know she should have a child ready to begin Kindergarten but trying to keep up with her little sister who was even younger than that had shown her beyond any doubt that she wasn't ready to become a mother.

Not yet.

"Don't let Penny change your mind."

"Hey, that girl runs me ragged." Catherine shook her head. She stood and stretched. "I need to get back to the apartment."

"Are you sure?"

"I have a lot of thinking to do, so yes, I'm sure."

"You don't have to drive all the way back to Millerstown to think."

"No, but I want to."

"Of course." He said this with an easy smile as he stood. "I'll walk you out."

It wasn't necessary, but it was kind, as was everything he'd always done for her.

His kindness weighed heavily on her mind as she laid in her bed that night staring up at the ceiling. It was what had drawn her in to begin with, even though she compared it constantly.

"Comparison is the thief of joy," she muttered, and rolled onto her side.

There was no comparison. Brad was here; Brody was not.

End of discussion.

Except in her mind, where she replayed Brody's kindness over and over, comparing it to the cold-hearted way he had ended their relationship.

Through a text.

A text to an 18-year-old girl who'd had her heart set on him being there to escort her to prom, only to find that not only was he not doing so, he'd made other arrangements for her.

Like that would be some way to console her.

And still, all these years later, he would cross her mind at the oddest times.

She'd sworn she'd seen him in the restaurant that evening, camera in hand, dark hair messed just right, blue eyes hidden from her.

But that couldn't have been him.

He'd decided upon taking up residence in Toronto with his biological father. For all she knew, he'd changed his name the way that JJ had, deciding to go by his birth name of Dimitri Kostopoulos despite the many times he'd sworn he wouldn't.

But he'd sworn their story wasn't over.

That had obviously been a lie.

Brody gave up sleep with a sigh. Hotel rooms were not his favorite, but the house he'd rented wouldn't be ready for another three days.

Brentfield.

It hadn't exactly been his home before, but the surrounding communities had banded together to rebuild the town after it was devastated by a tornado a few years earlier. With Brentfield thriving, the other communities began to thrive as well.

Valley High was no longer looked down upon, aside from its rival at Easton.

Thriving communities were sadly driving the rent up, as Brody found when he'd begun searching for a home. He was looking for the absolute best, though, in an area that he still could afford. It was in the same school district that he'd grown up in, the same one that Tyler and Sammi had started at.

The same school district they were in now.

Even though his mother had moved away shortly after he'd left, Frank had remained behind. From the gossip that had flowed from his aunt, he knew that Frank also lived in Brentfield, in a home that he'd built himself on a lot where an older home had been devastated, and eventually demolished. He lived there with his new wife, Delores, and on most weekends, his daughter, Penny.

And now, with his aunt's failing health, Tyler and Sammi were back with their father.

Brody had been overseas when this all took place, and he'd had no input. His aunt, it seemed, felt that he wasn't ready to be a father to two adolescents who had been through so much already. And their mother... well, she was less interested in being a mother than she had been years before when she'd sent her remaining children on their way.

His laptop was slow to boot up, reminding him that it needed replaced. Still, once it was going, it ran like a dream, uploading the files from his drive with ease. He wanted to look at the pictures he'd taken earlier objectively, and had planned to wait until first morning light, but 2 AM was as good a time as any.

"Cat."

His name for her was a whisper in the night, a dream he'd long given up.

He'd wanted her happiness, and knew he wasn't ready to be the person that she needed. He'd told her so years before over the phone, knowing there was no way he could do it in person.

"*I'm not asking you to wait.*"

"*I will wait.*"

"*No, Cat, don't.*"

And when she wouldn't listen to reason, he'd broken up with her through a text.

A text.

He hadn't been sorry when he'd made her promise to go live her life, to go to prom even though he wouldn't be there.

To date other people.

To live.

He examined each photograph with the utmost scrutiny, watching her expression, gauging her response.

He wished he hadn't followed her in.

Or did he?

Wasn't this the closure that he needed to move on himself?

His phone began to ring, its tone letting him know that Max was calling. What was he doing up at this hour?

Then Brody realized it was now after 4, and Max would be up for work.

"Hey," he said as he answered.

"Hey? Dude, you sound down. What gives?"

A sad smile touched Brody's lips. "Nothing. It's nothing. Thanks for the tip on the house, man. I will be there soon."

"Yeah? Cool. I could use more testosterone around here."

"You and Sarah really broke up?"

"Yeah, yeah, we were much better as friends. It's all good. Did I tell you about Em? How she's kicking ass in college?"

"So she's all grown up for real, and her letters weren't a load of bullshit?"

"For real. She's my roomie now. Cheaper than housing and she didn't want to go back to step mommy's house. She's cool as shit."

"Always has been."

"Now my house is clean."

Brody sat back with a smile. "Sure you won't kill each other?"

"No."

Brody finally let himself fully laugh. "Ah hell, Maximillian, I can't wait to see you."

"You sound like a chick. But yeah, same."

"Where are you working?"

"Running the bakery at Mack's. It's great because people think I own the whole store. But those pastries and cakes won't make themselves, so I gotta go. When will you be here?"

Brody stopped himself from telling Max that he already was. "I'll see you soon."

"Yeah, you've been saying that for a good five years now. Asshole."

That's exactly what Brody was feeling like at that moment.

An asshole.

He glanced over at his keys sitting beside his laptop, Catherine's surprised expression in the picture pulled up now holding his attention. "Soon," he repeated, knowing it was a matter of hours.

And as he hung up with Max, he studied the photos with more intensity.

Each and every one.

And he knew without a doubt what everyone else had missed.

She didn't say yes.

CHAPTER 2

Out of My Head

The sky was lightening, streaks of red breaking through the trees when Catherine left her apartment in Millerstown. She walked the short distance to her dew-covered car, climbed in, and closed the door with a sigh. Her eyes fluttered shut as her mind swam with memories that had invaded her dreams.

Brody.

How dare he enter her thoughts again, just hours after becoming engaged. Or sort of becoming engaged, as she still hadn't told Brad yes.

And it was if he didn't notice that.

That was one thing that bothered Catherine the most about Brad. He never seemed to notice the little details, the ones that had always captured Brody's attention. But Brad wasn't Brody, and Brody wasn't in the picture anymore.

Not since he'd called her and told her that he wasn't coming back. After all of his promises, after swearing going to meet his father was just a delay, all of a sudden, his life was headed in the opposite direction of hers.

Or so he said.

He hadn't given her the chance to voice her opinion, or to say she would wait for him.

And she would have.

He'd told her not to.

Then he cut all ties, changed his number, deleted his Facebook, and hit the road. The worst part was when she had found out he was still talking to his other friends but had decided not to talk to her. He made a name for himself, and his name kept coming up in the circle of friends she shared with him, but he'd shut her out completely.

"So, I moved on."

She said the words aloud as she wiped her fresh tears away. She didn't understand what had brought up his memory any more than she could understand her tears. She'd cried enough of them years ago—enough to last a lifetime.

She could still remember his phone call the day he left the facility, the excitement in his voice.

"I'm going to see the kids at Aunt Sheryl's before I do anything else. And Cat… he messaged me back. My dad wants to meet me."

"You're so going to, and don't give me your 'I don't know' because you do. You know."

"He asked about Brian."

"You didn't tell him?"

"I have his number, and… I can't even think about that right now. I love you and I miss you and I can't wait to come home to you."

"I don't have time for this now," she muttered as she put her car into reverse, using the onboard camera to safely guide her until she could turn her car around in the parking lot. Her mother had requested that she come straight over that morning, as she'd missed the dinner due to Penny's dance recital. Catherine was suddenly angry that she'd missed it. Brad had known she wanted to go, but he pulled his engagement stunt and…

And now she was obligated.

Or was she?

She used the drive to her mother's house to blare loud rock music and slowly talk herself down. Her temper was legendary, but it was one legend she would rather do without. It wouldn't serve her any better than it had in the past.

Unless Brody ever showed his face again.

She vowed silently to unleash all hell upon him should he ever be foolish enough to come back. Not that she was likely to see him, as she practically lived at Brad's big house in Easton and didn't feel comfortable around what she considered 'his' friends now.

"Get out of my head, asshole," she muttered as she finally made it to the house on the hill where she'd grown up. She sighed as she remembered Brody here, too.

He was everywhere.

The diamond ring that Brad had slipped onto her finger suddenly felt heavy even as it glistened in the early morning sunlight. She twisted it around a couple of times as she slowly walked up the steps to the front porch and let herself into the house, per her mother's instructions.

"Hello?"

"Catherine! You made it."

Her mother's smiling welcome felt foreign despite the fact that she smiled all the time now. This wasn't the same Theresa that

Catherine had grown up with. Now she smiled and laughed and played with her precocious little girl as if she didn't have a care in the world. She even extended her jovial moods towards Catherine, who didn't quite know how to take this change in her mother.

She wondered how different she would be, how her life would have been, had this been the mother she was raised with. She couldn't really say 'by.' Their housekeeper had done more for Catherine than her mother had bothered to.

But Theresa... she was different now.

She followed her mother into the living room, once off limits as a child, and noticed a few toys scattered about. Theresa merely pushed one off the couch and patted beside her for Catherine to sit down.

Catherine didn't know if she should laugh or cry.

"*Young lady, you know that no children are allowed in here.*"

"*But Mommy, I wanna,*"

"*No arguing with me, Catherine. Greta! This child needs something.*"

"Let's see," Theresa said to her, reaching towards Catherine's left hand.

"You knew?" Catherine asked, rattled a bit from her recollection, and even more so by the stark contrast of the woman before her to the woman she'd known most of her life.

"Of course, dear, he told everyone that he invited. Except Jen, of course, because we all know you two tell each other everything. Oh," Theresa gasped as she saw the ring. "That's beautiful!"

Catherine forced her smile, knowing she was good enough at this for it to look natural. "Isn't it?"

"Tell me everything. Would you like some coffee?"

Coffee.

Brody loved his coffee. And he drank it black. She should refuse, but she'd began to drink it her freshman year of college, keeping it on the sweet side, and realized she'd loved it, too.

And she never got to tell him.

"Of course," Catherine replied, keeping her tone light, pleasant. If her mother could be happy single and sober with a young child, Catherine could be happy to be engaged to marry a good man. And Brad was a good man—good with his job, good with his home, good with her.

Always good.

Never questioning.

And there was so much about her that he didn't know.

"So, did he do it how he said he was going to? Just get on one knee when you walked in the room?"

Catherine kept her smile even as she inhaled sharply. She'd always hated surprises, and yet Brad had planned all of this out anyway.

"Yes," she finally said. That's what she'd walked into, a room full of people and Brad down on one knee holding out the opened ring box.

All that was in Catherine's mind now was the man hidden in the shadows with a camera. Perhaps he was part of the surprise, taking pictures to add to albums that people were already wanting to see even though no date had been set, no formal announcement in the newspaper, no…

"Catherine?"

"Sorry," Catherine said with a forced laugh. "Mind is elsewhere."

"I'm sure it is. You know your grandfather would be pleased that you're marrying Brad. He really is a fine young man."

But that's what they'd said about Mitch, too.

What if Brad turned out just like him?

"Where's Penny?" Catherine asked, diverting the conversation to one that her mother loved to gush about.

"Sleeping, if you can believe it. She's so full of energy! I think... well, you were, too, but your energy was always focused. Mostly gymnastics, which I think Penny wants to do."

Catherine wondered for a moment if her mother ever spoke this fondly of her as a child, then smiled as naturally as ever. "Are you going to get her a private coach?"

"I'd rather see if she can handle a class with other children. She doesn't quite have the coordination that you've always had. Besides, it may be something she doesn't like."

"Is there really anything Penny doesn't like?"

Theresa laughed at Catherine's question. "I'm not sure yet. Have you set a date? No, wait, I don't suppose you have. It really is pretty here, especially in the fall, if you'd like,"

"It's fall now."

"I meant next fall. A long engagement is a good thing, so I've heard. Take your time to plan it. I will be more than happy to help."

Catherine thought for a moment as she stared at the ring on her finger. "I'll think about it," was the most committed she could get. "I need to talk to Brad."

"Oh, of course, of course." Theresa reached out and hugged Catherine, who stiffened momentarily before returning her mother's embrace

It felt strange still, even though Theresa had blossomed as a mother, as a human being, in the years since Penny was born.

As Catherine drove away that afternoon, she couldn't stop her tears from falling, wishing this was the mother she'd had all along.

Maybe then it would feel genuine to her.

But nothing had quite felt right since Brody had shut her out of his life. He'd abandoned her when she needed him the most.

She wasn't sure she could ever forgive him.

"Holy fucking shit!"

This was the greeting Max gave Brody despite the glaring looks from customers at the bakery in Mack's. Brody quickly found himself wrapped in a bear hug, gasping for air as Max picked him up off the ground.

"You're still a scrawny shit." Max grinned and gave Brody a slight shove.

"Not scrawny, you're just built like you still play football."

Max grinned. "Only a little these days. You prick, I didn't think you'd be here so fucking soon."

"I got in last night."

"Maria, love, I'm on break," Max called out as he motioned for Brody to follow him. "I'm surprised they let you in after punching that asshole."

"Yeah, well, that was five years ago," Brody replied as they passed the place he'd decked Mitch.

He'd do it all over again if…

No, sending him away was the best gift his mother had ever given him.

His freedom.

"Man, you should have been here last weekend," Max was saying. "JJ was in town, Mr. Hotshot top 10 album that he is. And you know what? It doesn't suck."

"No, it doesn't."

"But the party at Nan's… you fucking missed it. We even had the cops called on us. New sheriff," Max added before Brody could ask. "New neighbors, too, since they obviously had no fucking clue what goes on at Nan's."

"It probably hasn't for a while."

"The crowd got older." Max shrugged. "But JJ signed some autographs and shit and got us out of it. I'm guessing the neighbors joined in since they weren't called again and it got even louder. But man… it was great seeing everyone. And you! You with your big house, you're finally settling down?"

Brody shrugged and grinned. "Something like that. Just not traveling as much."

"Got a family we don't know about?"

"Nope."

"Just need three bedrooms for the hell of it? 'Cause if it's just you, fuck renting that big of a place. Move in with Em and me. We've got room."

"I have…" Brody paused as he thought of his brother and sister. "Plans."

"Please tell me those plans involve you stopping Catherine from marrying Brad fucking Montgomery. He's a total douchenozzle."

Brody sighed. "If she loves him and that's what she wants to do, it's…" *Heartbreaking. Soul-crushing.* "…not my business."

Especially since he was the one who'd let her go, who'd told her to move on, who'd urged her to live her life without him.

He didn't have the right to these feelings anymore.

"Maybe I'll invite her to your housewarming party."

"First of all, no. Second, what housewarming party?"

Max grinned. "There's no fucking way you're not having a housewarming party. Brentfield may be all stuffy and stuck up now, but it's you and you're back. Quite a few people have moved away, but we're older now. We have our own cars and lives and shit, but... c'mon, man. We missed out on college keggers, and on senior year, and everything. What's one little house party?"

"Max,"

"I'm baking. And I'll call everyone. And I'm inviting Catherine, too."

"No, you're not."

"Bet me."

Brody didn't need to bet him to know that Max would, and it stayed with him as he tossed in his hotel bed later that night. He couldn't stand the thought of her marrying this guy, but saying anything to her wasn't his place. He didn't bother worrying about whether or not she'd show up at his house, because he knew the answer was a firm no.

It didn't stop him from wondering what would happen if she did.

CHAPTER 3

Could Be

Catherine sat in silence staring down at the magazines before her on her dining room table. They'd arrived by courier, along with a single red rose and a note that Brad would be thinking of her while he was out of town. She pushed her hair back out of her eyes and secured it back with the rubber band from her wrist, and yet they still remained before her.

Unopened.

"What is the huge emergency?" Jen's voice filled Catherine's apartment as she slipped inside.

"This." Catherine gestured before her. "All of this."

"Why did you buy bridal magazines?"

Catherine huffed out a sigh. "I didn't. These were delivered here."

"Your mother?"

"Worse." Catherine looked up at Jen, her eyes full of dread. "Brad."

"Ugh, Catherine." Jen heaved her bag off her shoulder and it landed on the floor with a thud. "You didn't talk to him."

"Sort of. And this is what he sends to me by some courier company, and what am I supposed to do?"

"He's obviously thinking you're supposed to be planning a wedding. To a guy you wanted to break up with, just to remind you."

"I know." Catherine's voice was softer now as she looked at the magazines, remembering the day she'd picked one up imagining what her wedding to Brody would be like. It would have been fun over formal with a candy bar and Randall as their DJ. He would have asked Max to be his best man, who would throw out ideas for themes that would somehow stick. There would be a photo booth like the one she'd dragged Brody into at the mall, but bigger so many others could join in. There would be dancing and dares and so much laughter…

But Brody didn't want her.

"I'll talk to him when he gets back." Catherine looked at her table, dismayed as she knew exactly what kind of wedding Brad and his family would expect.

The same kind her mother would expect, and her grandfather, if he were still alive.

Formal.

Traditional.

The Catherine of old.

"Shall we round-file the magazines?"

"Round-file?" Catherine looked up at Jen, confusion in her eyes.

"The trash." Jen pulled out a chair and sat beside Catherine. "Nothing in these is going to give you the answers you need. But there might be something that will."

"What's that?"

"A totally stupid idea."

"Your stupid ideas tend to bring trouble." Catherine smiled fondly. "Like our senior prank."

"What was so bad about putting Mr. Weatherby's car on the roof?"

"After you had the shop kids disassemble it and reassemble it up there, you mean?"

Jen smiled. "They left the engine in the parking lot. Too heavy."

"We almost didn't get to have our prom."

"Almost doesn't count, because we did."

Catherine's smile faded. Prom… Brody was supposed to take her. It was going to be their reunion. Instead, he'd called Matt and had him all set up to take her.

Before he broke up with her.

"I know that frown," Jen said. "And I know the solution. Hear me out before you say anything."

"This can't be good."

Jen shuffled the magazines until they were all stacked in a pile. "I heard from Max today."

Max.

Brody's best friend.

"We've been invited to a house-warming party."

"Max moved?"

"Nope."

"If you say Emily, I'm going to decline. She was too happy that we'd broken up."

"No, but she'll be there." Jen inhaled deeply. "Seems the prodigal son has returned."

"Brody!" Sammi ran across the spacious living room and jumped into his arms. She was still small for her age, but her tiny body was solid muscle.

She loved her gymnastics, just like Catherine had known she would.

"This is a surprise." Delores, Frank's new wife, smiled at him. "I've heard so much about you."

Brody nodded as he set Sammi down. "Same. Sheryl speaks very kindly of you."

"As Frank does of you."

The words nearly knocked the wind out of him.

Frank? Speaking fondly of someone he'd tormented?

"He's so proud of you. He's kept every magazine and article your pictures have been a part of."

Wishing he had words, he merely nodded again. Of course it was about the pictures, his photos, the ones that had won awards and accolades and had older photographers angered at his success.

It was the success that Frank had sworn would never come to him.

"Tyler is at the batting cages with his friends." Delores was wiping her hands on a dish towel that she folded neatly before turning to go to the open kitchen and hang it on a rack to dry. "He should be back soon. Please, have a seat."

"Thank you." Brody had finally found his voice, his composure, and he took a seat on the plush couch where Sammi happily sat with a bounce beside him.

"What brings you to town?" Delores asked as she reentered the living room and sat in a straight backed accent chair. Her mannerisms reflected those of Theresa, although Delores emitted kindness rather than coldness.

He could have told her his plans—to take his brother and sister away from the monster that had held him by his throat and told him he'd never amount to anything.

Instead, he smiled. "Returning home."

"So you've moved here. How lovely. I know the kids have missed you."

"I have a gazillion things to show you!" Sammi's smile twinkled in her grey eyes.

"Is gazillion in your dictionary?" Brody teased before pulling her close with one arm and kissing the top of her head. "We're going to have all the time in the world, kiddo. I promise."

"I take lessons with Maxine, and I'm really good now."

Maxine.

Catherine's old boss.

He knew she didn't work there anymore as Max, Matt, and Emily seemed to make it a point to talk about what they'd seen or heard of her.

He should have told them he didn't want to know.

Maybe not knowing would take some of the hurt away.

"I've texted Frank. I hope you don't mind." Delores was smiling as she said this, and Brody felt himself stiffen at the mention of his name.

"Not a problem," Brody said, keeping his tone as friendly as possible.

"Dad will want to see you," Sammi piped in, her excitement showing. "And so will Ty, so don't leave yet, okay?"

"I'm not going anywhere," Brody replied as he took in the features of the girl before him, amazed at how much older she looked than he'd thought she would. Somehow he still pictured her as she had been when he'd last seen her the year before when he'd taken some down time and gone to Sheryl's.

"I go by Sam now," she said, sitting up a little straighter. "Dad still calls me Samantha, though."

"You'll always be Sammi to me."

"JJ was here, and he signed my CD. He's as big a deal around here as you are."

Brody brushed Sammi's hair back. "I'm hardly a big deal."

She giggled. "That's what he said, too."

"You look so different from your pictures," Delores commented, gesturing towards his mustache and beard, a full five days of growth. He was also slightly taller and his build, though still slender, was strong. Muscular.

Ready for any fight that could come.

Instead of replying to her comment, he said, "I'd like to take the kids out for ice cream."

"Oh." Delores looked shaken for a moment, but quickly recovered. "I already have supper started, but,"

"Please please please?" Sammi asked, her arms around one of his, squeezing tightly.

"We'll have to discuss this with your father." Delores was smiling when she said this, but Brody noticed the minuscule change in her demeanor. She went from kind hostess to protective mother in the blink of an eye.

Only she wasn't their mother. He wasn't sure where their mother was, and didn't know if Delores was privy to that information or not. He truly didn't care to see his mother any more so than he wished to see the man that Delores announced was on his way.

_____

"Are you telling me," Catherine said as she rose, "that Brody fucking Harris is back?"

Jen's grin was tight and she shrugged her shoulders, trying to fend off what was sure to be the fury of Catherine. "Could be."

"That rat bastard," Catherine began through gritted teeth as she began to pace. "He's back? Back how? As in just passing through on his whirlwind adventures that I was going to go on with him, but _no_, he decided he didn't want me there at all. Ever."

"It's a housewarming so,"

"Housewarming?" Catherine nearly shouted that word and she threw up her hands before her pacing continued. "Housewarming, he wants a housewarming? I should go kick his stupid perfect teeth in, how would that be for a housewarming?" Her hands balled into fists, her pace picking up as she continued. "How about I shave every hair off his head? Or... or... we get the shop guys to disassemble the car, the way they did with Mr. Weatherby's. Are any of the shop guys still around?"

Jen smirked. "Sure, I'll call them."

"Good." Catherine nodded. "Good. I just need to find out what kind of car he drives, and,"

"Wait, you're serious?"

Catherine paused, her cheeks flushed with anger. "Oh, you bet your ass I'm serious. He decimated me right before senior prom. And he talks to everyone, but me? No. No, I'm the one he discarded like a piece of trash. That boy is not getting away with treating me like trash, Jen."

"Okay, slow down, slugger." Jen stood before Catherine and shook her arms slightly to get her to loosen her fists. "He hurt you, I get that. I've heard so many times about what you would do to him if he ever showed up. But here's an idea you may not have thought of… Closure."

"Closure? What the hell would I need closure for?"

Jen gestured with her head towards the bridal magazines. "That's a good start right there."

Catherine huffed and walked back over to her table. "That's right. I'm getting married."

"You are?"

"To a nice, handsome, rich guy who worships me."

"I wouldn't go that far. I kinda think he's a dick."

"He isn't a dick."

"He's not very accepting."

Catherine scowled. "Yes, he is."

"No, I mean… of your old friends. He doesn't even like Audrey. It's like he thinks you should leave your high school friends behind, and you kinda have."

Catherine shook her head. "That was my doing."

"Why?"

Exasperated, Catherine threw up her hands. "He talks to everyone except me. He decided they were all good enough, but I wasn't. So, yeah, I'm going to have a problem talking to them."

"Is that why we're still friends? Because Brody won't talk to me?"

Catherine finally sat down. "No. We're best friends because we just are, the way we have been since you bumped into me."

"No, that was the other way around."

"Whatever. Brody couldn't change that."

Jen sat opposite of her, eyes narrowed. "Then everyone at school wasn't really your friend?"

"I don't know, Jen. I don't know if they really liked me."

"Wow, that shit from Davis really fucked you up."

"My therapist said that, too."

"Talk to her about this."

Catherine's eyes dropped. "I don't go anymore."

"Then talk to me."

"I'm not going to his housewarming, Jen." Catherine lifted her sad eyes to her best friend. "I can't see him, not now."

"You know what you need?"

"You're about to tell me."

"A triple fudge sundae from the Malt Shoppe."

Catherine let out a short laugh. "In Brentfield? Isn't that what we did when he broke up with me?"

"That's exactly what we did." Jen reached across the table, taking Catherine's hand in hers. "Let's get your mind off this for a little while."

Catherine squeezed her hand. "Deal."

Brody looked Frank in the eye as he stood, no longer the smaller boy this man had thrown around. In stark contrast to Frank's suit—he was now on the corporate side of construction—Brody was in a comfortable sweater and jeans with holes in the knees, and his Doc Martens had seen better days. Still, he stood tall.

Proud.

And his grip had more force than Frank's when he begrudgingly shook the man's hand.

"The beard suits you," Frank said.

"Thank you," Brody replied, knowing he'd be shaving it off the moment he returned to his hotel room.

"Hey, can I... Brody!" Tyler's question was cut off when he noticed his big brother in the room, and the hug they shared was warm with affection. For only 14, he stood nearly as tall as Brody, who surmised his little brother would tower over Frank someday. His build was slender, like Brody's, and although strong, lacked muscle definition that was sure to come in his later teens.

"Brody was asking if he could take them out for ice cream,"

"Dude!" Tyler exclaimed, giving his brother a high-five after he interrupted Delores.

"But I was saying that supper is being prepared."

"A little ice cream never hurt anyone," Sammi said as she stood beside Brody and looked expectantly at her father.

"Before supper it can." Delores's tone was firm.

"I promise I'll eat everything."

"Brody, son, you're more than welcome to eat with us."

Brody's stomach turned at the thought. "No, thank you. I'd just like to spend time with my brother and sister."

"Where are you staying?"

"In a hotel, for now," Brody said to Delores. "We'll be gone maybe an hour, just over to the Malt Shoppe."

Frank sighed.

Brody knew the sigh.

It was the one where he didn't want to be perceived as the 'bad guy.'

"I suppose," Frank finally said.

Brody stood in shock for a moment before he nodded once. "Thank you," he finally managed to say.

"Both of you need to promise to eat all of your supper," Frank added, and the kids readily agreed to.

Brody had expected a fight, he knew this subconsciously. A small trickle of sweat ran down his back beneath his sweater and he knew he had to get out of there.

Away from that monster.

"I'll bring them right back," he promised again as he wrote his phone number down, hating that Frank could call him now should he choose to. Then, without a backward glance, he ushered his brother and sister out the door.

"Are we really going to the Malt Shoppe?" Sammi asked excitedly.

"Yes," Brody replied with a smile. "Yes, we are."

CHAPTER 4

Closure

"Admit it," Jen said to Catherine. "The triple chocolate sundae does the trick every time."

"It's been so long since I've been here." Catherine looked around with a nostalgic smile. "Not much has changed."

"The kids keep getting younger."

"Yeah, I noticed that, too." Catherine smiled at a young couple in a booth across the shoppe. Her smile soon faded as she remembered Brody bringing her here, how he would smile across the table at her, take her hand just as the boy was doing with his girlfriend.

"Have you been back to this area? Aside from visiting your dad, I mean."

Catherine shook her head. "It's been too much, really. I live close enough as it is."

Jen leaned forward. "And aside from me, do you speak to anyone you went to high school with?"

One corner of Catherine's mouth lifted. "There was that time I cussed out Bethany for hurting you."

"Which was legendary, but seriously… since you went off to college, have you spoken with anyone else from here?"

Catherine's shoulders slumped. "Not really. I've been caught up in my own life."

"Your own life that included college and meeting this guy who's consumed your time."

Catherine scrunched up her nose. "He's kinda needy."

"Which is why you wanted to break up with him. And now you have bridal magazines that he's expecting you to go through that he had delivered to you. I mean, really, Catherine. He had them delivered."

"He has a courier at work." She looked around again before taking another spoonful of sugary, chocolatey goodness. "Maybe we shouldn't be here. I mean, he is back in town."

"Were we supposed to get these to go and have them all melted before we got back to your place?"

"We could have gotten a pint from the store."

"I'm trying to talk some sense into you."

"Yeah, well…" Catherine let those words hang in the air. She knew Jen was right; she'd wanted to break up with Brad over his neediness, his insistence that everything be his way, his questioning her choices which were hers to make.

But she would listen to him.

She would follow his advice.

She was losing herself in the process.

"Your spunk has been replaced with this haughty attitude, just in case you hadn't noticed," Jen pointed out with a grin.

Catherine of old was easy to slip back into, especially when circumstances called for it like business dinners and special occasions that always seemed to come up with Brad's work. She was always being called upon to entice the next client to listen, or to play the dutiful arm candy that her mother had prepared her for.

Her mother wasn't anyone's arm candy anymore.

Her mother was running the company her grandfather had left and still finding time to be a doting mother to a precocious toddler, one who reminded Catherine of Sammi so much that it hurt.

"So... Audrey and her husband just had another baby."

Catherine was able to truly smile at that news. "That's wonderful."

"And Randall DJs on the side still, even though he's a... what is he? A carpenter? A wood... something. He's been selling his woodwork at local vendor fairs and such. And we all know about Jase."

"JJ," Catherine corrected her.

"I can't call him JJ anymore, and he's my cousin. It just... it doesn't fit him anymore. He really has changed."

"At least he quit bleaching his hair."

"Amen," Jen agreed, lifting her spoon. "Max is the bakery manager at Mack's."

Catherine's smile was almost sad as she remembered her favorite ginger. "Have he and Sarah set a date?"

"They broke up a while ago. I can't believe you're actually letting me go on about people you've refused to let me mention for years."

"Yeah, well maybe I'm growing up."

"You say as you're devouring your sundae."

"Best sundae ever." Catherine smiled. "And you were saying that Max actually had you invite me to Brody's housewarming?"

"His exact words."

"So you have his address."

"I'm not taking you over to beat the hell out of your ex. That wouldn't be very grown up of you."

"I was just curious is all." She ate another spoonful of ice cream, her expression a bit too innocent.

"So are you coming with me to the housewarming?"

"Aren't you taking your girlfriend? I really don't want to be a third wheel."

"It will depend on if Deanne has to work."

"Besides, I'm not so sure I should go. I mean, I know you said it could give me closure, but,"

"Isn't closure what you want?"

She wanted to answer yes. She wanted to say that she was going there to tell Brody off once and for all.

The words never came.

Instead, she watched her 'closure' walk into the Malt Shoppe with his brother and sister in tow, all perfectly tousled hair, beard and mustache that had the nerve to make him look even better, and that grin on his face that she'd loved so much.

Jen followed her gaze and muttered the same words going through Catherine's mind.

"Oh, fuck."

Brody's chest ached as he caught Catherine's eye for one brief moment before she lowered her gaze. Frozen with a lump in his throat, he watched as Tyler and Sammi rushed over to Catherine, just as excited to see her as they had been to see him.

He loved this girl.

He'd always loved this girl.

But this girl had wanted to skip college and travel with him as he hopped from city to city, out of the country, and back again following one dangerous situation after another.

This girl had dreamed of starting a family when he didn't even know if he wanted to bring a child into this world, when he was so afraid of who he could become, when he couldn't be there because his work took him all over.

This girl... she sat demurely in her chair and showed off her engagement ring to Sammi and began gushing about her elaborate wedding plans.

"It will be held in a large church, of course," she was saying as he finally walked up, and he felt heat rush to his face.

She'd said yes.

"I'm thinking of teal and black. Your hair could match," she laughed at Jen, who quickly grinned.

"I could totally match my hair to the dress."

"And I'm thinking about white roses and... oh, we'll have the reception at the club."

The club.

The place her mother had taken Frank back when they were engaged, as Catherine was now.

As Catherine was now.

He was too late to tell her how sorry he was, and he didn't even know that he wanted to. He'd told her to live her life, and she had.

She had.

She'd graduated college, she'd gotten a job at a prestigious dance studio, she'd met the man of her dreams.

Oh, she couldn't say enough about him.

"Brad is the absolute best, Sammi, you would love him."

"Can I go to the wedding?" Sammi asked.

"Go? Penny's the flower girl. You could be a bridesmaid."

Catherine was happy.

Glowing.

Blushing as she went on and on about the love of her life.

Brody hadn't realized until that exact moment that he'd wanted her back.

He'd wanted her back.

But it was too late.

"Hi," he finally managed to say, but it was as if Catherine didn't hear him as she asked the kids how they were doing.

"Hey," Jen said with a nonchalant tone that hit Brody straight in his gut.

"Hi," he said again, hoping to get Catherine's attention this time. She glanced over her shoulder, then returned her attention to his brother and sister. Of course he'd be ignored; he'd ignored the both of them for the past five years, even though it had killed him.

And he hadn't realized it.

He'd kept going on with his own life the way that Catherine had gone on with hers, only now as he walked up to the counter to order did it hit him that he'd never gotten over her.

He'd never intended to.

Maybe he thought she'd wait for him, even though he'd told her not to.

It doesn't matter.

He said those words to himself as he watched the workers make the sundaes that he'd ordered. It didn't matter that he wasn't over her, that he'd never had the...

Closure.

He'd never had the closure he needed.

If he walked back over and wished her well, maybe that would do it. Maybe that would cure the ache in his chest, his sweaty palms, his racing heart.

He'd just wish her well.

Send her off with love, without saying the words that she didn't need to hear. He was a bigger man than that; he would never interfere in a relationship, never disrupt her happiness. This Brad person, the one with the stable corporate job who would give her everything she ever dreamed of—that was who she belonged with.

That was what she deserved.

With his order in hand, he inhaled sharply, ready to do the right thing.

But when he turned around, she was gone.

Tyler and Sammi had picked a table not far from where she'd sat, and he could still smell the light floral scent of her perfume as he joined them.

"Didn't she look pretty?" Sammi gushed.

"She looked beautiful," Brody replied, his voice choked with emotion.

"You've still got it bad for her," Tyler spoke up as he reached for his ice cream. "Thanks for this."

"You're welcome, and no, I don't."

"You don't still love her?" Sammi asked Brody, whose eyes looked down at the triple fudge sundae he'd ordered for himself.

Because it was her favorite.

"You can still love someone and not... *love* them," Brody tried to explain, but Sammi's perplexed expression let him know she didn't understand. "Like you love your best friend."

"Best friends talk to each other, though."

"Yeah, they don't avoid eye contact," Tyler interjected.

"I was not avoiding eye contact with her."

"No, but she didn't say anything to you. She was too busy going on about Brad." Tyler rolled his eyes. "Penny doesn't like him."

"She doesn't, huh?" Brody resisted the urge to smile.

"She won't say why, she just doesn't."

"Did you ask her why?"

"I did," Sammi replied. "Said he's icky. But Catherine seems to like him, so he can't be that bad."

"We can't judge him by that," Tyler piped up with a mischievous grin. "She liked Brody a lot, too."

"Yeah, yeah." Brody grinned. "Eat your ice cream."

Still, an alarm was sounding back in Brody's mind.

Catherine had liked Mitch, too.

Mitch had turned out to be the worst of the worst, preying on other girls when Catherine wasn't around, and forcing himself on her.

Was Brad the same?

Brody didn't have to ask himself the question again. He already knew he was going to do everything in his power to find out.

CHAPTER 5

Truth Bomb

"What the hell was that?" Jen asked as she drove Catherine back to her apartment.

"Payback."

"And now what, you'll marry Brad just for spite?"

Catherine watched the passing scenery with a heaviness in her heart. "I didn't think that far. I just reacted."

"Truth bomb?"

"Don't you always?"

Jen smirked. "Yes. If you were going for hurt, though, I'm pretty sure you achieved it."

Catherine glanced over at Jen, studying her expression and finding honesty there. "You think so?"

"I know so."

Despite the ache in her chest, Catherine replied, "Good," and resumed watching the scenery. Had she wanted to hurt him? Of course she had, considering the amount of hurt she'd been through over the years. It had taken her until her senior year of college to admit to herself that he wasn't going to change his mind and tell her he was wrong. Even that act had been painful, and she'd been unable to burn the letters he'd sent to her over the span of time that he was in the facility. Those were in a beautiful blue box tucked away in the top of her closet.

What would she do with them now?

"You didn't answer the most important question of all."

"Which one is that?"

"Are you going through with the wedding? With picking out dresses that damn well better not be hideous, and involving his sister of all people?"

"I've missed them, you know?" Catherine murmured.

"Missing them and asking his baby sister to be part of a wedding with a guy you wanted to dump don't exactly mesh."

"Maybe they do."

"What about closure?"

Closure.

The thing she needed the most from Brody that she could have gotten, right there in the Malt Shoppe.

Instead, she sighed and sat back in the seat, her eyes now facing forward. "You're right. I need closure." She looked back over at Jen. "Seems I'm going to this housewarming after all."

The following morning's air was crisp as Brody walked from his car to the door of the house he was renting. The couple who owned it actually wanted to sell, but Brody had talked them into renting for a while, just in case.

But his plan would work.

He would get Tyler and Sammi away from the monster who was sure to show his true colors any time now.

"Welcome." The real estate agent was a young blonde female with a bubbly personality that resembled Catherine's happier side. "I have the other rental agreement papers here for you to sign." She handed him a clipboard with highlighted spaces and little arrow sticky notes. He stood in the freshly painted living room, its soft grey walls welcoming as he signed and initialed on page after page. Once finished, he handed the clipboard back to her and was presented with two keys.

So similar to the ones he'd had in his pocket when he decked Mitch by the front door of Mack's.

"Aren't you going to take them?"

"Of course." He recovered with an easy smile. "Thank you so much for everything."

"You're welcome. It's all yours. The fridge has been turned on so any food you purchase is ready to be put in.

The agent left shortly after and Brody remained in the living room, looking around. It wasn't as small as the house he'd lived in with his mother and the kids, and there was plenty of room for the housewarming to take place, so long as it didn't turn out like one of JJ's parties. Max had insisted on a 'homecoming' theme, asking all to wear their old jerseys or uniforms.

Leave it to Max to come up with something like that.

Brody wondered if his old baseball jersey would still fit, but knowing that his other clothing did, albeit a little tighter, he was almost certain it would.

He also wondered if Catherine would show up in her cheerleading uniform.

Or if she would show up at all.

She certainly seemed intent on letting him know that yes, she was getting married, and that it would be an elaborate affair. Perhaps she'd reverted to her Lady Catherine days, with only the finest things in life being good enough for her.

Although that Catherine would never step foot in the Malt Shoppe.

Shaking off the hurt of the previous day, Brody walked down the hallway, redoing the inspection he'd gone through the day before. Each room was in move-in condition, ready for the furniture and décor he'd brought and bought. He'd bought dragonfly decorations for Sammi's room, and Tyler's would be in black and white, just the way he liked.

Brody's bedroom… well, it would be simple and plain, the way he'd kept it for years. He had no reason to buy anything extra for his sleeping space, and wouldn't even have a television in his room. He would have plenty of gadgets for the living room, though, where he could play games with the two of them when he wasn't on the road capturing just the right photos to keep that roof overhead. He'd made a good enough name for himself, and had stowed away everything extra just for this.

He was going to rescue them.

His attorney's number filled his screen, and he paused inside the newly remodeled kitchen to answer.

"Ah, Mr. Harris. I take it you're in town now?"

"Just signed the papers for the house today."

"Good, good. Could you swing by the office? There's a few things I wanted to go over with you to see how best to proceed."

Brody opened his empty refrigerator, knowing he'd be making a run at Mack's some time during the day. "When's a good time?"

"Now's as good as any."

"Okay, I'm on my way."

Catherine mumbled a groggy hello into her phone sometime after 10 that morning.

"I woke you?" Brad's voice held an edge of surprise, as Catherine had been an early riser for quite some time.

"Sugar crash," she replied as she stretched out her aching muscles. She'd worked out vigorously and had ended her night with even more ice cream while watching *Star Wars*, reliving parts of her life she'd best leave forgotten.

"Grab some coffee, sleepyhead. I have to stay another day out here, but I'll be back tomorrow. Did you look over the package?"

"You mean all the wedding magazines?"

"Not to pressure you," he said with a laugh, and Catherine rolled her eyes.

"Because that's not pressure at all, right?"

"Now, Catherine, you know I'm just being helpful."

Helpful. He always considered himself being helpful.

"I have a lot to think about," she admitted without quite admitting anything. She didn't need to tell him that she'd seen her ex, that she'd gushed about a wedding she wasn't even sure was going to happen, that she'd even invited his sister to be in her wedding party.

But Sammi was Penny's sister, too.

"Grab some coffee and spend your day off thinking," he suggested. "Go to the house if you need to."

Because thinking in a large house with a beautiful view that made her feel like she was living someone else's life would help. "I can get my thinking done here. But thank you," she added, knowing her mood wasn't all Brad's fault.

So much of it was her own.

And Brody's.

As she made her coffee, she pushed the magazines aside and covered them with the morning paper. She didn't want to think that morning, at least not about dresses and chapels and wedding nonsense. That's what it seemed like to her at that moment: complete nonsense. A huge show put on for everyone else, mostly people she didn't even care about.

Her thoughts this morning were elsewhere.

Why had he come back here, of all places? He hadn't moved to Chicago when the kids lived there. He'd never quite settled down, according to the gossip she would randomly hear, always choosing to live on the road, out of a suitcase.

Just like he'd always wanted to.

All of his dreams had come true while hers had to be altered, no longer including the boy who somehow still held her heart in his hands.

She had to know why he was back.

And the only way to do that was to speak directly to him.

"I understand your concerns, I'm just saying I'm not sure we have much of a case."

"Then what am I paying you for?" Brody snapped at his attorney.

"The truth, for starters. None of the charges ever stuck, it's his word against yours, and without other witnesses, I'm not sure you can prove to the judge that Frank was abusive towards you in any way."

He knew he couldn't rely on his mother, aside from not even knowing where she was. She'd always placed the blame of everything squarely on Brody's shoulders. Theresa wouldn't be any help, either; she'd decided that Frank deserved to have shared custody with their daughter despite the way Frank had treated him, or Catherine, for that matter.

Catherine...

"What if I could? Have a witness, I mean."

"How much did they see?"

"She saw him bash my head into a mirror, and that last fight— she was there for all of it."

His attorney nodded. "This is good, this is very good. And she'll agree to testify?"

"I don't know." Brody sat back with a sigh. "I mean, I can talk to her."

After he hadn't spoken with her in years, when he'd broken her heart along with his own. He'd had to cut her out of his life; if he hadn't, he would have relented, would have asked her to come with him.

Asked her to drop her entire life to be with him, in harm's way.

Isn't that what they'd both wanted?

No, he couldn't do it. Couldn't dream of it.

"I think with another's testimony you may have a shot. Talk to this friend of yours, and if she agrees, we will go forward."

Brody nodded, unsure if she would agree, but praying that she would.

CHAPTER 6

Are You Listening

Catherine had much better things to do on a Sunday morning than to listen to Brad rant about how he could do a better job running what was now her mother's company.

"She isn't shrewd enough to make the decisions that need to be made," he was saying as he flipped through the morning paper.

Catherine held her coffee in her hands and stared out his picturesque windows wishing she could just throw her running shoes on and explore. Anything was better than this rehashed conversation.

"Are you listening?"

She inhaled deeply and turned to look at him. "Is this what you asked me over here for? To tell me your incorrect opinion about my mother, who happens to have one of the best business minds out there?" She refrained from adding 'now that she's sober,' not wanting to share that part of her past.

There was so much of her past that she didn't want to share with him.

That wasn't quite the way for a relationship to be, let alone a marriage.

"I feel that Theresa just puts too much heart into her decisions. She takes the feelings of others,"

"What is so wrong about that?" Catherine cut him off. "She runs a tight and a fair company. It is entirely possible to do both."

"Her growth isn't what it should be."

"It's still growth." Catherine stood and stretched, her eyes back on the wooded area, suddenly realizing why it had captured her attention.

Because of the woods that bordered Brentfield.

Because of her time with Brody.

This wasn't good at all.

"I saw Brody," she said, stopping whatever comment he'd had that she wasn't paying attention to.

"Who?"

"Brody. My ex."

"You went to see your ex?"

"No," she said with a wave of her hand. "He was just there when Jen and I went to the Malt Shoppe."

"Ah, discussing plans with your maid of honor. Or is it matron? I'm not sure how this all works." Brad passed her, dropping a kiss on her forehead that nearly made her cringe.

He was not paying attention, truly, to what she was saying at all.

"It's maid, and… okay, yes, but not the point."

"Were the magazines any help?"

Catherine huffed out a "No" before taking another sip of her coffee. "I haven't technically said yes, just to remind you."

"Well, for when you do, I wanted you to be ready."

"You had them delivered to me like I was one of your clients."

"No need to be hostile, Catherine, I was merely helping you along."

No need to be hostile... she could show him hostile and probably have him sniffling and crying in a matter of minutes, had she wanted to. Instead, he continued drinking her coffee, staring out at the scenery, wishing she'd said something... *anything*... to Brody. No, keeping her silence had been better. The children didn't need to see her unleash all hell and fury on him, and...

"Are you listening?"

"Not really," she admitted to Brad.

Because that's who she was with.

Brad.

"I asked you over here to have coffee and conversation. Instead, you're a million miles away."

"Not quite," she murmured, thinking of how close Brentfield truly was, and the fact that she hadn't been back there in five years. Sure, she'd visited her father one town over in Groves Point, but Brentfield... no, that place had been off limits in her mind.

The tornado.

The pictures that started Brody's career, taking him away from her, changing his feelings to where she didn't even matter. Why else had he cut off all contact?

"So you saw an old crush. It's no big deal, Catherine."

He hadn't been a crush.

He'd shown her how to love.

She still wasn't sure if she was capable of loving anyone else. Sure, she cared for Brad, but it wasn't an all-consuming passion in any sense of the word. It was comfort.

Logic.

Someone to be there when her feelings of abandonment threatened to consume her.

But that was no reason to stay with someone, which was another reason she'd decided to end their relationship, which had been sidelined with the 5 carat rock on her left ring finger. It was showy. Flashy. All Brad and not much Catherine.

Perhaps she may have slipped a time or two back into that snooty, spoiled rich girl suit that she'd worn for most of her life, but she wasn't that person anymore.

Or was she?

"I have... so much in my brain, it's like an overload," she finally said. "And I need to think, and sending me bridal magazines isn't helping me actually *think*."

"Catherine." He drew her name out and she could almost hear Brody.

Lady Cath-er-ine

"You're wearing the ring. You're confiding in your maid of honor. You're already moving forward with this engagement."

Sometimes Brad was too smug, other times too smothering.

"I'll give you time to think, but right now..." He reached out and took her hand. "I need some time with the love of my life. I see you eyeing the grounds. Would you like to take a walk with me?"

That wasn't exactly what she wanted.

Hell, she wasn't sure *what* it was she wanted at that point.

Still, she flashed her million-dollar smile. "Of course."

"You mean to tell me you saw Catherine and she didn't castrate you?" Max asked as he hauled another box into Brody's house.

"All bits still intact. Wait… that one goes to the master bedroom."

"Yes, your royal pain in the ass."

"She ignored me while she gushed about her upcoming wedding."

"Wait, her what?" Max stopped halfway down the hall. "How did I miss this bit of information? Does Jen not know?"

"Jen was there."

"Hmm," was all Max said to that before taking the box the rest of the way down the hall. Brody returned to the kitchen, pushing back boxes of pots and pans to set down his new set of dishes. Being so used to living in hotel rooms, he'd had to purchase a lot of new things. Today, though, it brought back the sudden memory of his mother and how excited she'd been to get a dining room table.

He almost wanted to reach out to her, tell her he understood that feeling now.

Just almost.

Instead, he watched the movers bringing in his furniture as he and Max grabbed boxes and took them to their respective rooms. "The couch goes on that back wall over there," he said, pointing in the direction for the movers to see.

"Hey, I haven't heard back from Catherine yet," Max was saying as he came back into the living room.

"Heard back from?"

"You know, about the housewarming. I told her about the theme and everything."

"Theme?"

"Homecoming. You still have your baseball jersey, right? Anyway, I know that Jen's coming, so maybe you'll get your castration after all."

Brody let out a short laugh. "Yeah, no thanks. And you seriously invited Cat? Why would you do that?"

"Because both of you are being stupid. Besides, she's fun, and I miss her."

"Yeah, well, it's technically not *your* party." Brody was grinning still as a myriad of thoughts invaded his brain.

Would she come?

What would she say to him if she did?

Could he honestly endure hearing about how happy she is and how full and satisfying her life had become?

"So, the other two rooms,"

"Ty and Sammi."

"I'm guessing Sammi's is the one with all the dragonfly stuff?" Max asked, and Brody nodded. He wasn't quite sure what else to do for her, or for Tyler. He'd need to talk to them, find out what they liked now, how they wanted their rooms set up.

If they'd like for them to be permanent.

"You need to tell me more about this thing with Catherine."

"Not much to tell. She's engaged, she wants Sammi to be in the wedding, and,"

"Whoa, whoa, hold it." Max stopped Brody from taking a duffel bag of books to his room. "She wants Sammi in the wedding?"

"She is Penny's sister."

"Yeah, that's kinda Springer and all, but c'mon, dude. She was trying to get to you."

"No, she..." Brody's voice trailed off as he contemplated Max's words. "She wouldn't do that," he finally said, then he continued down the hallway, this time with a smile on his face.

She *would* do that.

Maybe she *had.*

He set his duffel bag of books on top of his unmade bed, opening them up as he remembered the first time he'd seen Catherine. He'd been carrying this same duffel bag, full of nearly the same books. He pulled out the one they'd never finished reading and flipped through its pages slowly, remembering... holding her in his arms, reading out loud to her, running his fingers through her hair as he did so.

He stopped as he came upon the bookmark he'd had in place.

The strip of pictures he'd taken with her at the mall.

He needed to talk to her, not only to ask her if she would be willing to testify.

He needed to tell her the truth.

She deserved to know.

CHAPTER 7

Homecoming

Another call from an unfamiliar number had Catherine hitting the button on her phone that sent it straight to voicemail. If whoever was calling her had something important they had to say, they could leave a message.

She had other things to think about.

"Homecoming, homecoming." She stood before her closet with her hands on her hips. Leave it to Max to come up with some absurd theme for Brody's housewarming party. No, that would have been had he requested 80's garb again. This should be simple; she could put her old cheerleading uniform on, throw her hair up in a ponytail, and be done with it.

But Brody had already seen her in her uniform, and besides… she didn't want to be dressed like anyone else.

Also, how foolish would she look if she changed her mind, as she had numerous times since she'd begun getting ready. No, her hair and makeup were too impeccable to waste. She'd simply find the beautiful tea-length gown she'd worn to prom along with the sash that he should have been there to see put on her.

Prom Queen.

"He has a lot of nerve," she muttered as she pulled the bagged garment out from the back of her closet where it had been since she'd picked it up from the dry cleaners. So what if she'd just done so yesterday, maybe she'd been planning to all along.

Maybe she was going to be making the short drive to Easton to Brad's house and surprise him.

Or maybe she was seeing if it still fit, which somehow it did so even better than the night she'd slipped it on despite not wanting to go to the dance. She was certainly eating better than she had back when her high school boyfriend had disintegrated her heart. He was probably going to be in his baseball jersey, which would show her they didn't fit together just as her grandfather had claimed.

How dare Brody prove her grandfather right?

Hell, there probably wouldn't be any wine, just a keg of beer no longer illegal for them to have.

"If I go," she said to her reflection. "Only if."

She'd received yet another text from Jen asking if she was on her way. There was no need to hold her best friend up when she was so adamant about going, so she replied telling Jen that she'd meet her there.

If she went.

She looked down at her old cheerleading uniform that she'd pulled from its storage just in case, then let out a huff. Nope, she wasn't going to change. And she would probably get halfway to the address already typed into her GPS and make a detour, choosing to go see her father instead.

In her old prom dress.

"They should have let me keep the tiara," she muttered as she carefully refolded her sash and placed it in her bag along with her old uniform.

She was the queen, after all.

Maybe Lady Cath-er-ine should make an appearance, just to show him what he missed out on.

Maybe she could give him the piece of her mind that wanted to scream obscenities when she'd seen him at the ice cream parlor.

Or maybe she should stick with her original plan, foregoing the entire housewarming altogether.

That's what she told herself she was doing as she slipped her diamond engagement ring back onto her finger, twisting it once for good measure.

"I'll just go see Brad," is what she told herself as she put her coat on and grabbed her bag, but she knew long before she put the key in the ignition that she was lying to herself.

She continued lying to herself as she stopped in at the mall to pick up her favorite lip gloss and asked the cashier if they sold tiaras, because it was just a joke. She didn't want one.

She lied to herself as she visited a novelty shop, referred by said cashier, and bought a small tiara, this one far less lavish than the one that had been placed on her head on the night that Brody should have taken her to the prom.

She lied as she silenced another call from the number she could almost swear was his.

She lied up until she missed the turn to go to her father's house, and followed her GPS instructions instead.

Brody hadn't expected a large turnout, having been gone for so long. Apparently those within driving distance, though, decided to come out to see exactly how well he had done for himself, most of which wanted to see his photographs and equipment. Luckily his equipment was out of harm's way, because he probably couldn't have kept tabs on it otherwise.

"Kegs are in the back yard," Max said as he walked up and placed a hand on Brody's shoulder. "Told you there'd be one hell of a turnout."

Most of the baseball team was there along with a smattering of cheerleaders. Audrey had declined, having recently given birth to her second child, and there was only one other cheerleader he'd wanted to see.

Only she hadn't made it.

"Jen's here," Emily announced. "And no, her sidekick didn't show. What is with all the costumes? Is this Halloween?"

"I told you, it's homecoming," Max said. "I'm going to tap the second keg."

"Excuse me," Brody mumbled, making his way back through the crowd back to the master bedroom. One more phone call that wouldn't be answered, but he had to try anyway. He'd been trying since he'd spoken with his lawyer, always stopping just shy of leaving a message.

He didn't want to talk to Catherine's voicemail.

He wanted to talk to her.

"She's not going to answer. You know, if you're the one who's been calling and hanging up." Jen had followed Brody down the hall and stood before him dressed all in black with her leather jacket still on. "Mind if I leave this back here?" she asked as she slipped the jacket off, and Brody shook his head.

"You can leave it on the bed here. Just don't have anyone else do that."

"Ah." She pointed to the bags and travel cases in the corner. "Hotshot has his equipment back here."

"I can show it to you," Brody said, wanting to keep the conversation going. "If you'd like."

Jen shrugged. "Maybe some other time. There's a keg out back calling my name."

"I have wine, too."

"That will make her happy."

She was coming.

She was coming.

Brody inhaled sharply as his adrenaline kicked in. "That's good to know. Is she,"

"Not bringing Brad, and don't ask me any more questions about her. Or him, for that matter." Her words weren't said harshly, but they hit him like a brick.

Don't ask about the girl... the *woman*... that he had loved so fiercely that he couldn't stand in her future's way. Was he over her? He'd told himself for years that he was.

And then he'd come back, watched another man slip a ring on her finger.

"Head out of the clouds, Harris," Jen said with a grin. "You have a house full of people to entertain, and no JJ to play his music."

Brody shoved his phone into his back pocket and followed Jen out of his room, shutting and locking the door behind him. "Let me know when you need your jacket," he said to her before she disappeared into the crowd. A loud roar of "Timmeh" let him know that another member of the baseball team had arrived, and he waved to Tim from across the room.

"How's it goin, Harris?"

Brody wasn't sure who had asked him the question any more than he was sure this whole housewarming had been a good idea. Leave it to Max to invite half the damn town. Leave it to the town with not much better to do to show up, some with alcohol of their own to add to the mixture of bottles in his kitchen area. With conversations overlapping, body heat from the myriad of people, and his own unease, Brody excused himself to step outside where, despite the kegs, seemed devoid of people.

A row of plastic cups were on the bench, still in their wrapper, and Brody grabbed one. Once full of beer, he took a long drink out of it, finishing with his second drink, and he filled his cup again.

"Whoa, look at you. Rebel." Emily was beside him, glass of wine in hand.

"You okay with that?" Brody pointed to her glass, and she shrugged.

"A glass or two on occasion isn't a problem. I see most everyone has outgrown the kegs of beer, though, and switched to the fancy stuff. They grabbed the other stack of cups and are actually drinking wine from them. Lucky I got here early." She tilted her head, reading Brody's expression. "You were looking for her."

"No, I wasn't," he replied a touch too quick, causing her to laugh.

"C'mon, Harris, she was your everything. Now you say she's getting married and it doesn't bother you?"

"I had to become my own everything, Em." Brody stared down into his beer. "As odd as that may sound, I had to be okay without depending on her. And I am."

"And you know I've supported that decision from the beginning. What's up with this house, though? It looks like you have kids rooms here."

Brody shrugged nonchalantly. "My brother and sister live close." And if he had his way... if he could just talk to Cat... it could be permanent.

"That's right," Emily said, not voicing her suspicion that was in her eyes.

"Dude," Max said as he stuck his head out the back door. "Matthew's on his way in."

"Cool," Brody replied.

"I'm pretty sure he's walking up with his date from the prom."

And Brody's heart skipped a beat.

His date from the prom.

Catherine.

Keeping his reaction to himself, Brody only nodded, staying in place on the back porch.

"Oh, come on." Emily grabbed his arm and pulled him towards his back door. "We're all adults now. Literally. You're going to walk in there, smile, greet your guests, and be the perfect gentleman. Got it?"

"Yes, Em. Whatever you say, Em."

She patted his arm. "Good boy. Now go."

One shove and he was weaving his way through the crowd, his eyes fixated on the vision that just walked through his front door.

CHAPTER 8

The Blue Shirt

Catherine commanded a room like no other. Even for one so tiny, her presence filled the entire room, and she graciously replied to each person who spoke to her, most with glowing compliments. Her shimmering green dress caught the light just so, the same way it had been when she was given the sash she was wearing now.

Prom Queen.

She'd even put the small tiara on.

It had been a happenstance that Matt had arrived when he did, and he so perfectly escorted her through the door and around the room. Being sure to keep eye contact with everyone she spoke with, she noticed that one face hadn't come into her view.

Oh, but this house... this was exactly what she'd pictured for him, exactly the way she'd imagined it would be decorated with photographs. She'd even imagined a dining room set close to the one she'd spied when she first walked in. Small, simple.

Perfect.

She was screaming inside as one person after another came up to her, her heart pounding so loudly in her ears that the words "gorgeous" and "goddess" barely made it through. One of the cheerleaders complained that she wasn't in uniform, and Catherine laughed softly.

"It's in my bag," she replied with her trademark smile.

But oh, she was faking it.

She was dying inside.

This was a home for a family, not some bachelor who was roaming from city to city. No, that person would have some studio apartment, barely furnished, no room for all of the guests that had gathered here. One glance down the hall showed her there were three bedrooms.

Three.

Was there something he wasn't telling her? Maybe he had someone, too. Maybe he had a whole family and…

And it didn't matter.

She was engaged, after all. Or… so she said. So Brody thought. So Brad wanted to be.

"Catherine!"

"Max, my favorite ginger!" She threw her arms around her old friend and welcomed his squeeze. "What is this about you and Sarah no longer being together?"

"She's here, but not with me. No, seriously." Max grinned down at Catherine. "We're the best of friends, as always. I didn't know Matthew was bringing you."

"Oh, he didn't. It was a happy coincidence."

"Well, happy coincidences are my favorite, Queen C. The man of the hour is lurking around somewhere. Can I get you anything?"

"White wine would be good, thank you." She began to follow Max towards the kitchen, but when her eyes locked with Brody's, she couldn't move.

His face was now clean-shaven, showing the features of the boy she'd loved that had grown into a man. His full lips curled in a half smile as he stood before her, broad shouldered yet lean as he'd always been. He filled his blue shirt out a bit more, and...

The blue shirt.

It was *the* blue shirt, the one she had bought for him.

"Hello, Catherine."

He had the nerve to sound like he was merely seeing an old friend again, and it struck her ire. She lifted an eyebrow as she observed him, her heart racing, heat threatening to overtake her. "You got taller," she blurted out, and immediately wanted to kick herself. He got taller? That was the best she could say to the man who'd shattered her heart?

"Most boys aren't done growing at 17."

And of course he came back completely smooth, completely unaffected.

"Nice house," was all she could say before excusing herself and walking towards the kitchen, begging her heart to slow down, her breathing to not be shallow. She accepted a plastic cup of white wine from Max with a smile.

"You okay?"

"It's a bit crowded in here," she replied. "I'm going to step out for some air."

She hadn't even been there for ten minutes and she already felt overwhelmed. Ignoring people's calls for her, she opened the back door and stepped out into the darkness, thankful as it enveloped her.

"You got taller?" she admonished herself out loud. "Good one."

"Well, he did."

Catherine let out a slight screech when she heard the female voice behind her, and she turned, startled. "Oh. Hi, Emily."

"It's nice to see you, too."

"You startled me. I'm just out here for a bit of air. This is almost reminiscent of JJ's parties."

"Minus the loud music and the benches from Randall's. Brody has his own. Beer?"

Catherine held up her cup of wine. "I'm good, thank you."

Emily moved closer, her head tilted to the side. "Homecoming queen? Is that what you're supposed to be?"

"Prom Queen," Catherine corrected her, pulling at her sash. Suddenly she didn't feel like wearing it anymore. "I need to find a place to put my things."

"I'll get the key," Emily offered and walked in with ease.

Did she live here, too?

No, Catherine was quite certain that Jen had told her that Emily was living with Max. Had that only been temporary as she'd waited for Brody? She knew that nearly everyone here had been in contact with him at some point.

Emily returned, holding a key up in her hand. "Follow me."

As much as Catherine would rather stand outside, she followed, her professional training taking over. She held her head high and smiled as she made her way through the crowd and down the hall, pausing with Emily as she unlocked a door to one of the bedrooms.

The master bedroom, Catherine noted, as she walked in, breathing in the scent that was all Brody. He must be using the same body wash he had been, Catherine noted, and she placed her bag on the bed beside a leather jacket.

Jen's leather jacket.

Catherine smiled as she recognized it, and she placed her bag and coat on the bed. She paused, then removed her sash and tiara, placing them in the bag where her cheerleading outfit was neatly folded, waiting. There was no need for any of the pomp and circumstance. She was there. She'd seen him.

He'd had the same effect on her that he'd had five years before, damn him.

Brody smiled as Emily came back and placed the key in his hand. "Everything good?"

"Grand," Emily replied. "She feels stupid over what she said to you, by the way. And you're welcome." With that, Emily was lost in the crowd leaving Brody feeling the heat rising to his cheeks.

Yeah, he was taller. His shoulders had broadened. He'd added more muscle carrying around his own equipment, not wanting to rely on anyone else.

Not wanting to put anyone else in harm's way.

Facing a Category 5 hurricane was nothing compared to the effect that Catherine had on him, the rush he felt in her presence, the way her floral scent could stir feelings in him that had long been denied. Her heart-shaped face called to him, her green eyes beseeching across the room. He wanted so badly to go to her, apologize to her repeatedly.

Beg for forgiveness.

His eyes stayed on her as she excused herself from the crowd and walked down the hallway, back towards the bedrooms. Despite the warning sirens screaming in his head, he followed, watching from a distance as she peered first in the room set up for Tyler, and then the one for Sammi, which drew her in.

Just as Catherine was drawing him in.

And like the fool he was for her, he followed.

He stood frozen in the doorway as she switched on the light and surveyed the room through wondrous eyes.

"Dragonflies," she said.

"They're her favorite."

He knew when the realization hit Catherine, when she turned to him with a knowing expression. "These rooms are for the kids, for Ty and Sammi."

He nodded as he entered, keeping his distance lest he get caught up in the moment, because that would only bring more hurt to him.

She was engaged to someone else.

"Aren't they with Sheryl?"

He shook his head. "She wasn't able to take care of them anymore."

"Well, I'm sure that your mother would be more than happy for you to take them sometimes. She certainly had you taking care of them before."

This time, he shook his head more slowly, and her eyes widened.

"Oh, you can't be serious! They're with Frank?"

"I can't leave them there," Brody said as he took a step forward. "You understand that, right? He can turn on them any minute."

"Well, good. Not good as in he'd turn on them, but good as in you're taking them. And you... obviously have someone in your life."

His voice was soft. "No, uh..."

"Nora?" Catherine nearly huffed the word. "Well, whomever this Nora is, she must not have a problem with Emily having a key to your bedroom. Do I know her?"

Brody laughed softly. "Nobody, Cat. It's just me."

"Don't call me that."

"Sorry."

"And don't smile at me, either. That's rude."

He put his hands up in surrender, unable to stop his smile. "Chill, Lady Cath-er-ine, I'm being hospitable."

"Well, I'm not in the mood, so,"

"There's something I need to ask of you, and I understand if you say no."

She crossed her arms and glared at him through narrowed eyes. "What?"

"My lawyer said I needed someone to corroborate my testimony."

"Fine."

"No, I mean, you would have to testify, too, and,"

"And I said *fine*. I'm not about to let those kids stay with Frank if there's anything that I can do about it. And no, Mr. Hotshot, this isn't about you. It's about them."

"I never said,"

"And furthermore..." Catherine took a step closer, her face upturned towards his. "If it's been you blowing up my phone, you need to stop."

"Your fiancé have a problem with it?"

"Yes, as a matter of fact, he does."

"I apologize, then. It wasn't something I wanted to leave in a voicemail."

"So I agree to do this, and you agree to stay out of my life? Because I'm happy, you know that? I have everything I wanted."

Her words shot daggers through his already wounded heart, though he vowed to never tell her. "Good. I've always wanted your happiness."

"And now that's settled, I need the key to your bedroom."

"Excuse me?" he asked quickly, unnerved by her statement as well as her holding out her hand.

"My things are in there. I need them to leave."

He nodded once and turned, motioning for her to follow. It was a short distance to the master bedroom, and he unlocked the door for her, pushing it open slightly, and he stood in the doorway watching her once more.

Don't leave.

But he couldn't say the words.

He could only nod at her as she pushed her way past him and stomped down the hallway.

"Catherine wait!"

The words came from Jen instead of Brody, breaking Catherine's heart a little more. She turned with her winning smile, though, facing her best friend. "What's up?"

"What's up? You just left a room with Brody huffing like you could kill somebody."

"The thought maybe crossed my mind." Catherine shifted her bag on her shoulder. "I really do need to go."

"What's the rush? There are so many people here who want to see you."

"They didn't come to see me, they came to see someone I'd rather not be around right now."

"So avoid him, the way you've avoided everyone else for the last five years."

Catherine frowned. "I haven't avoided everyone."

"Okay, so ghosted. The same thing that Brody did to you. You're better than that, Catherine."

Ghosted… yeah, that was one word she could use where Brody was concerned. She smiled at someone who said hello to her, then returned her attention to Jen. "I really don't want to be here."

Jen linked arms with her. "All the more reason to stay. I say you change out of your prom dress and into the uniform that someone said you brought with you. Mingle. Show that asshole what he missed out on. Yeah, I'm talking about you," she called out across the room where Brody stood silent.

Stoic.

His eyes locked on Catherine.

"I can't handle his broody stares right now," Catherine said, but Jen pulled her bag off her arm.

"C'mon, hot stuff. Show him what you've got. And keep flashing that ring around that's liable to blind someone. Make him sorry."

Catherine knew that she should say no, she should get in her car and drive back to her apartment and drown her feelings in tears and ice cream.

Instead, she smiled.

"Guard the bathroom door for me," she said to Jen, taking her bag back. Once emerged from the bathroom in her uniform, her dress over her arm, her entire demeanor had changed. Sure, she'd been confident in her dress and heels, but there, in her uniform, despite being barefoot, she felt more at ease.

More in her element.

More in her power.

She knew she had it in her to make Brody suffer for the hurt that he'd caused her. All she had to do was not look into his eyes, not see if there was sadness there.

Because she would falter.

She was sure of it.

"I just need a hair tie from my car," she announced before walking out the door, head held high, the Catherine of old coming forth. She quickly jogged to her car across cold pavement and colder, wet grass. Once there, she pulled a hair tie from her console and retrieved her running shoes and socks from the back seat where she'd placed them.

Just in case.

She could see his figure standing in the doorway, greeting others who'd arrived.

Watching her.

But she paid him no mind as she quickly put her shoes and socks on and jogged back to the house, waiting until she passed him to put her hair up in a flowing ponytail. She led the other cheerleaders out back and a few of the other guests followed out into the cool fall night air.

She felt his eyes on her with every move she made. With every kick, spin, flip, she felt his presence.

And yet he kept his distance as she stayed after her performance, mingling, doing shots with Tim and Randall before she grabbed her bag once again.

She knew he was watching.

She kept her head held high, her composure in check all the way to her car, holding it all in until she was two blocks away.

Then she let her tears fall.

She'd missed him so terribly, with every fiber of her being. She missed him still, even through the hurt, through the questions, through her conflicting emotions.

She was angry.

Devastated.

Happy.

Anguished.

She somehow managed through her tears, her sobs, to make it to the safety of her apartment where she tossed her bag to the side, noticing then that she'd forgotten her satin pumps, matched to her shimmering green prom dress, somewhere in the confines of Brody's home.

"Oh, how Cinderella of me," she sniffled as she grabbed a tissue. Brody was far from the Prince Charming of fairytales, and he wasn't likely to come knocking on her door to save her from this life she'd sworn she was happy with.

All of these calls, all of this time, and he wasn't even trying to tell her that he missed her.

All he needed was her help.

She left her shoes there.

Slowly—too slowly—people began to leave Brody's party, tell him how happy they were that he was back, promise they'd keep in touch.

She left her shoes there.

He'd watched her make her rounds, hold court with those in attendance, command attention from everyone in whatever room she was in. And she'd looked so perfect flitting about his home.

But she didn't belong there.

She belonged in the big house in Easton that she was talking about with Jen.

She belonged with Brad.

"You have some leftovers," Max was saying, snapping Brody's attention away from the small satin pumps. "Where do you want them?"

"Fridge is fine."

"I can get those shoes to Jen,"

"No, it's fine," Brody said a little too quickly, then he grinned. "I'll get them back to her." He had to see her again anyway, talk to her about his upcoming case to get his brother and sister into his custody.

"So that's twice you've been under the same roof and no one died. It's a miracle."

"I was thinking the same thing," Brody lied as he picked the shoes up and took them back towards his room. No, he'd been thinking as he'd watched her all night how well Catherine had done for herself despite her rocky start at Valley High. She'd made friends, gone on to excel in college, had the life of her dreams.

All she'd needed was to do it on her own.

Away from him.

Despite the ache in his chest, despite his arms longing to hold her, he knew then that staying away had been the right decision. Once this case was over, he would let her go again, off to her land of privilege that meant so much to her.

CHAPTER 9

The Right Thing

"Look at this text, Jen. Just look at it." Catherine held her phone out to where her best friend could see it. "Two whole days go by, and all Brody can text is 'I've got your shoes.' Like, what, he's holding them hostage?"

"Says the girl whose first words to her ex were 'you got taller.'"

"Yeah, well, that was spur of the moment. What is this shit?"

"That's a boy who has your shoes and doesn't think it's appropriate to say much more when he thinks your marrying someone else."

"Yeah, well, what would,"

"You told everyone you were, dummy. Have you actually made a decision?"

Catherine sat at her dining room table with a huff. "No. It isn't like I haven't thought about it, I just haven't given it as much thought as I should."

"So quit going mental about your shoes and talk this over with your maybe-fiancé."

"I'm talking it over with you right now. Ow! Quit squeezing my face." Catherine's words sounded muffled through her pushed-together lips, and Jen let go with a laugh. "My life isn't a... well, maybe it is a joke."

"No, I never said it was. Don't you have work today?"

"I'm taking over the afternoon classes starting this week."

"Ouch."

"Yeah, ouch." Catherine crossed her arms in front of her. "Morning and evening are where it's at. Afternoon classes are for those who don't take it quite as seriously. And really, there aren't enough students for me to get a decent paycheck."

"I didn't realize you began teaching dance and gymnastics for the paycheck."

"I didn't." She shrugged. "I love it."

"Not as much as you did when you worked with Maxine."

Catherine raised one shoulder. "It's hard to not love working there. Those students, it didn't matter what time their classes were, they really came to learn, not as some kind of hobby before happy hour. I'll pay my dues, though, and I'll get classes in the ideal times."

"Or you can go to Maxine's and enjoy whatever class you get."

Catherine frowned. "It's not that simple."

"You're avoiding all things that remind you of Brody."

"Okay, so maybe it is that simple. Besides, Brad says that... you know, I forget what he said." She sighed and took a sip of her coffee. "I'm making this more complicated than it is."

"What do you want to do?"

"Not obsess."

"Girl, I got news for you."

Catherine rolled her eyes. "Yeah, yeah, I've been obsessed since he left. Before that, even."

"And you turned that obsession to all things Brad until he started to annoy you."

"No, I didn't. And stop scrolling through your phone when we're talking. That's rude." Catherine stopped herself from smiling as she remembered telling Brody that he was being rude.

For smiling.

For being nice.

"I'm looking for something specific."

"Still rude," Catherine muttered as she picked up her own phone, staring at the text from Brody whose number she had saved as *Asshole*.

"Found it. You read this to me a couple years back, just before you met Brad."

Catherine turned to Jen as she put her phone down. "What's the significance now?"

Jen raised an eyebrow and began to read aloud. "Like his assumed father, the Oscar-nominated cinematographer Nicholas Paul, Brody is known for his temper and the short fuse associated with it."

Catherine frowned as she remembered the article that had painted Brody to be a temperamental asshole. It wasn't so much the hurt that he had carried part of Frank with him, or the assumption that maybe some of his temper came biologically.

It was his upcoming custody battle.

"Just a sec," Catherine said as she quickly picked her phone up again and shot a quick text to the ex who was pulling at her heartstrings in all the wrong ways.

We need to talk

She knew before he answered with his inquiry of when and where that he wasn't going to like what she had to say.

"Planning a clandestine meeting with your ex?"

Catherine's face turned a tell-tale shade of pink. "No, I'm planning on getting my shoes back."

"Does Brad even know you've seen Brody?"

Catherine crossed her arms again. "Yes," she replied, leaving out Brad's laughter and dismissal of something 'so trivial.'

"Okay, okay, listen." Jen leaned in closer. "You obviously haven't told Brad much about Brody, or I'd be listening to your tirade over his jealous streak. And you turning ten shades of red,"

"I did not."

"…means that seeing Brody again is more than just about the shoes. What gives?"

Catherine bit her lip slightly before answering. "Nothing gives," she lied.

It wasn't her story to tell.

"You're not even eating the doughnuts I brought over here to pull you out of your funk."

"I'm not in a funk."

"Have you broken up with Mr. Nonchalant or said yes to his proposal?"

"Neither. And he's not nonchalant." Catherine picked up a doughnut despite her lack of appetite. "I have a lot to think about."

And that was the truth.

Brody wanted custody of his brother and sister, wanted to take them away from the monster who had raised him.

The same man that Catherine's own mother raved about when it came to care of Penny.

The same man who had no record, aside from a dismissed case, of temperamental outbursts or violent tendencies.

But Brody... he did. There was a paper trail possibly a mile long dating all the way back to him being placed in a facility when he was 17. All of it would come out into the open, and what would happen then? Frank could easily bar him from ever seeing Tyler or Sammi again.

Catherine needed to do everything in her power to stop that from happening.

Brody's hands shook as he picked his phone up. He scowled at his response to Catherine's text that she would meet him that afternoon. What reason did he have to be nervous? They weren't high school kids anymore; they were both in their 20s and had more life experiences.

Their own life experiences.

He'd chosen long ago that the best thing for Catherine was for him to stay gone. Now that he was back, for reasons having nothing to do with her, he found that the mere knowledge of her close proximity was distracting. He needed her help, though, and he knew when she'd said she needed to talk, it was about his pending custody battle.

He was doing the right thing, though.

He was sure of it.

He was done reading through his emails and lists of potential assignments, none of which were as appealing to him as delivering a pair of emerald green satin high heels back to the girl who'd stolen his heart so long ago. He'd tried to forget, tried to move on, but somehow he couldn't.

No one compared to Catherine.

He wouldn't tell her this, of course. Not only for his pride, but also he'd seen shades of Lady Catherine the past two times she'd been in his presence. Had it been an act? He wasn't sure. But without any others around, perhaps she wouldn't put on a show. Maybe then he'd know that she'd held on to the values she'd grown to have.

"Fuck," he muttered as he shut his laptop. This girl would not leave his head.

But she needed to.

She belonged with her fiancé in the life that she'd built with him gone every bit as much as he belonged on the road, camera in hand, capturing the soul of the earth, of the people in every corner of the world that he'd had the privilege of visiting.

He thought as his phone buzzed again that Catherine was sending another text, instead he frowned at his biological father's name. What could he possibly want except to perhaps start another argument? The last one, where his father showed his true misogynistic behavior, left a bad enough taste in his mouth. He couldn't believe he'd come from a man who saw women as objects that he could treat however he pleased.

It was no wonder that Sandra had left him.

It was sad to say, but despite it all, Frank almost looked like a saint next to Nikos Kostopoulos, or as the world knew him, Nicolas Paul.

Brody preferred the term "asshole."

The text was only the words *call me.*

"How about blow me," Brody muttered as he pushed his phone aside. He had a couple of hours before meeting Catherine, and he figured a shower wouldn't hurt. Nicer clothes would be good as well. Maybe he'd try to do something with his unruly hair.

Or maybe not.

Maybe he would just show up in his track pants and t-shirt that he'd slept in and hadn't bothered to change out of. Maybe he wouldn't bother shaving the bit of scruff that had grown in after he'd shaved the beard that she seemed less than fond of. No, wait… he hadn't shaved it because she didn't like it. No, it was his decision.

He continued lying to himself as he showered, as he dressed in nicer clothes, as he glanced at his freshly shaven face in the mirror.

As he relived the moment he'd last kissed her, promising her that he would be back in three short months.

What if he had come back? What if he'd lied to himself and said his temper was in check, that he was nothing like the asshole who'd raised him, or even like the one who'd given half of his DNA.

How badly would he have damaged that relationship? How badly would he have damaged Catherine?

He already knew the answer.

It wasn't worth the risk, then or now.

CHAPTER 10

Touché

He had shaved.

That was the first thing that Catherine noticed as Brody walked into the Malt Shoppe. The second thing she noticed was his dress pants, his dark button-down shirt that fit so attractively across his shoulders. No, not attractively... he wasn't attractive to her... at all...

Yes, he was.

She sighed in resignation while he sat across from her, not because she was dreading the conversation, but because she knew.

She knew.

"The shoes," he said as he handed her a bag, her satin pumps peeking out the top.

"Thank you," she murmured softly.

"Nervous?"

"Hmm?" She wanted to kick herself immediately. "No, not at all." Instantly switching 'on,' she sat a bit straighter. "Thank you for agreeing to meet."

"Well, shoes," he said, gesturing towards the bag that she sat on the ground.

Was he blushing?

No, he couldn't be.

"Brody," she began as she pulled her phone out, "I have a question for you."

"Shoot."

"How true is this?" She had pulled up the article that Jen sent her the link to, and she pushed her phone in his direction. Watching his expression, she noted his frown and one muscle twitch in his jaw.

It was true, every word.

"Why are you showing me this?"

"Because of the pretense. Seriously, if you're going after Frank and he sees this?"

"It's in the past." Brody crossed his arms. "And it wasn't that bad."

"Brody,"

"I know," he finally said, and he ran his fingers through his hair. That one movement brought back a myriad of memories, each one attached to a feeling.

Grief.

Sadness.

The bliss of newfound affection.

She'd missed him terribly. She could admit that to herself now as she watched him shift in his chair uncomfortably.

"I'm just trying to say," she continued, "that if you can change, can't Frank? My mother says,"

"Yeah, well, your mother,"

"Stop." Her stern tone had his attention. "My mother has literally turned into Mother Theresa, okay? She has play dates and wears leggings, for fuck's sake, like, who is this woman? And she says that Frank has been nothing but amazing with Penny. I don't know what else to tell you, but these odds? They're stacked against you."

Brody lowered his head, hiding the sadness, the disappointment in his eyes that she'd already noticed. "I get it if you don't want to testify."

"I didn't say that. I will, absolutely, if that's the route you want to take. I mean, if the kids would rather be with you, then... why did you do that?"

"Do what?"

"You flinched."

He lifted his eyes to her. "No, I didn't."

"Yes, you did. I saw it. Do the kids want to be with you?"

"They, um..." He shifted again, his eyes downcast. "They don't know."

"Look at me."

He lifted his eyes and she felt her heart melt a little more. How could he do this to her with just a look?

"Brody, you need to talk to them before you even start this. Tyler will be straight with you, even if Sammi hesitates."

She watched as his shoulders dropped only a fraction of an inch. "I will. I'm waiting to hear if I can have them this weekend."

For the first time, she allowed herself to smile at him freely. "I hope they can."

One corner of his mouth lifted as he held her gaze, searing her to her soul, and she knew.

She knew.

"Funny how you picked here," he said as he glanced around, possibly remembering all of their times together there as she was. "I still owe you."

"Owe me?"

"A triple fudge sundae."

Because they'd gotten caught in the rain, and their date day had been cut short.

But he'd promised to make it up to her.

"What do you say?" he asked as he stood, his eyebrows raised as her silence wore on.

She should say no. She should decline not only because she'd already gone way over her caloric limit with all of her stress eating, but because it was him.

It was Brody asking.

"With an,"

"Extra cherry on top," he finished for her, and she waited until he turned to walk towards the counter before she exhaled. Her eyes stayed fixated on him, taking in how his walk now showed his confidence, far from the boy who'd been slump-shouldered and even a little skittish when they'd first met. He'd also filled out quite nicely in his absence, something she shouldn't notice but couldn't overlook. Even his shoulders seemed broader as he reached into his back pocket for his wallet.

Oh, she shouldn't have looked there.

Seeing him this way made her long for the days when he was stretched out in her old gymnasium in sweatpants and a torn t-shirt eating a slice of pizza with mushrooms on it.

But those days were long gone.

The seventeen-year-old boy was now a 22-year-old man, and as off limits to her now as he had been all those years ago.

She returned her attention to herself, to her hands that set clasped on the table, the glittering diamond making her stomach lurch because she knew.

She knew.

She couldn't marry Brad.

She still had feelings for Brody.

Brody's smile faltered while he walked back with their sundaes as the light caught the rock in the ring on Catherine's finger. It didn't matter that his heart longed for her, it didn't matter that he'd give anything to just kiss her. She wore that glaring reminder with pride, twisting it on her finger while her gaze in the distance showed him her mind was elsewhere. She was probably thinking about her fiancé, dreaming about the wedding that she'd asked his baby sister to be a part of.

"One triple fudge sundae," he said as he set it on the table in front of her. Did she thank him? If she had, he couldn't hear it above the rush of blood in his ears with each beat of his heart.

"You didn't have to do this, you know."

"I know."

"But thank you," she added with a smile as she took one of her cherries off and bit down.

He shouldn't have watched her do that.

He shouldn't be thinking of the clearing in the woods and the way the moonlight had shown on her tanned skin.

"So you said we needed to talk," he said, his eyes on his own sundae.

"And we did."

"That was it?" he asked as nonchalantly as possible. "You're concerned about an article that may or may not,"

"Bite you in your ass," she cut him off.

He resisted the urge to let out a laugh. "I can handle it, Cat."

Her eyes widened a fraction and a pink hue began to fill her cheeks, and only then did he realize he'd slipped and called her a name he only used as an endearment.

But she wasn't his Cat anymore.

"Sorry," he mumbled. "Habit."

"Is that what I am? A habit?"

No, she was so much more. "Of course not," was all he could say.

"So you get the kids this weekend."

"Maybe."

"And you talk to them about uprooting them again."

"Do you need to put it that way?" He watched as her composure faltered for a fraction of a second, and he immediately felt like an asshole for being short with her. "I mean... Catherine, I get it. It sounds on paper or whatever like a bad idea. But you only saw a few months of what Frank could do. I lived it for years. Yeah, sometimes it was good, but anytime that the slightest thing went wrong, he would snap."

"Like you?"

He opened his mouth to protest, but he couldn't.

She was right.

"I learned a lot these past few years," he finally said. He watched her nod and take another bite of ice cream. Damn, he missed kissing her. He could, right then and there, triple fudge sundae and all.

"So it took longer than three months," she said, her head tilting to the side.

"Touché."

"I have to get my digs in when I can."

"You always do."

She put her spoon down. "I can't do this. The ice cream, I mean," she added quickly, calming his heart that began to race. "I ate lunch before I got here and I am stuffed."

"I'd say take it home, but…"

She scrunched up her nose and his stomach took a dive the way it always had. "Yeah, that might make a mess."

"So you're in Easton," he threw out lightly, knowing that's where Brad was from. When she shook her head, his heart leapt with joy.

They weren't living together.

"I'm close, but not close enough."

"To Easton or here?"

Watching her swallow as her cheeks grew pink once more had him longing to reach out and grab her hand, tell her it was okay, she could trust him.

But could she?

"I should probably go," she said as she gathered her purse—designer, of course.

Of course.

"Are you sure?"

"Yes."

He nodded and looked down at his own sundae, which was far less appetizing than the woman who was walking away from him. "Wait."

She turned back towards him, her expression a mixture of puzzlement and hope.

Hope.

He gestured towards the bag she'd left behind. "Your shoes."

"Oof." She walked swiftly over to where she'd left the reason he'd texted her... no, the reason he'd broken down and contacted her, he'd wanted to for so long. "I'd forget my own head sometimes if I could."

"Since when?"

"Since forever. I'm so scattered."

"You're only scattered when something's wrong."

"Nothing's wrong." Her tone was a bit defensive, and he stopped himself from smiling.

Maybe she felt it, too... the familiar spark between them, the one that erupted into a flame so many times.

"Chapter thirty-one," he said, naming the chapter they'd left off on the book they'd been reading together.

"I have to go," she replied quickly, and she hurried her way out the door. Brody sat back, quite pleased with her reaction, and he finished up his triple fudge sundae before leaving the Malt Shoppe.

CHAPTER 11

Temper Tantrum

Catherine had intended to speak to Brad immediately after her epiphany at the Malt Shoppe but listened to her inner fear instead. It had been four long days where instead of going back and forth on her decision like her fear had told her she would, she was more steadfast in knowing she'd been right all along.

She should have never let him put that ring on her finger in the first place.

"We need to talk."

Catherine found herself saying those words to Brad, who was preoccupied with his newspaper. He always seemed preoccupied with something. He hadn't bothered to ask why she had declined spending the night as she had done many times before, accepting she would come over in the morning instead.

"Brad."

She heard him sigh before he set the paper aside with a smile that almost seemed forced. "Have you thought about setting a date, then?"

"No, and just... just listen to me, okay?" Catherine stood and began pacing the floor of his luxurious home. "I've just... I'm not ready."

"Oh, that's fine. We can discuss it some other time."

"No, I'm... put the paper down, please." She held her left hand out. "You haven't even noticed that I'm not wearing the ring."

"Of course I noticed."

"It's on your dresser in the box." She crossed her arms and waited for a response that didn't come. "I'm not ready to get married."

"Consider it a promise ring, then."

"You're not listening to me." She huffed and began to pace again. "I've had so much happen this past week and you've not noticed a single thing, or if you have, you haven't said a word."

"I figured you were inundated with plans."

"What plans? Brad, I never said yes."

"Now, Catherine." He stood and placed his hands on her shoulders halting her. "You didn't say no, either."

"I'm saying that now."

He let out a short laugh and tweeted her nose, irritating her all the more. "You just said you weren't ready."

"Why does it always have to be difficult to have a conversation with you?" She crossed her arms in defiance. "I just said no, and you're not listening."

"Why the change of heart, then?"

The fact that he was still calm and cool nearly set her in a rage. "I told you that I've been thinking, and I'm not ready."

"But,"

"I'm not over my ex, okay?" She threw her hands up. "There, I said it. I'm going to go now."

"Just hold on a moment." Brad's expression held a hint of amusement. "This mysterious ex whom you've never spoken about over the past two years?"

"I didn't feel like I needed to."

"It's called cold feet, Catherine. Now come, sit. We'll chat over coffee and take a walk along the grounds."

"You don't have grounds, you have a big yard. Trust me, I was raised in an actual estate, okay? And stop patronizing me! I'm telling you that I have feelings for someone else, and you find it funny?"

"I find it an excuse."

She growled in frustration. "Forget it. I'm out of here."

"Is that really the adult way to handle this?"

"To go off on my own, get over my anger, and figure out my life my damn self? You bet your ass it is." She grabbed her coat, her keys jangling in the pocket as she put it on, her words reverberating around in her head.

Maybe that's what Brody had been doing all along.

Brad sat down and picked his newspaper back up. "We can speak when you're over your temper tantrum."

She grabbed her purse and never looked back as she walked out of Brad's house. He thought this was a temper tantrum? She huffed out half a laugh. Brad didn't know her back in high school, wasn't aware that she could throw a tantrum that would bring him to his knees and beg for mercy.

Or so she'd like to tell herself back then.

"How's this for a temper tantrum," she muttered as she peeled out of his driveway, a smile firmly on her lips and a weight lifted off of her shoulders.

Catherine Garner was free.

She hadn't realized how she'd felt, at least in some ways, trapped into that relationship, going by the same set of rules that seemed to follow her everywhere, the ones that compared her was and her should be.

"No more should-be," she said aloud, cranking the alternative rock station she turned her radio dial to as she breezed down the highway towards her home, where she swiftly and decisively threw out every single bridal magazine that were scattered about her apartment directly into the dumpster. She shot a quick text to Jen letting her know the deed was done, and kicked back on her couch with a satisfied smile.

You slept with Brody?!?!

Catherine blinked several times and reread Jen's text. "What? No," she said as she typed the words. "Perv," she added, then was silent as she sent the next.

I broke up with Brad

Jen's response that she was coming right over with a bottle of champagne had Catherine laughing so hard she nearly had tears in her eyes.

Just nearly.

And from laughter.

Only then could she admit that Brody really wasn't the reason she'd broken up with Brad. Yes, her feelings were genuine, and yes, she needed to address them.

"But first," she said as she let her hair down, "I celebrate."

Brody returned home from a short assignment to Delores knocking on his door. "I'm actually… oh, didn't mean to scare you," he added as his voice made the woman jump.

"I was just absolutely nowhere near this side of town and thought it would be nice to drop by," she said with a sheepish grin.

"I'm just getting back." He pulled his suitcase closer as he reached with key in hand to unlock the door.

"How exciting."

It had hardly been exciting or worth much of his time when all he wanted to do was make his house a home. At least it was clean when they walked in. "I'm guessing you wanted to see the place before you let me take my brother and sister."

"For the whole weekend," she added, affirming his suspicions. "I'm rather protective of them."

He wanted to snap that she wasn't their mother, but instead he led her down the hallway where Tyler and Sammi's rooms were all set up, waiting for them. "Mine is just across the hall," he said with a gesture, refusing to let her into his personal space. He left his suitcase beside his locked bedroom door.

"My," Delores said, wonder in her voice. "You have dressers and everything. Isn't that a bit much? Or is it for other visitors?"

"I figure they will have things here," Brody replied with a shrug, not willing to elaborate further.

"I do love them, you know. Like they were my own."

"I never thought differently. Can I get you anything?"

"Some water, please." She followed him to the kitchen where he pulled a bottle of water out of the fridge. "Looks like you're ready for entertaining," she added, her eyes on the wine bottles he had on his counter left over from the homecoming gathering.

"I was."

"Is it wise to keep it around? I mean,"

"They won't have access to it, if that's what you're asking." He remained standing as Delores sat at his dining room table.

"Are you certain that… maybe just an overnighter? Or… oh, I'm not sure."

"What does Frank say?"

"Your father? I haven't discussed it with him."

"Why not?" Brody could feel his mood darken in a way that made him uncomfortable. He could handle this, handle anything.

Couldn't he?

"I'm not sure what he would say."

"Tell you what." Brody pushed off the wall and stood a little taller. "I'll discuss it with Frank if you don't want to. I would like a weekend with the kids. I'm…" His voice trailed off before he went on a rant about how he'd been the one to care for them for years.

"Frank's a good man."

Frank must have her fooled, Brody thought. "I'm a good man, too, Delores."

She nodded and looked down at the water bottle he'd handed her that she hadn't taken a single drink from. "I'm sure you are."

"So, it's settled. I speak with Frank so,"

"No, I'll do it," she cut him off as she stood. "I'm not sure what his answer will be."

Brody nodded. "Fair enough." If Frank denied him, he was sure he could work that to his advantage. Let his lawyer handle it, make it so that Brody had extended the olive branch and Frank had refused.

"I should go. I'm sure you need to get settled back in. All this travel, goodness, it's a wonder you've decided to go with such a large house."

Brody inhaled and forced a smile. "I want them to be comfortable here."

"I'm sure you do. It was good to see you again, Brody."

"You too, Delores." He followed her through the living room to the front door and once she was gone, he locked it.

She knew something was up, he could feel it.

He needed to handle this carefully.

He let it stew and stumble over and over in his head while he meticulously unpacked, the way he always did when he first came off of a job. Maybe she wouldn't mind some time with her husband without the kids under her feet.

Or maybe she'd grown so attached to them that she would fight tooth and nail to keep them.

And Frank... since when did he decide to be a 'good man,' a real father? Sheryl had said he'd begun to ask for them the moment that he married Delores, who had no children of her own.

Maybe that was it.

It didn't matter, though. He was going to stay the course, get the kids away from Frank. He didn't want either of them to feel the pain, the rage that had crawled through his own veins. It had taken him years of therapy, of mindfulness, of keeping himself in check until it became his way of being.

He wondered for a brief moment if Catherine would see him differently now that he wasn't an angry kid with a chip on his shoulder. Maybe with him this way, not needing to be fixed, she wouldn't be interested. He never did understand her love, even when he had it, as he'd always considered himself unworthy of it.

His phone began buzzing in his pocket and he pulled it out to see Max's name on the display. "Maximillian, what's up?"

"Dude, are you sitting down?"

"Let's say I am even though I'm not. What's up?"

"Jen called Sarah who called Randall who called me."

"Ah, shit, you have gossip?"

"We discuss, ass. She's free."

"So I know someone who was in jail?"

"No, man… Catherine. Your girl. She gave the ring back and everything. She's celebrating with Jen now."

Catherine.

Free.

No fiancé.

A smile began to cross his face as Max continued on in pure Max fashion, but he'd said everything that Brody wanted to hear.

His Cat…

For that one brief moment as he glanced around his darkened bedroom, he allowed himself to hope.

CHAPTER 12

Inevitable

It was inevitable that Catherine would run into Brody eventually, especially with her spending more time around her old neighborhood. That particular afternoon had her shopping for groceries at Mack's for her father, who was bedridden with the flu. She could feel the heat creeping up into her cheeks as she thought to herself that of course she would see him when she wasn't at her best. She'd been too worried about her father to even bother with makeup and was in jeggings and a baggy off-the-shoulder sweatshirt, and her hair was thrown up in a messy bun.

He still smiled his same smile at her, making her legs feel weak.

"Hey," he said to her, causing the fine hairs on her arms to stand up. She rubbed them absentmindedly.

"Hey," was all she could manage to say back.

"I didn't know you lived around here."

"I don't," she replied, regathering her senses. "I'm just helping my father out."

"How's Coach doing?"

He still called her father 'Coach.' It was equal parts endearing and annoying, or annoying that it was endearing.

"He's down with the flu. I'm getting a few things for him."

She watched as Brody's eyes fell to her basket and he surveyed the contents there. "You're making him chicken and noodles."

She hated that he knew her so well.

Or did she?

"I thought it might help him."

"You're a master at cooking."

"I have Greta's recipes." She shook her phone slightly.

"That's almost cheating."

"Well, she is busy working with her new family. She got her US citizenship, though. I was there for it."

She watched as he shifted his weight while he leaned on his grocery cart. His smile was warmer still. "Tell her I said congratulations."

He meant it, she knew.

She could also see it.

Brody had never been able to hide his moods or his thoughts, at least not from her. Once she knew him, she could tell his anger, his hurt, his jubilation.

He used to be able to do the same with her.

Could he not see that this small talk was tearing her up inside?

"Did you get the kids?" she asked, and he shook his head.

"I'm supposed to this weekend, though." He looked down at his grocery cart. "I'm not even sure what their favorites are anymore."

"Sheryl would know," she offered, knowing that Brody didn't want to ask Frank or his new wife.

His shoulders relaxed beneath his jacket. "I didn't even think about that. Thank you."

She knew she was blushing and damned herself for it. "You're welcome."

"Cat… Catherine, c'mon." He placed his hand on her arm with such gentleness. "It's me. We don't have to act like strangers passing, or even like we were mere acquaintances. You don't need to be tense."

"Of course I do," she countered, then lowered her lashes so he couldn't see the horror in her eyes at her own statement.

"I am sorry, you know?"

She inhaled sharply and lifted her eyes to his. "Good."

He let out one short laugh. "Good. Now we're getting somewhere. Do you need…" His voice trailed off, and she was suddenly aware of how naked her exposed left hand must look to him.

"I've got it covered, thanks."

What she couldn't cover was her next intake of breath, quivering as he took her left hand in his.

"Are you all right?"

"Never better," she replied with a conviction that she felt to her core, despite the rolling emotions threatening to overtake her. She pulled her hand back and lifted her chin. "How's Nora?"

His chuckle nearly sent her over the edge. "I'm telling you, I don't know anyone by that name."

So he hadn't been lying at the party. She could tell that now beneath the glaring lights of Mack's.

"I could help you get this all back to,"

"No, thank you," she cut him off.

One corner of his mouth lifted. "Tiny and fierce."

That's what he'd always said about her.

The familiarity hit every bit as strong as her urge to kiss him.

"I think I have everything," she said instead. "I should get going."

"Oh, yeah, sure. Hey, did... um, have you..."

"I talked to the lawyer yesterday. He has my statement."

Brody nodded. "Good, thanks. I'm not going to have them move forward until after I talk to Ty and Sammi."

"If you need me for the trial... well, I suppose your lawyer would let me know."

"Or I could."

Her heart fluttered in her chest. "Yeah, I suppose you could."

"Or we could just talk."

Oh, that could be bad.

Very bad.

Or it could be so good.

"Okay," she responded as she gripped the handle to her cart a little tighter. "I should go."

"I'll see you soon."

She couldn't stop her smile any more than she could stop from saying, "I'd like that."

She found herself muttering her curses after she'd checked out and was loading the groceries in her car.

"Seriously, self?" She put the first bag in, followed quickly by the second. "Stupid boy and his stupid smile that makes me act so... stupid." She slammed down the trunk and continued muttering to herself as she got in the car and made her way towards her father's home. "He had to look good, didn't he? Why does he always look good? Stupid... asshole... boy."

She finally ceased her muttering as she pulled up to her father's house and parked on the street. With one inhale, she switched gears, a smile on her face as she began to bring the groceries into the home. Her father was still in his recliner, kicked back, his face a ghastly shade of white.

"You didn't have to," he said as she set the groceries on the counter and removed the crockpot from its space.

"Yes, I do. I haven't met your latest girlfriend,"

"Charlotte."

"Yes, Charlotte, but the last one didn't meet my approval and you see how that went. I'm going to cook for you and,"

"I really don't want anything."

"Then it will be here for when you do, or when Charlotte comes over. Daddy, I never realized what a player you are." His laughter followed her as she placed the chicken breasts in the crockpot.

"I know that smile, though."

"What smile?"

"The one that says you were upset before you walked in here."

Her mouth twisted into a frown as she remembered how well her father knew her.

Almost as well as Brody once had.

"Did Brad say something to you?"

"Hmm? Oh, no," Catherine replied. "I haven't heard from him." Because she hadn't been taking his calls or listening to his voicemails and had his text messages going into the abyss on her phone.

"I never really liked him."

Catherine smiled. "I know. You never really like anyone I date."

"I wouldn't say that."

Because he'd been so fond of Brody, even asking her to forgive him for leaving. Her father had thought it for the best, and not because he didn't like Brody, but because he'd seen what Brody had been going through.

Forgiveness.

That was the one thing she knew she needed to do with Brody.

And the one thing she wasn't sure if she could.

Brody smiled to himself as he looked down at his phone. It wasn't Catherine's name, sadly, but there was a text from Frank.

The kids would love to spend this weekend with you.

Finally he could share his plan with Tyler and Sammi with the hopes that they would want what he wanted.

For the three of them to be together, under the same roof, until the kids were ready to venture off on their own.

He shot back his response, asking if Frank would be bringing them or if he could pick them up.

I'd like to bring them was Frank's response.

Brody knew this meant that, like Delores, Frank wanted to see where the kids were going to be, what their sleeping arrangements were, and if Brody's home was up to par. It didn't concern him, though, as he knew he was more than ready.

He'd been ready for anything Frank could throw his way for a long time.

He thought of the night he finally fought back in Catherine's basement, so tired, so angry, but determined to keep Frank away from her. He almost missed living in that house sometimes. Not the anger or the beatings, of course, but the way Catherine would sneak down those stairs in the middle of the night just to talk.

She was the only person he'd never had to hide from.

And now as he stared at the phone in his hand, all he wanted was to talk to her again.

He busied himself instead, editing photographs before sending them out to various channels. Each shot that he sent had to be perfect, the lighting just so, and still keep everything he wanted to show.

Loss.

Anguish.

Humanity.

Still, it all brought his thoughts back to Catherine, back to when he watched her fall to pieces and rise out of the ashes as a kinder, gentler, compassionate human.

Seeing a picture of a mother holding her child reminded him of holding her while she cried.

Seeing pictures of couples holding hands amid the wreckage reminded him of holding her hand that morning after Homecoming.

"Fuck." He closed his laptop and rubbed his face before sighing into his hands.

He needed to talk to her.

He needed that closeness they used to have, long before he'd ever kissed her.

It was eating him alive knowing how close she was, knowing she'd given him the okay to call her. What would he say to her? Would he convey his condolences over the ending of her engagement? Would he let her know that he'd never seen her say 'yes'?

Would he let her know he'd followed her into the restaurant that day?

Or would he congratulate her on knowing what she wanted, and knowing that it didn't include marrying someone that everyone else thought was right for her?

He stared down at his phone for the longest time, willing it to ring.

Willing it to be her.

When it finally did ring and Nikos's name flashed on the screen, Brody begrudgingly answered. "Hello?"

"Son." Nikos had been drinking; Brody could hear it in his voice. "Son," he repeated, "I've been trying to reach you. You don't return my texts. This hurts me. Why would you hurt your Pa like that?"

Pa. Nikos considered himself as 'Pa' despite giving up parental rights, despite leaving Brody and his twin to be raised by Frank instead.

"I've been busy," Brody replied, feeling the tension creep up his neck and throb at the base of his skull.

"Never be too busy. If you're too busy, you miss the life. You can miss all the pussy passing you by."

"Can you not?" Brody snapped, no longer willing to allow Nikos to speak degradingly about women. He'd put up with that long enough. He'd wondered if this was his legacy, if this was who he was going to become, if his temper and outbursts weren't just a product of nurture, but nature as well.

"Oh, poor sensitive Dimitri."

"Brody."

"Would Dante have been the same?"

Brody refrained from telling Nikos what he'd found out about his late brother and the boyfriend that he'd been so fond of. "Yes," was all he said, and it was true. Brian didn't like disrespect of others. Perhaps he had the dislike because of seeing how Brody had been treated, but Brody would never know the answer.

"You should come up to Toronto again, soon. I have a shoot and I could show you how to capture it with my kind of camera."

"I'm fine with mine."

"Why do you not want to come see your Pa?"

Brody rubbed the back of his neck, trying to relieve some of the tension there. "I'm busy right now, like I said."

"Soon."

"Sure." Brody sighed quietly. "Soon." He hit the end button on his phone, unable to deal with talking to Nikos any longer.

No wonder his mother had gotten as far away from him as she could.

But look what she ran to.

"Fuck, fuck, fuck, fuck, fuck!" He moved to throw his phone across the room, but stopped.

That was the way he used to be.

He refused to be that man consumed with anger now.

He drew in a shaky breath instead and dialed a number he'd known by heart since she'd given it to him. And when she answered, he smiled.

CHAPTER 13

Free

Catherine didn't want to speak with Brad, but the persistent phone calls were wearing her thin. That morning when her phone rang as she was getting dressed, she knew her time for avoidance was at an end.

As her conversation rehashed everything she had already told him, it began to wear her nerves. How many times would she have to tell him the same damn thing?

"Brad, it's over, okay? You aren't listening to anything I say, and for me, that's a deal breaker."

"I'm listening now."

"Then what did I just say?"

"Catherine, I think we should meet up, discuss this further in person."

She rolled her eyes. "I already told you that I don't want to."

"Well a few of your things are here. If we are over, as you've said, I'm sure you'll want them back."

"Send them by courier, then."

"So that's what this is about, because I had the bridal magazines sent by courier. I thought you'd want to look at them and was on my way out of town."

"And you thought I had nothing better to do than to plan a wedding I hadn't even agreed to?"

"I didn't say that, Catherine."

"I really can't deal with this right now, I have a lot going on." She looked around her clean apartment and her empty schedule before her, but refused to feel guilty. It wasn't as if she was lying; she had a lot on her mind and it consumed her every waking moment as well as her dreams. "Plus I have to get to work."

"I could meet you on your break."

"What part of 'no' doesn't resonate within your brain?" Now angry, she swiped her keys off the counter with force. "I have to go." She hit the end button before he had a chance to respond, and that soon her phone began to ring again. She huffed and turned her phone, then her breath caught in her throat.

Brody.

In spite of running late, she quickly answered with her most normal 'hello' that she could muster.

"I get the kids this weekend."

A smile touched her lips. This was Brody, always jumping right into the conversation. "That's wonderful," she replied, and she meant it with her whole heart.

"I think I'm ready, but I'm really nervous, you know? I guess I never prepared myself for if they said yes. Or if one said yes and the other said no. I mean,"

"Relax," she cut him off with an easy laugh. Everything with him flowed easily. "Get them settled, have some fun, and wait maybe until the end of the weekend. That way they don't feel pressured the whole time they're with you."

"Yeah, that's... that's actually a great idea, because I was gonna dive right in."

"Like at the pool."

He was silent for a moment before he said, "Yeah, like at the pool."

She wondered if he was lost in the memory the way she was, remembering his toned body leaping through and diving out as far as he could, coming up and shaking his dark hair, droplets of water clinging to his skin in the sun...

"Catherine?"

"Hmm? Oh, sorry." She was blushing, she could feel it. "Mind wandered."

"White bikini."

So had his.

"That was inappropriate of me, I'm sorry," he quickly said, and she shook her head. Always the gentleman.

"I'm the one who should apologize, since I can't stay on the phone. Work," she added, letting him know in her own way that was the only thing standing between them that day.

"How is Maxine?"

Catherine's smile faded. "I don't work with Maxine now. I'm at a studio in Easton."

"But that was your dream."

It had been her dream, to work with Maxine and eventually take over the studio when her mentor was ready to retire. "I suppose some dreams don't work out."

"Maybe they only get sidelined for a little bit."

"Or for a while."

She wasn't sure if she was talking about Maxine or Brody at that moment, until she heard him sigh.

She knew then it was all about him.

"We'll talk soon?" He worded it as a question, causing Catherine's smile to return.

"Yes, we will."

And her smile stayed with her all the way to her place of work, where she walked in with dread, feeling as out of place as she had her first day there.

The day had been a long one of phone calls and emails, getting his pictures to his manager, and assuring he would be compensated in a manner that would help his quest.

Was he overreaching? He still couldn't answer that question even as the sun set casting a red glow across his bedroom. Another night in, another night with not much else to do.

Until his phone rang.

"Dude," Max said the moment he answered, "JJ is in town tonight. Secret show, local friends and family only. It will be at the Basement."

The Basement, a small dive bar at the edge of Brentfield.

"It starts at nine. Get your ass there. And before you ask, Jen is letting your girl know."

Would Catherine be there?

"Yeah, yeah, uh… just let me get dressed dive-bar style."

"No suit and tie, Mr. High and Mighty."

Brody laughed. "Yeah, fuck you, too."

"I think everyone will be there. Except Kate, since we don't know where the hell she is. But seriously, we haven't been all together since your going away party."

"I'll be there, Max, I promise."

The hours couldn't move fast enough for him now as he busied himself around the house. There were things he wanted to change but couldn't without the landlord's permission, so he settled with washing the walls and pulling more photos out to frame and mount.

Only two hours had passed.

He pulled out the cleaning supplies and began the task of washing baseboards throughout the home, telling himself this was something Frank would be looking at.

Only another hour and a half had passed.

When it was finally close enough to the time, he showered and dressed in jeans and a t-shirt that clung to his shoulders, showing the work he'd been putting in on a near-daily basis. He shaved again, remembering the look of wonder in Catherine's eyes when she'd seen him last, and then cursed at himself for doing anything for someone else's benefit.

He'd walked away from her.

He had to live with that.

But she was free, as he'd been since he'd told her goodbye.

It was just after 7:30 when he arrived at The Basement, coming early per Max's request. It was going to be a stripped down acoustic show, with only JJ and his lead guitarist Damien, so setup wasn't going to be elaborate or difficult. That would also leave time for the boys—no, the men—to sit down and catch up.

With the smoking ban, The Basement didn't have the haze hanging in the air that it at one time had, only now smelling of stale smoke and spilled beer. The lighting was dark, as Brody had expected it to be, and only a couple of people sat at the bar, each having a beer and talking to the bartender as if they'd known her forever. Raucous laughter could be heard in the distance and Brody followed the sound towards a door with a sign that read Smokers Lounge, with a neon red 'Exit' sign above it.

"You must be Brody," the bartender called out to him and he blinked in surprise.

"Yeah, I am."

"They've been waiting for you," she said with a gesture towards the door, and he smiled.

"Thank you."

Leave it to JJ to be outside in this cold weather smoking like his life depended on it. Brody pushed the door open and was met with a blast of cold air and the smell of cigarettes.

He was also met with a huge bear hug from someone he nearly didn't recognize.

"Brody, my man!"

JJ stood before him, his hair now dark and longer, falling in waves and tufts to almost his shoulders. His face had filled out as had he, no longer the scrawny bleached blonde boy, but a man. His face bore about 3 days' growth of what would be a full beard, unlike the patchiness that kept him clean-shaven five years prior.

"Jeezus, JJ, I didn't know it was you," Brody finally said with a laugh.

"I can't get over the JJ," a young man Brody didn't know said.

"It's Jase now, dumbass," JJ said with a playful shove. "Want one?"

"Nah, I still don't smoke," Brody replied, and waved his hello to Max who was on the phone.

"Brody, this is Damien, my guitarist. Damien, this is Brody."

Brody shook the hand of the young man who was adorned with tattoos and piercings and an air of aloofness. Given his business, he was most likely accustomed to being introduced to many people, and Brody wondered for a moment how many of those wanted a piece of him to rub off on them, to benefit them in some way.

"Okay, so..." JJ took another hit off his cigarette. "Even Audrey is coming. Um, my brother Pete will have to be snuck in at some point since he's not 21."

"On it," Damien said with a sly smile.

"Pete's here?" Max asked as he pulled the phone away from his ear. "Dude, that's amazing. I haven't seen him since he was, what... nine?"

"Yeah, it was about 10 years ago," JJ replied. "Shana couldn't make it because of work, though."

"I bet your sister got hot. Ow," Max said, rubbing his arm where JJ had punched him.

"My sister's off limits."

Brody thought to himself that he knew someone else who was off limits.

Except she wasn't, not really.

"How's touring life treating you?" Brody asked, steering the conversation away from thoughts of Catherine.

"Man, we're going to have the sweetest setup in Cleveland," JJ replied with a smile. "I've got a suite and everything."

"Yeah, you've got a suite," Damien said with a good-natured smile.

"I'm gonna be there for a few days after the show, writing and recording." JJ bounced on his heels and had the most genuine smile that Brody had seen on him in quite some time. "Got some plans, if I can get them to work out."

"A hook up?" Max asked with a laugh, and JJ shook his head.

"Not telling, and that's all I'm gonna say."

"He's been doing this for weeks, by the way," Damien said as he pushed himself off the wall. "I'm empty. Anyone up for a drink?"

"Beer me," JJ said to him.

"Same," Max added.

"The road," JJ continued as Damien walked into the bar, the sound of the jukebox blaring through the opened door before being muffled, "is kinda monotonous. It's get to the venue, unload, although they have someone do that for us now, sound check. Break. Show. Meet people while your stuff's being broken down and loaded, head out."

"Stop acting like you don't like it, asshat," Max said with a laugh, and again JJ smiled.

"I fucking love it. Most of it, anyway. This tour's been long and brutal, though."

"But you are obviously seeing someone, so,"

"Not telling," JJ cut Max off. "How about you? I can't believe you and Sarah broke up."

"Yeah, well," Max shrugged, "better off as friends."

"You?" JJ asked Brody, and he shook his head. "No shit? No Catherine?"

Brody's heart fell a notch, weighing heavily in his chest. "No Catherine," he said, shrugging it off on the outside.

"I always thought you two were end-game."

"Same," Max added, then grinned as Damien walked out with his arms full of open beer bottles. "Dude, that was quick."

"Star treatment. Speaking of," Damien said as he passed the beers out, "there's some super-hot blonde that they almost didn't let in because they swore her ID was fake. She's a tiny thing, but damn she's just fucking gorgeous. That's my conquest of the night."

Brody felt his stomach tighten. "Tiny, huh?"

"Oh, but the mouth on her when she thought they weren't going to let her in." Damien laughed before taking a sip of his beer. "Yeah, she's a feisty one."

"Fierce," Brody corrected him, knowing exactly who he was talking about.

And exactly who wouldn't be a notch on Damien's belt.

"Hey," came a whisper from the trees behind the bar. "Coast clear?"

"Climb the fence and you're home free," JJ called out to his brother, who was two years shy of being old enough to attend the show, apparently regardless of the family ties.

"I'm gonna head in," Brody said, his heart hammering at the thought of who was behind the door.

"See you in a bit," JJ replied. Brody watched as Damien lit another cigarette, satisfied that his competition wouldn't be around.

Was it really competition?

Was he defending Catherine from being a 'conquest?'

Or did he want her for himself?

CHAPTER 14

Unexpected

Catherine was still fuming when she made it to the bar. "Will I need to show my ID again to get a drink?" she muttered, causing Jen to throw her head back in laughter. "Do I look 14? Seriously?"

"Do you really want an answer to that? Makers and soda," Jen added as the bartender looked her way.

"Just a beer," Catherine added, her scowl remaining as she turned back to her friend. "How many people did the bouncer get to look at that? I mean, really, I'm on the list and everything, aren't I?"

"It's a secret show, Catherine," Jen replied, still giggling. "Seriously, I needed that bit of humor today."

"So happy to be of service."

"Three o'clock, tattooed hot man giving you the eye."

"Why, does he think I'm too young to be here? Thank you," Catherine said to the bartender who set their drinks in front of them.

"Maybe it's because you wore a micro miniskirt leaving not much to the imagination. If you weren't my best friend and I didn't know you were straight, I'd hit on you, too."

A sly smile touched Catherine's lips. Maybe Brody would show up. Maybe he'd pay attention that she was showing off her legs, which before him she'd been slightly self-conscious about. Without the constant cheerleading, they were no longer as muscular as they'd once been, but were still trim and well-toned, the remnants of her summer tan showing in her every move.

"Can you even sit down in that skirt without showing everyone here your goods?"

"Ha ha, Jen, you're hilarious." Catherine's voice was flat, though her eyes showed a hint of laughter. "Let's find a table closer to the stage."

"Let's pause," Jen said softly in her ear, "and let your ex that just walked in the back door get a damn good look at you."

"Shall I turn this way?" Catherine shifted so that Brody could see the full view, but she kept her eyes on Jen. "Is he looking?"

"I think he just choked on his beer."

"Good. Let's grab that table."

"You're ruthless."

"That's why you love me."

Catherine knew just how to move to capture the attention of everyone in the room, and she made sure she did so as she and Jen grabbed the closest table that didn't say 'reserved' on it. She carefully crossed her legs at the ankles and eased herself into the chair, draping her coat over the empty chair to her left before Jen took the chair to her right. Feeling empowered even as others began to set their coats down, she turned to Jen with a smile.

"And?"

"And he's right behind you."

Catherine's smile fell. "Way to be subtle, Jen."

"And that's why you love me."

"Hi."

Catherine looked over her shoulder, smiling demurely at Brody. "Hello. I take it JJ and Max are already here?"

"Let's get these tables together," Brody said instead of answering, and began to move the reserved table closer to hers. "We'll be talking all night anyway, so,"

"We will, huh?"

"Yes, Lady Catherine. We always do."

"The star is my cousin," Jen said with a shrug. "It's part of the perks."

"Don't call him a star, it might go to his head," Brody quipped, his lopsided grin causing Catherine's stomach to take a dive.

Oh, this was going to be a long night.

"Jase? A big head? Nah." The tattooed man that Jen must have been referring to was beside Brody then, his hand outstretched in her direction. "Damien."

"Catherine," she replied, expecting him to shake her hand, but he lifted hers to his lips, leaving a ghost of a kiss on her knuckles. She could feel Brody's eyes on her as she smiled up at Damien.

"Well, that was unexpected," she said as she pulled her arm back and raised her bottle of beer. "To new friends." The clink of his bottle on hers was barely heard above JJ's loud exclamation.

"My favorite cousin!"

Catherine barely recognized him as he stood before her, no longer the scrawny boy with badly bleached hair, as he pulled Jen into a warm hug. "JJ?"

"I'm telling all of you, it's Jase now. This JJ shit confuses me," he said with a laugh. "I don't even know him anymore."

Catherine stood and gave JJ a hug, whispering in his ear, "I wouldn't have known it was you."

"I get that a lot," he said and he stood back. "You're as gorgeous as ever, Catherine."

She could feel herself blush under JJ's pull. He'd definitely changed. "Hell, look at you."

"Professional mandatory makeover." He shrugged and laughed before downing his beer. "Yeah, this is a whisky night."

"On it," an older gentleman who appeared in Catherine's line of sight said.

"You're a lifesaver, Jackie." JJ pulled a chair up backwards and straddled it. "Road manager," he explained with a grin.

"Spoiled brat," Damien said with a smirk.

With a rush, Catherine realized Brody's arm was on the back of her chair, and that she'd leaned back into it as she had countless times before.

And it felt so right.

She glanced shyly to her left, where Brody had moved her coats and had slid into the seat beside her, and his eyes… oh, those blue eyes.

She was lost.

So lost.

And then he smiled, and she knew.

She'd loved him always.

Brody kept getting pulled away, first to do shots at the bar with JJ and the bartender, then to say hello to various high school friends who'd made their way to the tiny hole-in-the-wall bar on a week night. His eyes were on Catherine every moment he could catch a glimpse, and sometimes share a glance.

Most of those times were when she was sharing some banter with JJ's guitarist and her newest admirer, Damien.

He couldn't tell if his blood was running cold or if it had changed to boiling over with jealousy from one moment to the next.

"What is up with you and Catherine?" Max asked. "One minute you look like you need a room, and the next it's looking like our boy Damien is going to get his wish."

"He's not 'our boy,'" Brody said before downing the rest of his beer. It wasn't that he disliked Damien; it was simply because he'd thought of Catherine as no more than a conquest that he was determined to win.

That simply wouldn't do.

"Excuse me," he mumbled to the people crowding around the bar before the show, ensuring that their drinks would be full for the time when Jase Warner took the stage. He saw Jen talking with JJ, but Catherine and Damien had disappeared. The closing door to the outside smoking area was a hint of where he would find her, and he was happy that not only had he, but it had several people alongside of them as Damien lit his cigarette.

"I probably should have worn something warmer," Catherine was saying, and silently while Brody enjoyed the view, he agreed.

"I like your dress," Damien replied, as smooth as silk.

"Isn't it the best?" one of the girls asked, and Brody smiled to himself as the conversation now included two girls from high school who could also turn Damien's head.

If he would just look the other way.

Brody eased his way up behind Catherine and spoke softly in her ear. "Would you like me to bring your coat?"

She turned her face to his and he bit back a smile as she crinkled her nose. "Would you?"

"Of course."

He wasn't staking his claim, as Damien seemed to want to, but merely helping her out as he went back inside for her longer tan colored jacket. JJ followed him outside for one last cigarette, and as he let Damien know it was almost time, Brody helped Catherine slip into her jacket.

"Thank you. It's freezing out here."

"So why did you come out?"

"It's hard to hear in there," she replied as she pulled her jacket closed around her. "How are you? Are you ready for this weekend?"

"As ready as I can be." He shrugged. "I took care of them for years, how hard can one weekend be?"

"They're older, and if they're anything like you, probably mouthier, too."

Brody smiled down at her. "I don't know what you're talking about."

"Sure thing. Ugh, it's too cold. I'm going back inside."

"Here," he said, taking a few steps back before opening the door. "Ladies first."

Much to his chagrin, every lady that was out there stepped through that door, putting more space between him and Catherine, who had walked back to their adjoined tables and placed her coat aside. Damn, she looked beautiful.

"I'm not stepping on any toes there, am I?" Damien asked as he finished his cigarette.

"How long have you two been apart? Years, I know, but,"

"A long time," Brody cut JJ off, who shrugged.

"Years seem to blend together after a while. I'm glad you're here. Hey, Damien, did I tell you that Brody was Brian's twin?"

Damien shook his head. "Man, that's harsh. I don't think I could have handled it."

Brody's heart ached over the loss of his brother still. "Losing a brother is the hardest thing I've ever dealt with." And he continued to daily, unable to bear the thought of anything happening to Tyler or Sammi now.

That's why he had to get them back.

Jackie stepped outside, and with a nod he let JJ and Damien know that it was time.

"Okay, let's do this," JJ said, clapping his hands together as Brody walked past Jackie back into the dimly lit bar. He quickly found Catherine and noticed the seat he'd been sitting in now held her coat. When she saw him, she removed it with a smile.

She was saving his seat for him.

"So Jen said that Audrey wanted to come but her baby is sick," she said into his ear just as the jukebox was cut. "Sorry if that was loud," she whispered.

"I hope everything's okay," he replied.

"Yeah, me, too."

Small talk.

Was that what had been going on between Catherine and Damien? Brody doubted it with the sly grin that Damien flashed Catherine's way as they took the stage to thunderous applause. No, she was probably telling him about her hopes and dreams, ones that used to include him.

But they'd also included working with Maxine until it was time to take over the studio, and she instead opted for a flashier position in Easton.

They'd included going on the road with him, but he'd shot that down.

He had done so much damage in cutting her off, he knew this.

Still, as JJ and Damien began to play and she settled back beside him, he placed his arm around her, resting it on the back of her chair.

Did she just sigh?

Was it from contentment or annoyance?

He stole a glance down at her smiling face, unable to tell if her eyes were on JJ or on Damien.

This was going to be a long night.

CHAPTER 15

Jealousy

Catherine silenced another late-night call from Brad as Jen pulled up in front of Nan's house. "Feels surreal to be back here," she said as she exited the car.

"She's not my Nan, so same, I guess," Jen replied. Other cars were pulling in one by one including a black sedan driven by JJ's road manager.

"Come in, come in," Nan said with a grin, her door wide, and Catherine watched as she took JJ into her arms, hugging him tight. "Everyone, come. And hurry, it's cold as shit out here."

"Is shit cold?" Damien asked as he appeared beside Catherine and guided her in with a hand on the small of her back. She didn't know if she should feel flattered or offended, but she stuck with flattered and flashed her dazzling smile in his direction.

"Out there? Probably. Thank you," she said to JJ, who took her coat along with several others.

"Just put them back on your bed," Nan said to him. "And make sure they stay there. No funny business under my roof. Beer is in the fridge, whiskey is on the counter."

"And you can say that legally to us now," Max quipped as he entered with Brody close behind.

"How many are coming?" Nan asked as Damien brought Catherine an opened beer.

"Some had to work tomorrow," Brody said from behind her, and she could feel his eyes on her. "But there will be a few more. I don't think any of the other patrons who just happened to be there will swing by."

"You know how it is," JJ said to Nan as he passed her and left a kiss on her cheek. "Had to dance on the bar. Had to. Nan, I got Pete to do it, too. You should have seen him, it was priceless. Hey, do you still have the sheriff in your pocket, or do we need to keep the music down?"

"You should keep it down anyway so everyone can catch up. Catherine, dear, I would love a rematch."

"Rematch?" Damien asked.

"Beer pong," Catherine replied over the music which, of course, JJ had turned up loud. "Nan's the best."

"My eyesight is going," Nan said with a shrug as she pulled the folding table out. Brody took it from her to set up. "I should have had this set up already, but I didn't know you'd be coming."

"Catherine's slumming it again with us," Max grinned. "Now that she dumped her snooty boyfriend."

"Brad isn't... okay, maybe a little snooty, but since when do you use that word?"

"Since always," Sarah said as she entered. "That has to be Max you're talking to."

Old waves of nostalgia hit Catherine full-force as the first five were all together again—her, Brody, Sarah, Max, and Jen. Jen was the first person she'd met on her way to class on her first day at Valley High, where she had been shocked to see Brody. It was during that first class that she'd met Max and Sarah, and the four of them—eventually including Jen—had been nearly inseparable for months.

Would she have changed anything knowing that Brody would destroy her heart a year later? She doubted that, as his eyes met hers and he smiled knowingly.

Maybe he felt it, too.

"First, I get my rematch with Catherine," Nan announced, "and then I take on any challengers."

"You sure you're going to beat me?" Catherine asked with an easy laugh.

"My dear, you look out of practice."

And out of practice she was, losing the first match without much fanfare. Demanding a rematch, she won the next two before retiring, declaring herself officially the all-time champion who needed to slow down her drinking. More than a few others had shown up at this point, and while the living room wasn't nearly as full as it had been during the parties Catherine's first summer in the Valley, there were still scores of people for her to catch up with.

"I've decided," Jen said, throwing her arm around Catherine's shoulders, "that I'm adopting Nan, so our visits here will be far more frequent."

Catherine glanced into the brightly lit kitchen where Nan stood with JJ, Max, and Brody, glowing with pride at the men the boys had grown into. Catherine felt the pride as well, marveling over how far they'd all come in the past five years.

"Hey," Damien said as he walked up to her, "another beer?"

"No, thank you," Catherine replied. "I've had my fill with beer pong. Ugh," she added with a laugh. Jen had drifted away, talking to someone else they'd gone to school with. "It was a great show tonight."

"You should see us when we're a full band. Come to Cleveland."

"Oh, I couldn't." Catherine shook her head. "I have classes to teach."

"Some other show, then."

Catherine smiled at him. "I'd like that."

"Jase is going to be in Cleveland writing for a few days. I'd like to fly back here, take you out to dinner."

Catherine's mouth was slightly agape for a moment before she regained her senses. "Dinner?"

"You don't seem the type to come back with me to my room tonight," he added, and her eyes widened.

"You're right about that."

"I'm not trying to offend you, I'm just not used to actually having to ask a girl out."

Catherine once again could feel Brody's presence.

Brody, who had avoided her since they'd arrived here at Nan's.

Brody, who had been so close to her and barely said a word at the Basement.

"Dinner? You'd fly out here for... dinner?"

Damien's grin made him look slightly less intimidating. "Yeah."

"Okay, then," she replied smoothly. "It's a date."

Her heart fell when Brody said nothing, only moving further away from her to talk to someone he'd barely spoken to when they'd all been at Valley High.

All but Damien, who looked so out of place amidst the people gathered there, talking about how they needed to leave, get up for work the next morning.

Catherine didn't feel a spark. She didn't feel much of anything in Damien's presence. Perhaps it was cruel of her to agree to dinner when she didn't see anything coming of it other than a musician racking up more frequent flyer miles.

But as Brody turned his back to her once more, she lied and told herself she'd done the right thing.

Jealousy was not an emotion that Brody was used to, nor was it one that he liked. But with every glance stolen between Damien and Catherine, the more it crept into Brody's head. And when Catherine agreed to a date, it moved to his heart.

With a sigh, he eased back, leaning on the counter in the kitchen, nursing his beer and his wounded pride when Max turned the corner and saw him. "Dude," Max said quietly, which was a feat for him, "how are you just gonna stand there and let someone take your girl?"

"She's not my girl, Max," Brody replied, just a quietly, though his quietness came from a resolve that he was losing her for good.

"Like hell she isn't. And while you're at it, stop avoiding her. You're acting like the douchebag ex who wants to prove she doesn't mean anything."

"You spend too much time with Emily."

"Em's a great sounding board. Newsflash for you, Harris; if you don't man up, I'm calling her."

"No," Brody said with a shake of his head. "Nope, let Em sleep."

"I say let Emily berate your ass for being stupid. And if I'd known JJ was sneaking Pete in, we could have gotten Emily in the same way."

"Where is Pete?"

"I guess he's back at the motel," Max replied with a shrug. "Not sure. But Nan's not his nan."

"She's everyone's Nan," Brody said, smiling at the older woman who'd won another round of beer pong. She had taken each of the boys under her wing and instilled as much wisdom as they would allow her to, her words of comfort meaning more to him than he could ever convey to her.

"That she is," JJ agreed as he entered the kitchen with a genuine smile. "Man, I needed this night. The tour has been so fucking hard this time around. It's one thing to be an opening band, it's another entirely when it's on you to carry the show."

"But you're Jase Warner," Max said with his easygoing grin. "Making the ladies swoon."

"Yeah, yeah." JJ looked a bit embarrassed, surprising Brody.

"Isn't that what most musicians want?" Brody asked, and JJ shrugged.

"Yeah, but they want the persona. That's not... well, it's who I am, but *not*."

Brody nodded slowly. "Makes sense."

"I'd still take advantage of it," Max added.

"Not saying I haven't," JJ admitted with a grin. "But it gets old, and that's just not what I want anymore. I mean, I never had a steady home other than here. But that's what I want, a home to go to."

"Home meaning,"

"That's it." Jase's grin widened. "A home. Not a house, not a place to crash, not random women wanting Jase Warner the rockstar."

"Rockstar," Max laughed. "I'm so calling you that now."

"I just want to be me."

"So just JJ," Brody said.

"Nope. Jase is what Michael used to call me, and it's what I go by now. But... hey, where's Damien?"

"Go look for Catherine, he'll be there," Brody said dryly, and JJ only laughed.

"He's a player," was all JJ said before exiting the kitchen.

A player, who was playing Cat like she was his own personal instrument.

"Go find her," Max said, his tone again soft, only for Brody's ears. "Make sure you're the one who drives her home."

"She came with Jen."

"Dude." Max shoved him slightly. "Go. I'll take care of Jen."

With a growl, Brody shoved off the counter and went in search of Catherine, weaving through the people still there, still scrambling to get closer to JJ, whose smile was much less genuine now. Catherine wasn't in the living room, so he went down the hallway, searching each empty room for her. Conceding that she must have left, he resigned himself to rejoin the party and its hangers on.

The front door opened, and Catherine emerged into the room, her cheeks flushed. Was it from cold? Or was it from the tattooed guitarist following in behind her? Tattooed wasn't the best way to describe him, especially as JJ had plenty of tattoos as well, but Brody couldn't place what it was he didn't like about him.

Yes, he could.

It was the way his hand was on the small of Catherine's back, as if he owned her.

He had to put a stop to this.

CHAPTER 16

Yes

Catherine had wanted time alone outside to think and get a breath of fresh, crisp air. Instead, Damien had followed her, telling her of the loneliness of the road. She hadn't quite known what to make of it, cutting his stories short by telling him she had to get in from the cold. Was he trying to get her to leave with him? If that was the case, he would be disappointed. She'd never been that girl.

She wasn't about to start now.

As they entered the home again, she heard Jackie announce that it was time for them to leave, to catch their next flight back to their actual tour. Was that relief she felt? She couldn't be sure. She felt more alive than she had in years, but was that because of the attention of a rockstar guitarist?

Or because she locked eyes with Brody the moment she turned her head?

The heat in his gaze sent shockwaves through her body, and she inhaled sharply as she turned away from him. Her only other option was to walk across that room and kiss him the way he'd kissed her that day in her father's SUV.

When he had promised he would return to her as quickly as he could.

But no, he'd returned to get his brother and sister back years after he'd demolished her heart.

She could be strong, she could hold her head high and...

"Where's Jen?" Catherine looked around the living room, not seeing her teal-headed best friend.

"Ah, Catherine, I'm so sorry," Max said as he threw his arm around her shoulders. "I thought you were taking off with Damien."

She felt her face heat up. "No, and thanks, that was my ride you sent home."

"We could give you a lift," Damien offered.

"We're running a bit behind," Jackie said with a look at his watch.

"Oh, no worries," Max replied with a wave of his hand. "I could give her a lift. Or Brody could. He wouldn't mind, would you, Harris?"

Brody's eyes were on Catherine when he answered, "I can give you a ride home."

Did her temperature suddenly spike? She couldn't tell, but the living room was suffocating her now. "Thank you," she managed to say.

What was she thinking? She should have told him no, should have taken Max up on his offer since he was the one who screwed up.

But that little voice inside of her, the one telling her to run, was on Catherine's last nerve. She was a grown woman now, not some sniveling high school girl who thought that prom was her right of passage. Just one high school dance that wasn't somehow associated with drama had been the only thing on her mind back then, back before Brody broke her heart.

Still, as she sat in the passenger seat of his car, she felt that high school girl creep back in. Crossing her arms, she remained silent as he started the car.

"I need the address."

He had the nerve to sound sexy when he said that, didn't he? She softly spoke, telling him which apartment complex she lived in without giving her exact address away.

"Thank you."

And he thanked her. There he went, being the perfect gentleman, full of manners. At least he wasn't scowling and cursing the way he seemed to always do when they'd first met. Then again, she wasn't the spoiled brat demanding everything be her way and her way only.

They'd both grown up.

"He seems nice."

Perhaps Brody had grown up more than she had, as she only nodded at his comment. Damien did seem nice, and very shy when he wasn't around a crowd of people.

"You can talk to me, Cat. You know that."

"Stop calling me that."

"Sorry, Catherine. You can talk to me," he repeated.

"I'm surprised you speak to me at all, you know?" She wasn't quite sure where her sudden boldness had come from. "I was an insolent little bitch to you for quite a while."

"Ah, the good old days," Brody said with a laugh, and the corners of her mouth lifted in a smile. "See? I knew you had a smile in you. How do you like Millerstown?"

She shrugged. "It's okay. I don't venture out much."

"Why don't you work with Maxine, Catherine?" Brody asked suddenly. "I just can't get it out of my head how that was your dream, something you were going to work your ass off for. When you weren't spouting off about putting off college and,"

"Spouting off? Seriously," she snapped. "I hadn't seen you in forever, you decided to ditch the remaining of your senior year for your GED and your camera and your real father. I wanted time with you."

"But you were going to sacrifice your own future."

"That was my decision."

"And I couldn't live with that, okay? I couldn't." She watched him run a hand through his hair as they pulled up to a stoplight close to the complex. "I couldn't let you do that."

"So, what, instead of having a conversation with me, like we're having right now, you decided to break up with me?"

She'd been joking when she said it, albeit angrily.

She hadn't been prepared for his answer.

"Yes."

He hadn't meant to tell her that, not there in the car. His eyes were on the road as he drove the remainder of the short distance to her apartment complex, but he could still see her in his peripheral vision. She remained silent, her arms still crossed, but held more tightly to her chest, as if she was hurt.

Of course she was. All he'd done was hurt her for the past few years.

"Are you going to say anything?" he asked, and he heard her clear her throat.

"Turn in by the sign and follow around to the back parking lot."

She was choosing to avoid the subject, or perhaps a bit stunned at his admission. Or maybe she was angry with him all over again; he couldn't tell which was the case. Her arms were crossed a little tighter and her breathing was deep, each breath reaching into Brody's soul. He longed to know what was going through her mind as he followed her directions and pulled into a parking spot, but the buzzing of her phone interrupted what should have been the conversation he needed to have with Catherine.

Instead, she answered her phone with a breathy "Hello."

In the stillness of the car, only the purr of the engine filling the cabin, he could hear the caller's voice.

Damien.

Damien, who had her attention nearly all night long.

Damien, who was confirming their date this upcoming Saturday.

"Of course," Catherine said, her tone light, almost happy. "Yeah, I can't wait, either."

Brody's eyes slid shut and his head dropped, his eyes on his hands that still held the steering wheel. He could reach out to her, touch her, remind her that he was still there, tell her that this was tearing him apart.

"Of course you can call. No, middle of the night is not entirely out of the question. I work afternoons."

Late night calls, like they used to have, back when they would share their hopes and dreams with one another.

"I will see you then," Catherine finally said, and if Brody had wanted to see her expression when she hung up, he would have been even more disappointed than he was with himself. She exited the car without so much as a 'goodbye' to him, and he watched as she moved with the same grace and ease that had always enthralled him all the way to her door. No looks over her shoulder, no wave, she simply entered and shut the door.

Shutting him out.

He knew he deserved it; he'd shut her out for years. And what for? To force her to follow a dream that she'd laid aside to work with a richer clientele base.

Silently, he drove putting distance between them, his breath labored. It wasn't until he made it home, entered his own empty, lonely house, that he realized that tears were on his face.

"Fuck," he muttered as he pulled his coat off and tossed it aside. He swept his hand across his face and shook the wetness to the ground.

He had no one to blame but himself.

CHAPTER 17

Unspoken Words

Catherine waited until the door was closed, until she was free from being under Brody's penetrating gaze before she let her tears fall. Over the shock, the denial that he'd admitted the reason that he'd broken her heart was to force her to follow her own path, the anger behind her tears was sudden, all-consuming.

How dare he?

It wasn't his place to make this decision for her. She could have easily gone to school after a year off, on the road with him. But no, he hadn't wanted her there.

As the night wore on and her anger waned, she began to wonder if maybe… maybe this meant that he was ready to accept her into his life as she was now. This would spark her anger all over again, fresh waves of tears over years lost, years they could never get back. Out of tissues, she found an old t-shirt of his and tore it into small rags, using those for her comfort, then crying anew that she'd never wear that shirt of his to bed again.

"Fuck this," she said, muttering a curse that rarely left her lips. Early morning light was beginning to peak into her windows, and she cursed aloud again, knowing she'd had a sleepless night and was going to be a wreck for her classes that afternoon. Maybe she could get another instructor to take over, feign illness.

Would she really be feigning?

Her heart ached in her chest and she wondered if maybe, just maybe she should call him, give him a piece of her mind, but she was too tired and distraught to bother. Instead, when she picked up her phone and saw the question marks and winky face from Jen, she shot her a message.

Max lied to you. Had Brody drive me home.

She tossed her phone aside and began to make a pot of coffee, remembering how she'd teased Brody over it when they were younger. Stupid boy with his stupid moral compass being stupid and hurting her the way he did. She hoped the guilt was crushing him.

No, she didn't. She couldn't bear the thought of him hurting.

In the next breath, anger renewed, she decided that hurt would be the best thing for him. She hoped he'd found himself bereft and crying, too, although she couldn't see it.

Yes, she could. She'd been witness to him breaking under the weight of all the bullshit he'd been dealt with as a child.

"Shit." She brushed her new tears away and picked up her phone, more question marks from Jen. She typed back that she couldn't talk about it right then, and that was the absolute truth. Even a cup of coffee later, she was brushing away new tears and scowling at her swollen eyelids in the bathroom mirror. She looked like hell.

Jen's face when Catherine answered the door showed that yes, she indeed looked as bad as she had assessed. "What did that asshole do to you?"

Catherine shrugged, her bottom lip trembling. "He told me the truth."

"It better be that he has a wasting disease, or he's going to be short his testicles." Jen guided Catherine into the living room where she sat curled up in her chair.

"He didn't want me to go with him."

"Go? Go where?" Jen asked. "Hold that thought, I'm getting a cup of coffee, too. Refill?"

"Please." Catherine handed Jen her empty cup and pulled her knees up to her chin, her arms wrapped around her legs. "I hate him. No... no, I wish I hated him."

"Let me do all the hating."

Catherine sniffled. "Deal."

"Okay, now..." Jen returned with their coffees and handed Catherine's back to her before she sat on the couch. "What did that asshole say?"

"I'd wanted to take a year off college and go with him, on the road. And he'd decided on his own to break up with me instead." Catherine shrugged and wiped her tears away. "So maybe I didn't state that I would eventually go to college, but I would have. I just wanted time with him, and he wasn't going. So..."

"So he forced you to go instead," Jen finished for her, and she nodded.

"It sounds stupid."

"It is stupid."

"But I didn't press him for any details, because why? Five years later and now he decides to do this."

"What did you say to him after he told you?"

"Nothing," Catherine replied. "I answered a call from Damien instead. And I confirmed our plans for this Saturday."

"Plans, what plans?"

"He's flying in, taking me to dinner."

Jen's mouth was opened to reply, but she waited for a beat before she did. "Damien. As in my cousin's guitarist. Flying in for dinner?"

"Yes." Catherine wiped more tears away. "So I've got to get over this whole asshole opening up old wounds and,"

"It's okay to be sad. You don't need to just get over it, Catherine, it changed your life."

"Yeah," Catherine sniffled, "it did." She'd gone ahead to college, getting her degrees in business and teaching so that she could be a dance instructor. But instead of going back to Maxine, she'd followed Brad's advice and stayed at the studio in Easton where she'd done her student teaching.

Where she wasn't nearly as happy as she'd been back in high school, even when she was only cleaning up and assisting a little with form.

"So, what are you going to do now?"

Catherine nibbled on the inside of her lip as she looked at her best friend through tear-soaked lashes. "Take today off."

"Smart move. You look like shit."

"Thanks."

"And then what?"

Catherine inhaled sharply as she thought of her upcoming date with Damien.

And she thought of the unspoken words between her and Brody.

"I don't know, Jen. I honestly don't know."

Friday had snuck up on Brody before he'd known it, and he walked around his house with nervous energy. He hadn't heard from Catherine, nor had he reached out to speak to her. That day, he had other things on his mind.

Tyler and Sammi were coming for the weekend.

Frank had promised they'd be there by 7 PM, already having dinner, and he'd have them until 5 PM on Sunday. It was more than he'd expected, and he was ready for them.

Or was he?

He did another check of their rooms, of his food supply, of the games he had for the systems that he'd set up in the living room. Everything was in order, down to his camera equipment being securely locked up. Still, he found himself on edge as Frank pulled into his driveway behind his Jeep. Maybe it was Frank himself, the memories of all he'd put Brody through, that had Brody's heart pounding in his chest when he opened the door.

"Brody," Frank said as he walked past and entered the living room. Tyler and Sammi were all smiles, so grown from the last time he'd been the one in charge of their care.

That day when the tornado had touched down not far from where he lived now.

Brody remembered himself at their ages, how he only smiled that way when he'd been far away from Frank. He hadn't even had a cellphone the way each of them did until he was working and had purchased one for himself, only to have it be taken away before they headed for the house on the hill. His brother and sister were a far cry from how he'd been.

He was almost envious of them.

"Mind your brother," Frank was saying. "Do what he tells you to."

"Yes, sir," was Tyler's response without missing a beat.

"Okay, Dad," was Sammi's. "Wow, this is my room?"

Brody smiled at her. "Yep."

"You certainly have things in order," Frank's voice came from behind him as he surveyed the kids' rooms.

"I try to." Brody couldn't stop the tightness in his throat, perhaps from the memories of all the times that Frank's hand had been there.

Like when he shoved Brody's head into the mirror in Catherine's gym.

"They're good kids," Frank continued as he walked slowly back towards the living room.

"They always have been."

"You weren't so bad yourself."

"Funny, you never gave me that impression." Brody couldn't stop himself from making the comment. Frank only nodded as he continued on to the dining room and kitchen area.

"No alcohol?"

"None where they can get to it," Brody replied, gesturing with his head towards the locked liquor cabinet that he'd purchased just for this.

Just so Frank wouldn't have a reason to take them from him.

And Brody knew as he showed Frank out the door that once the kids were with him on a permanent basis, that would be the first thing Frank would try to do—take them.

"Can my friends come over and see this?" Tyler asked with pure glee in his face when he surveyed the gaming setup in the living room.

"I was thinking it would just be us tonight," Brody replied.

"Yeah, cool."

"Hey, Ty."

"Yeah?"

Brody paused as he surveyed his brother's tall form, his shoulders up and squared. "Is everything okay at home?"

"Yeah, yeah, it's great."

Once upon a time that had been Brody's answer, but he'd never looked as confident as Tyler looked now. Maybe Frank was going through one of his good phases, the ones where he showered the children with affection and gifts.

"Why?" Tyler asked, and Brody shrugged.

"Just checking."

Just checking because he wanted so badly for them to want to be with him full-time, not just an off weekend here and there. He needed to know that they were in a loving, safe environment always, not just when Frank was in a good mood.

"I have room to have friends over!" Sammi exclaimed, and Brody smiled as Tyler told her that it would be just them that evening. "Dad doesn't like a lot of people coming over," she added.

Of course he didn't.

Either they could see the truth, or they knew the noise would set him off; that had always been Frank's way. That was why most of Brody's time when he wasn't taking care of the kids had been spent with Max, or with Max, Brian, and JJ at Nan's.

"Can we play?" Tyler asked, gesturing towards the console.

"Of course," Brody replied with an easy smile, his heart warm as he watched them start their game, the same one he'd taught them how to play when they'd been far too young to. This version was newer, of course, but the nostalgia still lingered back to that last summer with them, when they'd had the Xbox from Catherine and they'd take turns playing, Brody teaching them the ins and outs and Max teaching them how to get to the cheats.

Max would probably fall over if he could see them now, practically grown, laughing at each other in Brody's living room, and his heart ached as his thoughts returned to Catherine, that summer afternoon where she sat on his lap trying to help him find his birth father.

Neither of those situations had ended well.

"Is Catherine coming over?" Sammi asked. "Penny's mom said she's not getting married, but I want to see if we'll still go shopping."

"Dad would kill you," Tyler commented with a laugh.

"Yeah, probably." Sammi's voice wasn't full of fear, but instead amusement.

How different their lives were from his.

"I see more controllers," Tyler said to him. "You've always been the best at this game. I want to see if I can beat you."

"Without Max's cheats?" Brody teased as he walked up and chose his controller.

"Will we see him this weekend, too?" Sammi asked excitedly.

"Yeah, probably," Brody answered. All he had to do was call, and Max would be there, swearing that Emily was grating his nerves with her point-blank statements calling him out on everything.

"Let's see who's the best at this now," Tyler challenged, and Brody smiled. Maybe he'd hold off on his talk with them, let them have one night of fun before he dropped his question on them, asking them to choose between Frank and him.

"Game on."

CHAPTER 18

Clear

Catherine stood before her full-length mirror in jeans and a cute top thinking to herself of the night Sammi had crashed into her with her full glass of cherry Kool-Aid. She'd never imagined herself the slightest bit interested in Brody, thinking incorrectly, irresponsibly, that he was beneath her.

How could she have been so wrong... so wrong about everything?

She'd been sure that he had wanted to move on, to see other girls, that perhaps he'd already found someone. Instead, she now knew the truth.

He hadn't wanted her to give up her dream.

"Fuck," she muttered as she swiped at an imagined smudge of makeup beneath her eye. Here she was getting ready for a date with a musician, one who was flying in from Cleveland to take her to dinner. "I don't even know how to dress for this." She walked into her bedroom and sat on the edge of her bed in a huff.

She hated surprises.

She hated how surprised she'd been at Brody's admission.

She hated that she hadn't said a word to him since then.

Her phone laid on her dresser, silent. Brody hadn't reached out to her, either, not that Catherine could blame him; he'd left the door open for her.

Or had he? Was he just clearing his conscience, or was he opening that door?

It didn't matter, though, she reminded herself as she took one last look in the mirror. She was ready for her date that wouldn't be in the state for several hours. Why she'd gotten ready so early, she couldn't know. But her restlessness was getting the best of her, and she began to pace.

"What am I doing? No, I know what I'm doing. I'm going on a date with someone who is interested in me and spoke up about it, that's what I'm doing. Is Damien interested in me? Or does he think he's going to get some, because that's not happening. I shaved my legs because I always do. I did my hair and my makeup like this because I like it. I'm doing this for me." She paused her rant-filled pace to glance at her phone, which was now buzzing on her dresser.

Damien.

"Hello," she said in the friendliest voice she could conjure. "Everything still in place?"

"Yep," he replied, his voice stronger, more confident. "Just waiting to board the connecting flight."

The connecting flight which would bring him closer, which would have him picking up his rented vehicle and using his GPS on his phone to find the restaurant she'd picked to meet at, because she was not going to give him her address just yet.

"That's good. More adoring fans at this airport?"

She heard him laugh softly. "Nah, it's not as crazy as it is when Jase is around. His face is out there more."

"It's still weird hearing him called that."

"It's his choice, though."

"Yeah," she said slowly. "It is. Thank you for reminding me; I'll be more careful next time."

"I didn't say it to offend you."

"No, no," she said with a wave of her hand. "You're right; he's chosen to be called Jase, and we should respect that."

"It's what his brother called him. Michael, I mean. Pete does, too, but it was more about Michael." Michael, who Catherine knew had passed away not long after Brian.

"I was the newbie," she replied. "I only met J... Jase the summer before he moved away. Jen is my best friend."

"Ah, his cousin. I figured you met him through your ex."

"Him, too." Catherine's voice was soft when she'd said this. "But the parties at Nan's were really where I got to know him."

"And you're the only one who can beat her at beer pong."

"Yeah, that's something for my resume." Catherine smiled at the memories of that summer so long ago.

It seemed like a lifetime to her.

It was a different life, though, one that had revolved around Brody and whatever she could do to help him, his mood, his life's direction, and...

And she had started to lose herself in his world.

Only when she joined the Valley High cheerleading squad did she feel she had something of her own again.

"You still with me?" Damien asked.

"Oh, yeah, yeah... I'm... Okay, no. I missed what you said last," she admitted.

"My phone's about to die. I need to find a place to charge it. I'll let you know when I'm in the air and on the way."

Again, she was smiling. "Sounds good."

As she said her goodbyes, she knew she was only bound to wear a hole in her carpet from all of her pacing, bound to let her racing thoughts get the best of her, so she grabbed her keys, phone, and her purse.

Maybe a drive around town would help to clear her head.

"So… um, I just wanted to talk to you two for a little bit." Brody sat on the coffee table facing Tyler and Sammi, who were on the couch, wide-eyed. "No, you didn't do anything wrong, so no worrying, okay?" He watched them both relax, although Tyler was looking at him with wariness.

"What's this about?" Tyler asked.

"Here." Brody gestured around him. "This place. I want to know what you think."

"Are you kidding?" Sammi asked. "This is great! And you're sure I can have Tina spend the night next time?"

"I promise," Brody replied with a grin, then turned his attention to Tyler. "Ty?"

"What's the catch?" Tyler asked. "There has to be one."

"None. Not exactly, anyway."

"What's that supposed to mean?" Tyler seemed to be full of questions, of suspicion.

"It means…" Brody's voice trailed off and he sighed. "I like having you here. I… I just want to know if you like being here is all."

"Yeah," Sammi said quickly.

"We've been here less than 24 hours," Tyler pointed out.

"I just... Here's the thing." Brody leaned forward, his elbows on his knees. "I'd like to have you here permanently. I won't do or say anything if you don't want to be," he added quickly, noting the shock in both of their faces.

"But you're gone all the time," Sammi said softly.

"Not all of the time. I'm here now, aren't I?"

"What would you have to give up?" Tyler asked. "Jobs? Would you be able to keep us here and still work?"

"Yeah, I'll just..." Have to take local jobs. Lose a lot of money. Have sitters lined up for the big jobs that he couldn't say no to. "...work it out."

In Brody's mind, he couldn't imagine anything other than glee, joy of the three of them being back together, all living under the same roof. He'd never thought of tears in Sammi's eyes or Tyler's glare, full of skepticism.

"What about Dad?" Sammi asked, and Brody's heart constricted. For all that she'd seen, she still loved her father.

"You can see him whenever you want."

"Yeah, but..." Sammi blinked a few times before wiping her eyes. "He doesn't want us?"

"No, that's not what this is."

"Sure seems like it," Tyler interjected.

"He doesn't know," Brody said as he sat up straighter. "I didn't say anything to him because I wanted to talk to the two of you first. If this isn't something you want, that's okay. I'll understand."

But he couldn't understand, no matter how he tried to wrap his head around the concept. How could they want to stay with a man they'd watch beat their big brother? A man whose temper could turn on a dime?

"So, what, you're bribing us?" Tyler asked. "With bedrooms done how we would like and promises and video games?"

"I'm not trying to bribe you," Brody promised. "This is how it always was, right? I'd just be end game, the one you answer to instead of him."

"But you went away," Sammi said slowly, "because you were acting just like him. That's what they said. And Dad, he's been really good."

"Strict, but good."

A muscle in Brody's jaw twitched at the word 'strict,' but he refrained from asking for further definition or examples.

He could only imagine the fear they must be living in.

"He really is great right now," Tyler added. "We have to do chores to earn video time, but it's good."

"I'm learning how to cook," Sammi said proudly. "Can you cook yet?"

Cook... well, that wasn't one of Brody's specialties, but he could get by. Could he teach them how?

"I'm learning how to do stuff around the house," Tyler added. "It's cool. I like it."

Of course Frank could teach him those kinds of things; he worked in construction, and had for years, aside from the time he'd bribed his way into Theresa's father's company. Could Brody do work around the house? Well... minimal things. He knew when to call an expert.

Someone like Frank.

"What if we think about it?" Sammi asked quickly, possibly honing in on Brody's defeated expression.

"Yeah," he agreed with a smile. "Think about it, but have some fun."

"Do you want me to cook tonight?" Sammi asked. "I just need adult supervision; I can do the rest."

Brody smiled and mussed her hair. "Yeah, I'd like that."

"Can we look at some of your pictures?" Tyler asked, and Brody blinked a couple of times in surprise. He didn't think that was something they'd be interested in.

"Yeah, of course. I'll get the laptop. They're all backed up," he added as he stood, "so don't worry if you click on something wrong, or if the laptop decides to take a dump."

They were on that laptop still an hour later as Brody busied himself around the house in between answering questions. The last thing he wanted to do was hover, especially when he'd asked them to take on a weight that children their age shouldn't have to—choosing who they wanted to live with. He wished he hadn't fucked up so royally with Catherine, because he wanted nothing more at that moment than to talk to her, tell her everything that had transpired, ask her opinion on their reactions and what he should do next.

Mostly, he just missed her.

"Is that Catherine?" Sammi asked, and he shrugged.

"It may be; I took a few pictures of her." At her surprise engagement party, the one he'd crashed from the sidelines. He exhaled as he remembered how beautiful she'd looked, not just that night, but the night of JJ's show, when he'd dropped her off at her apartment.

"It is!"

"What?" Brody was genuinely confused by Sammi's excited reaction until there was a soft knock at the door.

He knew her knock from anywhere.

He was closest to the door, and his hand was twitching as he reached for the knob.

It was Saturday.

She had her date with Damien that night.

And when he opened the door, all words failed him as he drank in her mere presence.

Her tone was light, casual, but her words held his heart in a vice grip.

"We need to talk."

CHAPTER 19

A Few Minutes

"I'm not sure why I came this way," Catherine said as she stood in Brody's doorway. "But I ended up here at your home, and I need... we just need to talk."

"Sure," he finally said, and she couldn't tell if she was frightened or relieved. Her heart was pounding an uncomfortable rhythm as she entered his home, as the children who were now taller than her came to greet her.

"I'm 5'4 and a half," Sammi said proudly, over an inch taller than Catherine who could still see the lost little girl who'd showed up at her house on the hill over 5 years before. Tyler, who she knew would be tall like his father, nearly towered over her at almost Brody's height. She hugged them both, her smile genuine as she heard of their time with their brother.

"Do you still play?" Tyler asked, gesturing towards the controllers, and Catherine shook her head.

"Not really," she admitted. "Not anymore."

Not since she'd given up her Queen C username, abandoned everything that reminded her of her time with Brody. With that thought, she turned back to Brody, watching the pride in his face as the kids began naming their accomplishments, from Sammi's dancing to Tyler's excelling in academics.

Brody truly cared for them, about them.

He'd gone to great lengths to bring them back into his life.

It was one of the million things she could think about that equally warmed and devastated her.

Why couldn't he have gone through those lengths for her?

"I can't stay long," Catherine began, then stopped as she saw the laptop on the coffee table, opened, revealing pictures of her.

Pictures from the surprise engagement party, the day when Brad had literally popped the question on one knee in front of everyone.

She paused, her eyes wide as her glance went from the laptop, to Brody's guilty expression, and to the laptop again. "You took these?" Catherine couldn't hide the disbelief from her voice, and she didn't miss Brody's sharp intake of breath.

"Could you two give us a few minutes?" Brody said to the kids, who agreed to go outside rather than to their rooms, but not without giving Catherine warm hugs on their way out. She returned each sweet embrace, her heart aching as they walked outside and she turned to Brody. "I can,"

"What, explain?" Catherine snapped. "Please do."

"I saw you and Jen turn into the parking lot and I followed."

"And instead of letting me know you were there, you, what? Hid in the shadows and took creepy pictures without my consent?"

"There's nothing creepy about them."

Catherine crossed her arms and her eyebrow jumped. "Is that so?"

"The pictures themselves. I would have given them to you."

"When? When you decided to come clean about stalking me?"

Brody sighed. "I wasn't stalking you, Catherine."

"Really? Because these photos say otherwise."

"I didn't know what else to do." He shrugged, his eyes tired and sad. "So I stood there and watched this guy propose to you, slip a ring on your finger, and I took pictures of it. It was wrong, and I'm sorry."

"What about the rest of it?"

"What rest of it?"

She crossed her arms, her hands balled into fists. "The rest of it. You know, where you dumped me, ghosted me for years. Are you sorry about that, too?"

Brody lowered his head for a moment before meeting her eyes. "More sorry than you know."

Was that the answer she'd been hoping for? She couldn't tell. All she could feel was pain ripping through her heart.

"It was my decision to make, Brody. Mine. And all you had to say was 'no.' All you had to do was talk to me, but instead you shut me out." She took a step closer, her arms uncrossed, her hands clenched into fists at her side. "For years you acted like I didn't exist, and then... what? You see me and decide to take pictures without saying hello, or even better, asking permission."

"You hate surprises."

"I hate surprises?! Is that the best you can do? Why did you shut me out?"

"I had to."

"I asked why, pay attention."

She watched intently as Brody licked his lips, his eyes shining with unshed tears. Part of her wanted to reach out, take his hand, tell him she loved him and always had, even when she had given up all hope of him coming back. The other part of her longed to strike out at him, hurt him in the way he'd hurt her.

She couldn't do either.

Instead, she stood her ground, the dripping of the faucet the only sound in the room. She tilted her chin up as he replied.

"If I heard from you, if I saw you, you wouldn't be where you are now. You wouldn't have your degree, you wouldn't be a dance instructor, you,"

"Oh, how the hell would you know that? Huh? How do you know that I wouldn't have gone on to college if you had just talked to me?"

"Because I would have taken you with me and never looked back."

His admission stole her breath and a rush of tears filled her eyes. "You bastard."

Somehow, even though Brody had expected her anger, her reaction still caught him off guard. Or maybe it was her use of one word that Frank had rammed down his throat for years. He felt his own flash of anger, one that he'd worked years on to keep at bay.

"You... you ripped my heart out because you couldn't deal with the ramifications of hurting me?"

"That's not it."

"No, that is it, Brody. You were too much of a coward to face me after what you'd done. So instead of following your heart, you listened to the side of you,"

"That didn't want to hurt you," he cut her off. "You don't understand what I've been through, what I've had to learn. Hell, what I've had to unlearn. I had to be whole again, or maybe for the first time. I just..." He ran his hands through his hair, his eyes on the carpet as he began to pace back and forth, back and forth. "It was bad enough to be raised by Frank, to be nurtured, or... or not really nurtured in an environment when I was treated like shit. And then I find that my birth father is a real piece of work, a misogynistic asshole who thinks women are good for the bed and the kitchen, and that's it. Then... *then* I figure out I can't control this bullshit temper that I have, and it takes years... *years*, Cat, and I don't even know if I have a handle on it or not. That article?" He stopped and faced her, his breathing shallow and rapid. "That article was all true, all of it. I've been a total asshole and you deserve better than that."

The silence spread out between them and his heart splintered as he watched a tear drop down her cheek.

"You shut me out," she said slowly through clenched teeth, "because of your temper? Because of the same temper that I lived with all those months that we were together? Do you not remember the horrible bitch from hell that I was when we first met?"

"You deserve better," he repeated as he took one small step in her direction. "And if it isn't Brad, then maybe it's Damien. Just be careful with him, please, because you're not... you're not some conquest, okay? Don't let him treat you like one."

He caught her wrist before she could strike him, and they stood there motionless, his hand wrapped around her tiny wrist, both of them breathing shallowly.

"I wish I could hate you," she finally said between tears. "God, I wish I could. That would make my life much simpler now."

"If it would help, I'm not a big fan of myself." He slowly released his grip and pulled away, resisting the urge to take her into his arms.

"You need to be. You'll never achieve your goals if you don't believe you can reach them."

"Why aren't you working with Maxine?"

"This isn't about that, or about me." Catherine brushed her tears off her face. "This is about you not believing that you could be with me."

"I don't deserve you."

"You know what? You're right. You don't. You ripped my heart into a million pieces and left them to carry off in the wind. You changed your number. You deactivated your Facebook. You never responded to a single email that I sent, so either you blocked me, or you got a new one. You don't even deserve me standing here telling you how much I wish I didn't love you."

"You what?"

Her eyes grew wide as she seemed to only realize what she'd said at that moment.

"Cat…"

"Don't call me that," she snapped as she took a step back.

"You moved on."

"You left me no choice."

"I never did."

"What do you call Nora?"

He couldn't help but let out one soft laugh. "I said 'no, uh.' There's no Nora, I told you. There's no one. I couldn't." Almost as much as he couldn't believe he was actually saying this to her. "I came back here for the kids. I knew you'd moved on. I asked about you, I heard. I also know you never asked around about me."

"Why the hell would I? And you asked about me? Not to me, but about me?"

"I know I don't have the right to ask for forgiveness,"

"Damn straight you don't."

"But I'm going to anyway. Can we just... can we be friends? At least?"

This time it was Catherine who let out one short laugh, and not the least bit friendly. "Friends. You... fuck, I can't believe I'm ruining my makeup over this."

"There's Lady Cath-er-ine." He said this with a sad smile, one that showed his regret.

"You haven't seen the half of it." She stood taller, her chin up in defiance. "They all loved me, you know that? Even after you left me, they still loved me. They loved me even though you told me that you didn't anymore."

He reached out and took her hand in his, holding it tightly so she couldn't pull away, his next two words holding more meaning than he could convey. "I lied."

He watched another tear fall down her cheek. "Why?"

Unable to resist anymore, he reached out and caught the tear with his thumb, brushing it away. "I had to," he said, his hand lingering on the side of her face before reaching back into her soft hair. "I had to," he repeated as finally... *finally* he lowered his lips to hers.

CHAPTER 20

Shockwave

Catherine was unprepared for the shockwave that went through her when Brody's lips lightly touched hers. He was leaving soft, gentle kisses on her lips that she responded to a little more each time, and with a sigh she surrendered to him, opening up, their tongues touching gently, his nips on her lower lip making her tremble.

This is what it should be like.

Gentle, sweet, no rush as they tasted each other, reacquainting themselves with curves and valleys, muscles and softness. When her fingertips touched his cheeks, it was his turn to sigh. And when he gathered her into his arms, lifting her with ease, she wrapped her legs around his waist.

"Oh," she breathed against his lips.

"Cat," he whispered in return, his gentle nibbles drawing tiny moans and sighs from her as he explored her neck.

And they were moving.

He was walking with her in his arms, their kisses never stopping as she heard the rattle of a doorknob.

He's taking me to his room, she thought.

I shouldn't do this.

But I want to.

Her mind was warring even as her body surrendered to his touch, his fingertips roaming her body as she felt the softness beneath her.

His bed.

He paused then, holding himself up on his arms as he gazed down upon her, his eyes full of emotion more than the lust she was used to seeing in Brad's face.

Brad.

No… no, she and Brad were through.

She watched as Brody's eyes lowered, as he began to move away from her, dejected, and she couldn't bear it anymore. Reaching up, she grabbed fistfuls of his shirt and pulled her to him again, kissing him with all the passion, all the love that had been burning for him all this time.

With sure hands, they began to undress one another, each caress, each touch of skin a piece of heaven they'd been denied for far too long. His fingertips brushing over her body had her sighing, and her own touch on him drove them further, closer to where their bodies, their hearts longed to be. All of Catherine's senses became heightened, alive.

The soft cotton sheets beneath her bare body.

The smell of his bodywash.

The taste of his mint toothpaste.

The soft caress of his hands as he sought and found the places on her body that were most sensitive to his touch, his lips, his teeth, his tongue.

The love in her heart that she shared with him as she explored the planes and valleys of his body.

The grip of their clasps hands as they soared high, together.

The cry that tore from her throat as she found the sweet release she'd been missing without him.

His tender kisses dropping on her face afterward, and the smile they shared, the one that let her know he felt it, too.

He felt it, too.

"I love you, Cat," he whispered against her lips.

Love... that's what this was. And it made the world slip away, leaving only the two of them wrapped up in each other. The tears that left her eyes this time were ones of joy, ones of knowing they'd found their way back to one another.

This was real.

This was...

"Brody?" Three knocks on the door from his little sister interrupted them, and Brody let out a soft laugh.

"Yeah?"

"Is Catherine okay?"

This time it was Catherine's turn to laugh softly, a blush covering her entire body.

"She's fine, moppet," Brody replied.

"Why's the door locked?"

"We're busy." Brody was trying not to laugh as he said this, and Catherine ran her fingers through his tousled hair.

"Oh. Can I ride your bike?"

"You need a helmet."

"Okay," Sammi replied, and Catherine heard her footsteps fall away.

"I don't suppose now is the time to tell her I don't have a helmet."

"So 'do as I say, not as I do?' You're ready to raise them," Catherine teased, then sighed as he gathered her into his arms. They were silent for a stretch, only their breathing heard as they both slowly returned to normal.

"Was this too soon?" Brody asked, his voice tinged with worry.

Catherine contemplated his question for a moment. "I don't... I don't know, I don't think so. Why?"

"No, no." He kissed the top of her head. "I don't want to screw this up. I wasn't... I didn't think I'd ever get the chance to hold you again."

She smiled against his chest and left a kiss there. "I know."

"Catherine?"

"Hmm," she said sleepily.

"I think you're late for your date."

Her date with Damien. She laughed softly, sleepily. "I'm good where I'm at," she said before sleep took over.

Brody had always loved watching Catherine sleep, even in their earlier days when they'd been the bitterest of enemies. She looked peaceful, angelic. Back in the beginning when she'd passed out in his bed, he'd watched her, wondering if he would ever see her look at him with the serenity her features held while sleeping.

He knew what that felt like now.

He didn't want anything or anyone to stand in their way again.

He gently pushed her hair back as he vowed to himself that this was it—this was end game. He and Catherine were meant to be together. That must be why she'd come to him that day, because she knew it, too.

Or did she come for closure?

Was this her way of saying goodbye?

Her eyes were still closed when a smile began to form on her beautiful face. "You're watching me sleep, aren't you?"

He smiled in return. "Guilty as charged." He placed a soft kiss on the tip of her nose. "Cat?"

"Hmm?"

"Are you okay with this?"

Her eyelids fluttered open, and her gaze of love nearly took his breath away. "Of course I am. I wouldn't be here, like this, right now, if I wasn't sure."

Her reassurance lifted his heart out of the depths of insecurity. "Are you hungry? Sammi said she's going to make dinner."

"Really now? I'm intrigued."

"I don't know if I'm intrigued or worried."

"Her cooking can't be any worse than yours," Catherine teased, and he laughed.

"I'm going to agree with you on that one." He kissed the tip of her nose and moved out of bed, gathering his clothes as he went. "I'm going to take a quick shower. You game?"

"I'll follow." He watched as she crinkled up her nose in that way he'd always found endearing. "I have an apologetic text to send."

He nodded, saving his smile until he'd turned from her and was in the bathroom.

When they'd both emerged—showered, refreshed, rejuvenated—only Tyler was in the living room playing a video game. "Where's Sammi?" Brody asked, and Tyler shrugged.

"She took your bike to Tina's, I think."

"My... fuck." Brody said the curse softly, despite cursing freely in front of the kids when they were younger.

"I thought you told her no," Catherine commented, smiling as Brody offered to make some coffee. "Yes, please."

"Technically I said not without a helmet, which I don't have."

"I think that's why she was going to Tina's," Tyler offered, and Brody sighed with a grin of his own. She was a sly one.

"How long ago was that?"

"Whenever she asked you." Tyler shrugged again. "Don't know."

"She should be back by now," Brody said. "Do you have Tina's number?"

Tyler shook his head. "Delores does. Dad, too."

Of course they did, because they thought about things like that. "Okay, I'm going to call for that number. Go outside, see if you can find her. And if you do, tell her it's time to start making dinner."

"Yes, sir... Brody, I mean." Tyler paused his game and went outside as Brody finished putting the coffee grounds in the maker and turned it on.

"Will that get her in trouble, if you call for the number?" Catherine asked.

"Not sure." Brody frowned as he thought of how this could look, with him calling for a number he should already have. Sammi may not have thought that far, and he certainly didn't want her in trouble, but when Tyler came back in and announced he didn't see his sister, Brody bit the bullet and called anyway.

No answer.

He tried their cellphones and they didn't answer those, either, so he left a message with Delores asking for Tina's phone number. "She'd said she wanted to make dinner," he reminded Catherine.

"She may have just lost track of time. We were teenagers not too long ago."

It felt like a lifetime ago to him, but he agreed. "Hey, Ty, do you know where Tina lives?"

"Not really."

"I'll make dinner," Catherine offered, "and you two can round up our missing chef."

"You don't mind?" Brody asked her as he gathered her into his arms and gave her a kiss on top of her head.

"Not at all."

"You could call her cellphone," Tyler suggested, but when Brody attempted to call it, there was no answer. "Frank has a GPS deal thing; you can call him."

"I tried. No answer. C'mon, kiddo," Brody said to Tyler. "Let's go find your sister."

The walk around the plat showed nothing, no kids on bikes anywhere. Tyler guided him to the neighborhood where Sammi and her friends would play, but she was nowhere to be found.

"Maybe she went back to the house already," Tyler said.

"Let me check," Brody said, and he called Catherine's cell. "Hey, has she come home?"

"Not yet," Catherine replied. "Dinner is almost ready. Are you heading back?"

With a sigh, Brody glanced over at Tyler. "I need to find her."

"Maybe she went home," Tyler replied. "To our home."

"I need to check with Frank and Delores," Brody said to Catherine, making a sharp left turn towards their house before hanging up the phone. "Does she do this often?"

"Honest?" Tyler shrugged. "Yeah. Dad says she's a wanderer."

"We've checked the park already."

"Nah, not at the park. They go to some fort."

Brody could feel the blood drain from his face. "What fort? C'mon, Ty, it's getting dark out."

"Dude, relax. I don't go with her. I hang with my friends. I'm sure she's fine."

Neither Frank nor Delores were home, and neither were answering their phones as Brody headed back to the house to drop Tyler off. "I'm going to keep looking," he said to Catherine, even as Tyler laughed it off.

"She'll be back. She always comes back."

"It's not..." He stopped himself from saying that it wasn't safe, it wasn't okay. "I'll try her cell again."

This time it went straight to voicemail.

"I'm telling you," Tyler said as he sat down at the table, ready to dive into his spaghetti, "there's no reason to worry."

But that little voice in the back of Brody's mind—the one that had found his twin brother dead—was telling him differently.

CHAPTER 21

The Protector

Catherine felt lost as Brody left again in search of his sister. The sun was starting to set, and despite Tyler's insistence that Sammi did this all the time, she was beginning to worry as well. Perhaps it was because of Brody's mood affecting her.

Or perhaps it was the guilt she'd seen in Brody's face, the look that said that they shouldn't have gone back to his room, shouldn't have been making love as his sister took off on the bike.

The only text she had on her phone was one from Damien, a curt "ok" after her apology for not showing. Nothing yet from Brody, but he hadn't been gone too long, either.

"You mind if I play some more?" Tyler asked, gesturing towards the video game. "You could play with me."

"Yeah," she said with a smile. "Yeah, that's a good idea."

To pass the time while they waited for word.

Catherine had wanted to go with Brody, but he'd asked her to stay with Tyler, unwilling to not have an eye on him, too.

"Did you know?" Tyler asked her as he pulled up the game.

"Know what?"

"That he wanted us to come live with him." He handed her a controller and she sat down on the couch with it.

"He'd said something about it, yeah," she replied nonchalantly. "What do you think about that?"

"That I need to think about it."

Catherine paused for a moment, looking over at Tyler, whose eyes were on the game. "Is everything okay?"

"Yeah, yeah, everything's fine."

"With your dad, I mean," she clarified.

"He's been great. Sammi has always been a daddy's girl, even when he was being a dick. I don't know if she'd want to."

"And you?"

Tyler was quiet for a moment as he took out a couple of bad guys on screen. "I go where Sammi goes."

The protector.

Just like his big brother.

"And it's all good, you know? Dad's been great. He's got a good job. He's strict, but really he's been great. Just like Brody's been great. I think Dad got his shit together, too."

Catherine hid her shock over Tyler's cursing. Knowing his brother the way she did, she shouldn't have been shocked at his language. Still, though, she saw him as the frail boy who'd taken over her game room at that house on the hill, the one who'd never really opened up to her.

Just like she saw Sammi as the scared little girl searching for someone to give her the love and attention that she needed.

"Sammi's a lot like Brody," Tyler continued. "Brody used to sneak out of the house, go wandering. That's what Dad said."

Still, she was only… what, twelve? Thirteen? Catherine wasn't sure. But as the skies grew darker with still no word from Brody or anyone else, Catherine knew in her heart it was time to worry. She shot a quick text to Brody asking if he'd heard anything, and her phone began to ring.

"Sorry, Ty, I need to take this," she said as she exited the game. He shrugged and continued playing. "Hello?"

"Nothing," Brody said, causing an icy grip to take hold of her heart. "But Frank is about to meet me at the house. They were out. He'd figured they were safe with me, Cat. She should…"

"She's fine," Catherine tried to reassure him.

"Her phone's going straight to voicemail," Brody said as the headlights of his car shown in the house. Brody continued talking, even though he was just outside. "What if what I asked of her… what if she ran away?"

The line went dead as he walked in, his eyes conveying the unspoken message: don't say anything about that in front of Tyler. "Hey," she greeted Brody with a warm embrace and a soft kiss.

"Tyler, Frank is on his way here."

Tyler shrugged. "Do I need to get off here?"

Brody shook his head. "Just… if you know anything, please tell me."

"She does this all the time."

"For this long?"

"Sometimes longer. Dad has the GPS thing; he'll be able to find her with a quickness."

If her phone was in range.

If her phone was on.

Frank's demeanor when he entered Brody's home a short time later was guarded, his voice low and even as he spoke. "Her phone isn't on, but I have the coordinates of where it last pinged. I've checked with Tina's family, Debbie's, and even Destiny's. She was last seen at Tina's house, where she had gone, but Tina wasn't home. She's on your bike, I'm guessing, since hers is at home."

"Yes," Brody replied as he squeezed Catherine's hand.

"I should have warned you about her... tendencies," Frank said, his hand still gesturing in the air for a moment. "She's like you."

Catherine felt Brody stiffen. "What's that supposed to mean?"

"She's a dreamer. A wanderer. She would chase dragonflies if she could get away with it. She's currently grounded from her bike for disappearing like this. And if I'm not mistaken," he held his phone up, "she's gone to the exact place I told her not to go. Would you like to come with?"

"Yes, I would," Brody replied, then he turned to Catherine. "Can you stay here with Ty?"

"Dude, I'm old enough, I don't need a babysitter," Tyler spoke up.

"He just doesn't want me doing better than he does in the game," Catherine said with a smile. "I could go with you," she added softly, and Brody shook his head.

"I've got this."

Without another word, he left the house with Frank in search of his baby sister.

"The GPS says she's around the edge of the woods," Frank said. "Or that was the last place."

Brody nodded, his eyes out the side window as he searched, silently pleading for her to be riding around, on her way back already.

"Is there anything I should know?" Frank asked, and Brody stiffened. He wasn't ready to share his plans, not now.

"No," was all he said.

"I'm not angry with you, you know."

Brody's jaw clenched as he stopped himself from saying 'that's a first.' He kept his eyes on the passing scenery, hoping.

"She does this more often than I'd like to admit," Frank continued. The streetlights were now on, illuminating the darkened neighborhood. "It's part of the reason that I put the app on the kids' phones, the one where I can find them when I need to."

"And they don't mind you keeping tabs on them?"

"Not if they like having their devices," Frank said, and either he missed Brody's biting tone, or he was choosing to ignore it. "They're great kids, don't give me much trouble. Well, other than times like this." He chuckled softly. "I know they're with you this weekend, and your rules are your own. Just go easy on her."

Go easy? The man who'd shoved Brody's head into a mirror was asking him to go easy? It was so hard right at that moment to keep from screaming at the top of his lungs that he was nothing like Frank, so no one needed to worry about Sammi in that way. Go easy on her... he scoffed as the words went through his head again.

"What was that for?" Frank asked, and Brody didn't take his eyes off his surroundings to answer.

"You already know."

"Listen, son,"

"Turn here," Brody said abruptly, interrupting whatever Frank was going to say to him. He saw a couple of kids riding bikes, but they were too far away, and it was dark. When Frank pulled up to another stop sign, Brody got out of the car and ran in the riders' direction. "Hey! HEY!"

One of them was his bike. He'd know it anywhere.

But it wasn't Sammi riding it.

Instead, it was a teenage boy asking Brody what the fuck he was doing yanking on the handlebars that way.

Brody kept his grip firm, his expression angry. "Where did you get this bike?"

"Dude, this is my,"

"It's *mine*, now where the fuck did you get it?" Brody demanded. "And where's my sister? Where the fuck is my sister?"

"Dude, I don't know what you're talking about."

"This is my bike and she was on it and she's... where is she?"

The teenager began to stammer. "I... I don't know nothin' about no girl, okay? I found the bike."

"Where?" Brody shouted.

"Over there."

The boy pointed towards the woods.

"It was just up there, man, I swear. I just,"

"Get off the bike. Now."

"Dude, I don't know anything!"

"Brody." Frank had caught up to him.

"This is my bike," Brody said quickly, and he pushed it in Frank's direction. "Get it in the car. We need to go."

"Where?"

"The woods."

Frank muttered a curse. "Get the bike in the car; I'll be right there."

174

Brody didn't know why Frank insisted on staying there, getting the boy's name and number before returning to the car and driving down to a dead end street. Brody's heart kept pounding harder and faster with each passing moment.

The woods.

She went into the woods.

Or did she? He couldn't be certain, other than being told about the fort that Sammi and her friends would go to.

As soon as the car was parked, Brody was out of it like a shot, running up the hill towards the woods that separated Brentfield from the town he'd grown up in. He couldn't run fast enough, or keep his footing as well as he normally did. The ground was softened from the rainy week that they'd had, only making matters worse.

He pulled his phone out and turned the flashlight on, noting the tire tracks on the hill. He followed them up farther and farther to the edge of the woods where they stopped.

Where it looked like the bike had been laid down.

"Sammi?!" He was shouting, hoping for the sound of her voice to follow. "Sammi!"

There was a crunch beneath his foot, and he pulled back, shining his light down on the ground.

Her cellphone.

Broken.

Had he broken it, or had something happened to it before?

"Fuck... FUCK!" He dropped to his knees and carefully picked the phone up, examining it, noting how it wouldn't turn on.

Her calls had begun to go to voicemail long ago.

The battery must have died, or the phone had broken.

It was so long ago.

"What did you find?" Frank asked, and Brody held the phone up, his eyesight blurring as tears threatened. "Come with me."

"We have to find her."

"We are going to need help," Frank said as he pulled out his cell and dialed 911.

They needed to issue an Amber Alert, he said.

Sammi was missing.

CHAPTER 22

Just In Case

Catherine poured a cup of coffee for Brody as he greeted the officers at the door. "How quick can we make this?" she heard him ask. "I need to get back out there."

"We will make this as quick as possible. I'm Officer Warren, this is my partner, Officer Raines."

"Thank you," Brody murmured to Catherine, and she noted the slight shake in his hands as he took the cup from her.

"Delores is at the house, in case," Frank said as he entered without knocking—they were past that point that night. "Sorry I'm late, I just wanted to check one other place."

Catherine could feel bile creeping up in her throat and she excused herself from the dining room. She couldn't believe that this was happening. How could Sammi just go missing like this? Was she lost?

Was foul play involved?

The wave of nausea over the fear of it all had her retching as silently as she could, damning herself for eating at all at a time when who knows what was happening to that innocent little girl. With trembling hands, Catherine rinsed out her mouth and went in search of some mouthwash.

"No," she heard Brody say, "there was no way she was running away. She asked if she could take my bike and I said not without a helmet."

"But she took it anyway," Officer Warren said, and the sounds were muffled again as Catherine shut the door to Brody's bedroom, assuming correctly that his own bathroom was where she would find the mouthwash. She knew that the officers were being thorough, but a child was missing, a child who wouldn't run away. Of course the officers wouldn't know that without knowing Sammi first, but time was of the essence. It was dark, it was beginning to rain again, and Frank and Brody both wanted to get back out there and look for her.

So did Catherine.

And this time she wasn't going to let Brody tell her no. She needed to be with him just in case...

She couldn't finish her thought.

She walked back out to the dining room and stood behind Brody, her hands on his shoulders where she could feel the tension.

"But you didn't see her take the bike?"

"I know she did," Brody continued, "because Tyler told me."

"And where were you?"

She felt him stiffen. "I was back in the bedroom," he replied.

"We were talking," Catherine added before the officer could ask what they had been doing when Sammi left. She couldn't tell if his expression gave away that there was so much more than that going on, but she felt him stiffen at her words.

"What about earlier in the day? Was there anything she could have been upset over?"

Brody was silent for a moment, all eyes on him, the tension in the room so thick that Catherine could feel it weighing her down. "We had a talk earlier," Brody replied.

"Was she in some sort of trouble?"

"No." Brody inhaled sharply, then continued. "I asked her and her brother if they'd like to come live with me."

Out of the corner of her eye, she saw Frank stand. "You did what?"

"And what was her response?" Officer Warren asked.

"They said they'd think about it."

"Why would you... jeezus." Frank turned then, his hands in his hair as Brody continued on.

"They're my brother and sister, I wanted... *want* them to come stay with me."

"So that's what this was?" Frank asked angrily.

"Sir, I'm going to ask you to calm down now," Officer Raines spoke up. "Now is not the time."

Catherine squeezed Brody's shoulders only to feel a shock go through her as he shrugged her off. "She didn't seem upset when she asked to ride the bike."

"This is the bike that you saw another young man riding."

"Yes," Brody replied as Catherine walked into the kitchen. From her vantage point there, she could see the pained expression in Brody's face, see the unshed tears in his eyes. "We just need to get out there and find her."

"We already have a search party out there."

"But they're nobody she knows," Brody said with a shake of his head. "It's dark, and... and what if someone... fuck, what if someone..."

"We're not going to jump to any conclusions right now, okay? We're going to find her and get her to her home."

"My home," Frank said sharply. "Tyler, get your things."

"But, Dad, I want,"

"Now," Frank cut him off. "You can stay with Delores while we're looking for Samantha."

Catherine recognized that tone; he'd used it often with the children when they'd all lived in the house on the hill. Her stomach dipped uncomfortably, especially when she saw the anger flare up in Brody's eyes. *Not now* she thought. *Please not now.*

"Sir, I understand your frustration, but I'm going to have to ask you to remain calm," Officer Raines said to him.

"Calm?" Frank shot back. "My daughter is missing, their brother was conspiring to take them away from me, he was back in the bedroom with his girlfriend *talking* when she took off, and you want me to remain calm? I'm taking my son home and I'm going out there to find my daughter."

Tyler shot past Frank and went down the hall, the rustling of him gathering his things together heard above the notes that Officer Warren was jotting down. "I only have a few more questions," Officer Warren said softly.

Catherine watched a muscle in Brody's jaw twitch as he nodded. "Okay," he said.

"We have her picture, we have a description of what she was wearing. We know she's on foot now. How long from the time that she took the bike until you discovered that she was missing?"

"We didn't know she was missing until we found the bike," Brody tried to explain. "They said she likes to wander and kept telling me that she does this all the time."

"Okay, okay," Officer Warren said, his tone soft and kind. "She easily could have wandered and gotten lost in those woods. Let's go find your sister."

"I'm coming with you," Catherine said to Brody, expecting him to protest, ask her if she would stay at the house. Instead he nodded, his tear-filled eyes turning to her for the first time since the officers had shown up.

"Thank you."

The officers had asked one of Sammi's friends if they could show them where the 'fort' was that the girls would like to go hang out at. Unfortunately, with the week's rains, most of the trails were difficult to pass, and a couple of them had been washed out.

There were scores of people who had shown up with flashlights, hiking boots on, searching for the girl who loved to wander, who adored dragonflies, who just hours before had ridden her bike to the top of the hill and laid it down beside the woods. The calls of her name in all of its forms could be heard, almost like echoes, one after another.

"Sammi!"

"Samantha?"

"Sam!"

"Sammi, you're not in trouble," Brody called out. "Where are you?"

He held his flashlight on the treacherous ground as he and Catherine maneuvered their way down one embankment and up another while most people stayed on the trails themselves. More than once he'd had to help Catherine up the side of a hill, her grace failing her on the muddy ground.

"Are you okay?" he asked her, and Catherine nodded.

"Let's just find her," she said.

It was cold, wet, and dark, and all Brody could think of was Sammi being out there alone and scared.

The alternative was too frightening to fathom.

No moonlight was visible to guide them, so they relied on the flashlight in Brody's hand as they went through one ravine after another. It didn't matter to him that he'd been up almost 24 hours; he wasn't stopping until he found her.

All teams had been given whistles in case they found something, some clue, or better yet, Sammi herself. But as the night drug on, no sounds of whistles could be heard. Only the distant calls of her name ringing throughout the dense patch of trees.

"Samantha?"

"Sammi! Where are you?"

There was no sign of her at the fort or along the trails that could be reached leading to it. With warnings of the other trails being washed out, those were occupied by police and rescue workers to keep the harm to civilians at a minimum. One couple had to be taken to the hospital after falling, causing Brody's worry to ramp up all the more.

He thought of his sweet baby sister and the way she always smiled up at him, her grey eyes dancing with laughter more often than not.

All he wanted was to see that smile again.

He wanted to get her home where she would be warm and safe and dry, and he didn't even care at that point if it was his home or Frank's.

"Samantha?" Frank could be heard bellowing, and Brody turned away from the sound, stopping himself from screaming out at her father to stop sounding so angry, maybe it would scare her.

That anger should be directed at Brody himself.

It was his fault.

All his fault.

The intensity of the raindrops grew as grey morning light seeped through the trees. The sun was rising and she still hadn't been found.

"Brody?"

"Let's go this way," he said to Catherine, shining his light on a trail that had been ravaged and deemed nearly impassable.

"Are you sure?"

"Please." He turned to Catherine, seeing the worry in her eyes. "We'll be okay. Just follow my lead." When she nodded, they carefully began to maneuver the rain-soaked trail, mud sloshing beneath their feet.

The incline on either side of the trail was steep and riddled with rocks and fallen tree limbs. Their pace was slow, and Brody kept the flashlight on as the density of the woods thickened.

One step. Slip. Two steps. Grab a tree branch. One step further.

Slowly they walked the trail, looking down each embankment, Brody not knowing if he should pray that he find her here or that he didn't.

"Please," he whispered more than once.

"Sammi," he called out repeatedly. "Sammi, it's Brody. We're coming for you."

The sound of Catherine falling stopped him and he turned around, the flashlight showing on her rain-soaked form. Her face held pain, a pain that gripped his heart.

"Are you okay? Here," he held out his hand to her, expecting her to take it.

Instead, she handed him a shoe.

Sammi's shoe, caked in mud.

Yes!

No, no, no, no

"Sammi?" Brody screamed turning around in a circle, his flashlight reflecting off of something down the steep embankment, in the bottom of the ravine.

"Sammi!"

The sound of the whistle that Catherine was blowing drowned out his grunt as he slid most of the way down, mud covering his jeans as he stood slowly, turning his flashlight back towards where the light had reflected.

On a zipper.

A zipper on the opened coat of the slender form that lay twenty feet from him, face down.

In a puddle.

"No, no, no, Sammi!"

He ran to her as fast as he could collapsing to his knees as he turned her over.

And her grey eyes stared up at him.

Lifeless.

CHAPTER 23

Help Me

Catherine felt Brody's agony-filled bellow deep in the depths of her soul as she braved her way down the side of the hill, sliding down much as he had before her, barely missing a large boulder embedded in the ground. "Sammi," she whispered as she finally reached them, where Brody was wiping his baby sister's face.

"C'mon, baby girl," he said, laying her down. "C'mon." He turned to Catherine. "CPR. You know CPR, right?"

Catherine stood in shock, staring down into Sammi's lifeless eyes. "Brody," she began, but couldn't finish. The smell of earth, of rain, of metal was overwhelming.

Metal.

Blood.

She was suddenly queasy at the smell, the realization of what it was.

"Help me!"

"Brody," Catherine said, reaching for him, but he cut her off again.

"No! No, she... she can't. She can't die. She. Cannot. Die." He breathed into her mouth as Catherine knelt beside them, reaching for Sammi's hand. It was twisted up, as if she'd landed on it wrong.

She was cold.

So very cold.

"Brody, she's gone."

"No, come on sweet girl." His tears were dripping down as he caressed her unmoving face. "C'mon, moppet, don't die. Don't die."

But she was already gone, Catherine knew from the blue of her lips to the coldness of her touch.

There was no bringing Sammi back.

"You have so much to live for," he continued, his voice broken. "You have boyfriends that I'm going to hate, and school dances, and cheerleading. You have dancing, and gymnastics, and Tyler, and... and me."

Catherine moved to comfort him, but he shrugged her off as sobs wracked his body.

"Baby, please." Brody scooped her up, holding her against him. "C'mon, sweet girl, it's time to wake up for me. You can wake up for me, right?"

"Brody,"

"No!" He held Sammi tighter. "No, Sammi, no, no, no, no."

Catherine blew her whistle again as she heard voices coming nearer, but she couldn't take her eyes off this man whose whole world lay in his arms. Even as he roared to the heavens, she was picturing them years before in that house on the hill, Brody carrying his baby sister in his arms, telling her it was all going to be okay.

He couldn't promise her that today.

"Why?" His question punched through the air even as rescue workers showed, climbing down the ravine with much more skill. "Why her? Why not me? Take me! TAKE ME!"

"Sir, I need you to step away,"

"No!"

Catherine's own tears were falling as she watched Brody cling to his sister's body, brushing her hair back from her face, dropping kisses on her forehead that she'd never feel.

"Just come back to me, Sammi. Just come back."

"Samantha?"

Catherine's attention snapped to Frank, his shocked expression from the top of the hill. He dropped to his knees as behind her the rescue workers were trying to reason with a man so stricken with grief that he seemed unable to hear them.

"I'm so sorry, I'm so sorry. I'm sorry, I'm sorry, I'm sorry." He repeated the words over and over as he sobbed into Sammi's matted hair.

It took two strong officers to pull Brody back, his guttural howl of agony as his sister's body dropped to the ground unlike anything Catherine had ever heard before. Through his sobs, he turned his face to her.

"Why wouldn't you help me?" he demanded, dropping to his knees as the rescue workers said to call it.

Call her.

Dead.

"We need everyone to clear the area." That was Officer Warren, and Catherine noted his sad, tired eyes as he spoke.

"I'm not leaving. I'm not leaving," Brody repeated. He moved closer to Sammi, moving to pick her up, but was stopped by the officers.

"We need photographs."

Photographs.

Catherine thought she was sure to vomit, but nothing was in her stomach to come up, her own tears blurring her vision as Brody was restrained again.

"Please, let him be with her," she said to anyone who would listen.

But no one did.

"Was she like this when she was found?"

"No," Catherine answered for Brody. "She was face down, over there, in that puddle. I found her shoe at the top of the hill, where I tripped on a tree root."

"Can you show us?"

She glanced at Brody, wanting to go to him, wanting in some way to comfort him, but instead was guided by officers back up the hill, Brody's sobs echoing below.

"What made you come this way?" Officer Warren asked.

"Because nobody else was," Catherine replied with a sniffle, thanking a stranger who handed her a tissue before being led away. "Please let him be with her."

"He can't move the body."

The body.

Sammi was reduced to being 'the body.'

Catherine's eyes moved over the thinning crowd and came to rest upon Frank, who hadn't moved from his spot on the hill. He was ghost white and trembling, silent tears rolling down his cheeks, and she thought back to how he snapped at Sammi for having her Kool-Aid out of the kitchen.

That was a lifetime ago.

And now that little girl, so full of life, of hope, of promise, was gone.

She was 'the body.'

"I need to get back down there," she said. "Please, he needs me."

Officer Warren looked like he was going to deny her, but instead he nodded once, telling her to be careful as he and his partner looked around at the scene. As she made her way to the best path, one that was now clear with the grey filtered light, she heard Frank's murmurs.

"I have to bury another child. I can't... I just can't..."

But her heart was with Brody who knelt beside his sister, inconsolable.

"Baby girl, please. Let's just...let's do today over, okay?" He reached out a trembling hand but was again asked to not touch her. "Let's go back and I won't ask if you want to stay with me. And... and we'll play video games and dress up, and you can wear the red swooshie if you want to."

Catherine knelt beside Brody in the mud, the cold and dampness seeping through her jeans. "I'm so sorry," she whispered as she reached out and ran her fingers through his dripping wet hair. "I'm so sorry."

"You should have gone on your date," he snapped, and she recoiled from the harshness in his voice.

"What?"

"God, what have I done?" Brody cried. "What have I done?" He reached out, touching his baby sister's twisted hand, disregarding the commands to not touch her. "Sweet girl, what have I done?"

"Brody,"

"Leave," he snapped at her. "Just leave."

Brody couldn't bear the thought of life without his baby sister in it. In his mind over and over, he pleaded with a god he didn't know to switch them, to take him instead, but his prayers went unanswered. The coroner arrived, stating what they already knew, stating that he would need an autopsy to determine the cause of death.

They were going to cut his baby sister open on a cold metal table where she would be all alone.

"Please," he said to unhearing ears, "please don't hurt her anymore. She's..."

"She's gone, son," Officer Warren said to him, placing a hand on his shoulder. This time he didn't shake it off.

"You don't understand. She can't be. She... she has so much to live for, see? She's just a kid, and she still has growing up to do. She has... she has her whole life ahead of her, and she brings so much light to this world."

There were paramedics on the scene, ones with bags full of life saving equipment that wouldn't do any good for his Sammi.

She'd been gone for hours, they'd said.

This isn't happening, this isn't happening.

He couldn't turn away as they closed her eyes for the last time.

She'd been awake, probably aware.

What had happened to her before she landed in that puddle?

"It looks like she hit her head on this rock back here," he heard an officer say.

Click, click, click

More pictures.

Pictures.

His camera.

He never wanted to hear that click again.

"Son, is anyone with you?" Officer Warren was beside Brody again as two other men carefully placed Sammi in a black bag and began to zip it up.

"Wait!" He scrambled over in the muck and the mud to get closer. "Please..." He leaned over, kissing Sammi's forehead. "I don't know how to live without you."

He felt another hand on his shoulder, assuming it was the officer, until he heard Max's voice.

"It's going to be okay, alright?"

One last kiss.

And another.

And another.

"I failed you," Brody whispered. "And I'm so sorry."

"Brody," Max said softly, and Brody felt the squeeze on his shoulder. "You need to tell her goodbye."

The rush of tears, harder than before, broke forth, and he sobbed into his sister's shoulder. "Please forgive me. Please."

Max's arms were around him then, gently pulling him back. "Let's go, okay? Let them take care of her now."

"We will take good care of her," he heard a woman say. "Your father will be setting up arrangements."

Arrangements.

For a little girl who never even experienced high school or the pangs of first love.

"I have to let you go with them now," he whispered into an ear that would never listen to its favorite sounds again. One last kiss on her forehead, and he stood, supported by Max on one side and Emily on the other.

This isn't happening. This isn't happening. It's all a bad dream that you need to wake up from.

"I'm so sorry," Emily said as she gave him a hug.

Sorry.

He couldn't hug her back.

He needed to be alone.

He needed Sammi back.

The walk up the hill was slow, so slow, mechanical, one step, another, one slide, another step.

Why had she taken this trail?

Oh, right. It was the most direct to their fort.

Their fort that was 100 yards away in a clearing.

She'd been so close.

Passing Frank, he heard him say, "But I just got her back."

And I was going to take them, he thought. *I was going to take them and keep them safe.*

But he had failed.

And life would never be the same.

CHAPTER 24

Selfish

Catherine let herself into Brody's house—he'd kept it unlocked, just in case—and she busied herself cleaning up. She had to do something, *anything* to keep her mind off the horrors that she'd seen. She pulled up music on her phone to counter the silence that was screaming at her from every corner of the house that should have had two adolescents running around in it.

The first thing she had to do was shower and change, thankful for the bag she always carried with her even after her breakup with Brad. Washing away the mud couldn't get the image out of her mind.

Sammi.

Catherine had already run the dishwasher the night before, so once out of the shower and dressed, she washed the pots and pans, she did her best to put everything back where it was supposed to go. Brody would have enough on his plate without having to worry about a clean house, or about cooking, either.

After she made a quick list of things to buy to prepare a few dishes, she proceeded to the living room.

Not much was out of place there, aside from Brody's laptop. She took it back to his bedroom, pausing at the door to what was Sammi's room for a moment.

He shouldn't have to clean that up, either.

After she'd stripped and made Brody's bed, placing the sheets in the washer, she slowly made her way into Sammi's room and turned the light on. Her things were still strewn about, as if she'd changed clothes quickly and hadn't bothered to pick up after herself.

Now she never would again.

They wouldn't go shopping for dresses, which she'd intended to do despite the lack of upcoming wedding.

She wouldn't be there for her little sister, who was probably too young to understand why Sammi was never coming home.

Still, Catherine stood there, looking over the purple and the dragonflies and the small desk in the corner.

Her books were on it, still, where they'd remain untouched, homework undone, stories unfinished.

Her life cut short.

Catherine didn't realize she was crying until she walked over to the desk, its contents blurred through her tears. With the sadness, the disbelief she was feeling, she knew it would be a hundred times over worse for her brothers, her protectors.

How would Tyler react?

Did he even know yet?

She didn't want to turn on the television, to hear that the Amber Alert had been canceled, to hear the details that the reporters on the scene had been trying to get when she left, when she called Max to break the news and beg him to go to Brody.

He'd been so broken.

"What the hell are you doing?"

She jumped at the sound of Brody's voice, and the venom in the words, and she turned to face him in the doorway, covered in mud as she had been.

And blood.

Sammi's blood.

"I just want to help."

"I told you to go home, Catherine. This is not your home."

Ignoring his biting words, she said, "I was helping clean up around here, and,"

"Get the hell out of her room!" Brody roared, his hands clenched. "You... I don't want you here."

"Brody, I,"

"I was stupid and selfish, and it cost my sister her life," he continued, two large tears spilling down his face. "I can't look at you right now."

"Hey." Emily was suddenly beside him. "This was an accident, it's not Catherine's fault."

"No, it's mine," Brody said softly as he turned and walked towards his bedroom. "It's mine."

"Brody," Catherine began, but he cut her off.

"Get out of her room, and get the hell out of my head, out of my life."

He said this through tears, but with so much conviction that cut through Catherine's soul.

He blamed her.

He blamed her.

"Go!"

"Hey, man," Max stepped in, "go get cleaned up. We've got this here, okay?"

"Make her leave, Max," she heard Brody say as she pushed past him and quickly walked the hallway to the living room.

She hadn't known what to expect, but it wasn't this.

It wasn't the man she loved, the man she'd held only a few short hours ago, whispering promises of 'this time' and 'love' and 'together.'

"We're staying here with him," Emily said to her as she gathered her bag that she'd brought in, now with clothes in desperate need of washing.

"Good," was all Catherine could manage through her tears.

"Hey, look, I know you and I have never been on the best of terms, but he's dealing with a lot right now. We need to do what he needs. He'll come around."

But Catherine knew him, knew how deeply this man felt to the core of his soul.

"We'll see," she finally said, and she walked quickly out to her car, slamming her door shut with a curse, peeling out of the plat at too high a speed. Right at that moment, when she knew he needed her the most, he was shutting her out. Blaming her, blaming himself for what the authorities believed was nothing more than an accident.

An accident that took someone Brody loved more than life itself.

She made record time getting back to Millerstown, calling off work, making the phone call to her best friend, begging her to come over.

"Jen, please."

"Give me ten minutes. Just like JJ says, call in reinforcements. I'll be there before you know it."

Instead of holding Brody, letting him pour his grief into her, she laid with her head on Jen's lap and let her own grief over losing everything take hold.

Brody sat down on Sammi's bed and held her pillow close.

It still smelled like her.

With Max and Emily out in the living room making calls, finding out arrangements, he sat alone in this room feeling closer to her than he had when he'd been holding her lifeless body.

How could she be gone?

"Hey," Emily's voice broke into his thoughts, but he kept his eyes closed, inhaling deeply.

"Yeah?" His voice sounded weird, broken.

"They're meeting over at the funeral home at 3 to go over arrangements. Delores called Max and let him know."

No one had called him.

Why would they?

It was his fault that Sammi was gone.

"I can drive you over there, if you'd like to go. They still... well, the service probably won't be until later in the week, depending."

Depending on the autopsy, the outcome.

"Max is getting ready to make some food."

"I'm not hungry."

"Brody, you need to eat. You need to keep your strength up."

He didn't want to.

He didn't want to.

What had he done?

All because the woman he loved had stood before him, letting him kiss her, and all he'd wanted was to make her stay. He hadn't meant for it to go as far as it did, as quickly as it had. He just wanted her to know how much he loved her, and this was his payment.

His sister's life.

"So Max is cooking, and I'm going to give you your space. But you need to eat. And if you want to be at the funeral home, I'll take you."

Brody nodded once and heard her walk down the hall, leaving him alone in his sister's room. He'd been sure he had no more tears to cry, but still they came. One by one they hit his hands which held his sister's pillow to his chest.

Still, they couldn't take away the pain.

He wanted Catherine.

But how could he ever look at her without knowing what he'd done? Without knowing the last time he would ever hear Sammi's voice was when she asked a question through the locked door and he hadn't said a firm no? Why hadn't he just asked her to wait until he was back out in the living room, or just told her to stay close to home? Instead he'd made some comment about not without a helmet, and she'd gone anyway, possibly in search of one.

Now she was gone.

Brody declined food when it was finished, remaining on Sammi's bed that she'd only gotten to sleep in one night, its covers in disarray, her scent still on the pillow that he held in his arms.

"I'm so sorry, moppet," he whispered as he laid on his side. "I'm so sorry."

He couldn't go to the funeral home and face them all, knowing for certain they'd be looking at him with blame and contempt. He didn't know if he could ever face Tyler again, let alone the monster he'd wanted so desperately to protect them from. In the end, they hadn't needed protection from Frank; they'd needed it from him.

He'd never be able to forgive himself.

"Brody, it's time," Emily said, but he shook his head.

He wasn't going.

He didn't want to leave this room that he'd had decorated just for her, this room that she'd loved and couldn't wait to show to her friends.

"Hey." Emily knelt beside the bed. "I think you should go."

"I just need some sleep," he said, his eyes still closed, Sammi's lifeless eyes boring into his mind. He felt Emily's hand brush his hair back.

"Okay, I'll let Delores know."

Delores.

Not even their own mother.

Did she know she'd lost another child?

He brushed the question off as he turned, the pillow still wrapped up in his arms. What did it matter if Sandra knew? She'd given the children to her sister and never looked back, only visiting a handful of times. He hoped she did know, and that she was just as eaten up with guilt as he was.

If only she'd kept them.

Would Brody have gone back after he'd gotten out of the facility? Or would she have told him to stay away?

It didn't matter.

None of it did.

All that mattered was the world had lost an incredible soul that day, and all the wishing that the universe had taken him instead wouldn't change a thing.

CHAPTER 25

Making Lists

Catherine wasn't surprised when Brody failed to answer her calls or texts. She wanted so badly to be there for him, but with the overwhelming guilt that he felt, she knew that she was the last person he wanted to see. Still, she sent a simple *I love you* to his phone in hopes that he would read it, would know that he was on her mind.

Instead of being with Brody, she was in her own home with her best friend helping her gather ingredients and begin the task of making dinners that could be reheated.

"Okay, so you're out of garlic powder and paprika," Jen said. "I'm going to the store, so,"

"I have a list." Catherine sniffled as she pulled up the list on her phone. "I can send it to you."

"Are these going to Brody, or to Frank?"

Catherine looked over the list, adding garlic powder and paprika to it before forwarding it to Jen. "Both."

"Okay, I'm also going to pick up some disposable pans. That way you don't have to worry about dishes and such coming back."

Catherine nodded. "Thank you. And Jen?"

"Yeah?"

Catherine's lower lip trembled. "Can you hurry?"

"I will, I promise."

Once alone, Catherine busied herself with anything she could come up with to keep her mind from wandering, but still it did. She'd never seen a body before, never experienced the kind of grief that she knew Brody and his family were going through. It was difficult to think of much else, and she found herself making lists of what was to come

The visitation.

The funeral.

The entire community had rallied together in the short time that Sammi had been missing, and Catherine was sure there would be many attending.

Would she sit with Brody?

Would he sit with his family?

Did they blame him?

She had no way of knowing as she had no contact information for Frank or Delores. And what about Sandra? Did she know?

Did she care?

Her phone pinged with a message, and in hopes that it was Brody, she quickly looked. Instead, it was from Max.

Visitation Thursday from 7-9 and Friday from 10-noon. Funeral at noon. Dawson's on Main Street.

That was a long time to wait, but Catherine remembered the autopsy had to be performed, and they probably needed time to get family in from out of state.

Her aunt, Sandra's sister, who had raised the kids for five years while Sandra was out doing whatever she wanted, and Frank was...

What had Frank been doing? Getting his own shit together the way Brody had claimed he was doing?

Brody...

She shot a quick text back to Max, asking about Brody, about how he was doing.

He's not.

Oh, that hurt her heart.

I want to be there for him she sent back and wasn't surprised at his reply.

Now's not the best time.

But when would be?

She asked Max to convey her love, her condolences, her heart for her since he didn't want her there to tell him herself.

We won't leave him alone, I promise Max sent back.

"Good," she said aloud, her voice sounding odd with how congested she was. She'd cried more in the past 12 hours than she could remember, even more than when she'd lost her baby on her seventeenth birthday. She looked up at the ceiling, wondering if spirits and angels were real. "Take care of my baby, okay Sammi?"

Her phone began to ring, her mother's face lighting up the screen.

Oh, no.

Penny.

Penny had just lost the sister that she absolutely adored.

"Mom?

"Oh, baby," her mother breathed. "Your voice is breaking my heart. Are you okay?"

No... no, she was far from okay, and hearing her mother's sympathetic tone only pushed that button inside of her, the one who had longed for her mother to be there for her.

"Catherine?"

"Mom, I need you."

"Hang tight, baby. We're on our way."

Brody woke with a start, not recognizing his surroundings. The light was still on, and he was still in Sammi's bed, still clutching her pillow. It was dark outside; he could tell by the opened curtains. Sammi always loved having the curtains opened, seeing the world outside even when she wasn't out there.

Now she always could be.

Slowly, he unfolded himself, his muscles stiff and sore from the hiking, the sliding, the climbing that it took to get to her.

To her body.

He'd been too late.

He made his way robotically to the bathroom, not recognizing the pale face staring back at him in the mirror, the one with the dark circles under his red, puffy eyes.

"Fuck," he muttered before losing what little content he had in his stomach. Max was baking; he could smell it.

That only made his nausea worse.

"Hey, Max," he said as he walked down the hallway. "What the hell are you doing?"

"Cooking. It's hard to do without basic ingredients, so I sent Emily to Mack's to pick some up. Are you really living on frozen dinners?"

"Yeah, well." That was all Brody said in return as he sat down at the kitchen table with a drawn-out sigh.

"I'm making some chicken Alfredo," Max continued as he stirred what Brody assumed was the sauce. "And there's pizza casserole in the fridge, if you're hungry now. You can freeze this stuff and have something decent to eat. You'll need it."

"Not much up for eating now." Brody noticed a short note written on the table and he picked it up, tears welling in his eyes.

The arrangements for Sammi.

"I think you should call Delores," Max said. "She was asking about you. And Catherine."

"No."

"Look, I don't know what happened, but I can guess because I know you. And you're going through some shit right now, I get that. But shutting them out isn't going to,"

"It's my fault, Max."

"It was an accident."

An accident that could have been prevented had he not been so fucking selfish.

Had he not been consumed by the woman he loved.

He'd never forgive himself.

Max didn't understand.

"I let them know that you're alive and breathing and that's about it."

Alive. Breathing.

"She's not alone, you know." Max walked over and sat down in a chair close to Brody. "She's with Brian, and we know he's taking good care of her. He's probably throwing her all over a pool up there."

A pool.

Sammi had been the best swimmer.

Sammi had drowned in a puddle of water.

The world began to spin, and Brody put his head on his arms, resting them on the table.

"It kinda makes me mad at him all over," Max continued. "He chose to leave."

"And she didn't," Brody finished for him.

She didn't.

She had so many things she wanted to do, to finish. She had been excited about her upcoming dance recital, about entering junior high, about boys and dragonflies.

She loved dragonflies.

"You need to eat something," he heard Max say, his voice further away as if he'd gone back to the kitchen. He heard the whirring of the microwave soon after, the smells of pizza casserole drifting out to where he sat.

Pizza casserole was her favorite.

"Em and I talked, and we're not leaving you alone."

"Maybe I need to be," Brody replied.

"Nope. You'll have one of us or the both of us. Deal with it."

But he couldn't deal… he couldn't wrap his head around the past 24 hours.

He'd been so happy.

Then it all went to hell.

"Mom," Catherine squeaked out as Theresa entered her apartment, and for the first time since she was a little girl, she cried into her mother's shoulder, inviting the warmth that Theresa offered.

"Hey, Ms. Garner," Jen called out from the kitchen where she was preparing a late dinner.

"Hi, Jen," Catherine heard her mother say as she continued to hold her.

"Mom, it was so awful, so awful."

"I know, baby," Theresa said soothingly, and in smaller hushed tones, "Penny's with me, sweetheart. I'll get the details later."

"Hi," Catherine said to her little sister as she wiped her tears and stepped away from her mother.

"Are you sad because of Sammi?" Penny asked, her big blue eyes brimming with tears.

"Yes, baby, we all are." She hugged Penny then and kissed the top of her head. "How are you?"

"I want to see her."

No, you don't, Catherine thought. Not the way Brody and I did.

"I brought your coloring books," Theresa said softly. "Go on to the table and I'll get them for you."

"Will she see my colors?" Penny asked, and Catherine blinked back more tears as Theresa ruffled the little girl's hair.

"All of them," Theresa replied, and Penny walked slowly, sullenly to the kitchen table. Catherine took her place on the couch as she watched her mother pull coloring books and crayons out of her expensive bag.

They seemed so out of place.

Everything seemed out of place.

"I'm almost done with dinner," Jen announced. "If you'd like something to eat."

"Mommy said there'd be lots of food," Penny replied.

"How are you?" Theresa asked Catherine as she sat beside her and took her hand, which Catherine squeezed.

"Not okay."

"How's Brody?"

Catherine sniffled as fresh tears began. "Not talking to me," she said, and thanked her mother for the tissue that she handed her. "He says he blames himself, and I suppose me as well."

"Why you?"

"I went to see him."

Theresa almost smiled. "You never could stay away from that boy."

Catherine shrugged. "I love him, Mom. I love him and we were..." Her voice trailed off and she looked down at her hands. "We were back in his bedroom when Sammi left."

"Oh." Theresa drew the word out, and Catherine felt her hand push hair back from her face. "This isn't your fault, sweetheart. This was an accident. All of the reports on the news are saying she fell and that there was no sign of foul play."

"But it doesn't matter," Catherine cried. "It doesn't matter because she left, and we weren't out there, and he... he said he can't even look at me right now."

"Give it time. Give him time."

But Theresa didn't understand, not the way that Catherine did. Brody always let his emotions overtake him; he'd been that way since... well, if he'd been that way before he'd opened up to Catherine, he never let it show. But for someone who feels everything so deeply, there was no way of her knowing if giving him time would make things better.

She feared it would only make them worse.

CHAPTER 26

I'm Just Not

By Wednesday, the only text Catherine had received from Brody was a curt *I can't deal with this right now*. She accepted that not only because he'd lost his baby sister, but also because it wasn't a flat-out ghosting the way he'd done before. It didn't make the separation any easier, but she understood.

Or she told herself she did.

It also helped that Max was keeping her and Jen in the loop, letting them know how things were going, making sure the food they'd made was delivered to Brody and also to Delores and Frank. The only thing he didn't really know was how Tyler was doing, but Catherine could only imagine the pain he was going through.

Catherine also found herself back at work that Wednesday, feeling as though she were in a fog. She'd already requested that Friday off, and when she went in to ensure that it had been taken care of, she was angered at the site on the board. Two other instructors had the day off, but Catherine was scheduled during the time of Sammi's funeral.

"No," she muttered, then inhaled sharply. This wasn't going to do at all.

Katarina, the studio's owner, was in her office when Catherine went to knock on the door which was partially open. "Come in," she heard her far too perky boss say.

"I was wondering why I'm on the schedule this Friday," Catherine said, keeping her tone as light and casual a possible.

"The girls were wanting to go to that funeral," Katarina answered, her eyes still on the paper before her.

"That funeral? Samantha Harris?"

"Yes. She was a dancer, it turns out."

"Hey, look at me! Samantha Harris is someone I knew, someone I introduced to dancing and gymnastics, and I'm going to her funeral."

"Are you related?" Katarina asked coolly.

"Are they?"

"Look, Catherine," Katarina set her papers aside, "I like you. I really do. You've been calling off a lot lately, and that's not okay."

"I was with her brother when he found her," Catherine continued, her anger spiked. "I'm not going to apologize for that. And I will not be in here this Friday, period."

"If you're not happy here,"

"You know what?" Catherine snapped, interrupting her. "I'm not. I'm just not. I have seniority over the both of them, the turnover here is shit, you're giving them time to go to a funeral of a girl they don't even know, and you ask me if I'm happy? I'll work my classes today, but after that? Fuck you."

Katarina blinked in surprise at Catherine's outburst, but recovered quickly. "No, you can leave now."

"Done."

Catherine grabbed her dance bag and her purse and headed out the door of Katarina's studio for the last time, not even looking back as she got in her car and drove away. Could she afford to quit? Technically, no, but with her mother's recent understanding attitude, she was sure she could get some of her trust fund money before the date it reverted to her name.

"I'm so done with people right now," she muttered as she drove the short distance from the studio to her apartment, remembering as she pulled into the back parking lot the night that Brody had driven her home.

The night he'd confessed that he couldn't see her or talk to her all those years ago because he knew that he'd relent, he'd want her back in his life.

She sat in her car nibbling on her bottom lip as she realized she'd finally be seeing him the next day.

She had no idea what to expect.

"It's so kind of you to let me stay here," Sheryl said to Brody as she poured herself a cup of coffee.

"It's no problem, really," Brody replied. Max and Emily had finally left when Sheryl arrived that morning. He couldn't contain the guilt that consumed him when he thought of their own lives that they'd put on hold.

Of Sammi's life, which had been cut far too short.

"You've been so quiet," Sheryl commented, and Brody shrugged. "When do I get to meet this Catherine that you couldn't stop talking about?"

Even when he'd cut her out of his life, he'd always talked to Sheryl about her.

"Brody?"

"She'll... she'll probably be there tomorrow."

Tomorrow.

Sammi's viewing.

When he'd have to face not only saying goodbye to his sister, but seeing the woman he loved so desperately. How could he face Catherine knowing their actions, his actions, was the reason his sister was gone?

"Max said that some of this food came from her."

Brody nodded, his eyes still on his coffee cup. "Yeah, the enchiladas, and... something else, I can't remember."

"That was very nice of her."

"Yeah, she knows I suck at cooking."

Sheryl laughed softly. "I think it's more than that."

She'd told him that she loved him.

She'd showed him.

And it had cost him everything.

"It might be," was all he said. "I need to shower."

"Yes, dear, you do," Sheryl replied teasingly. "Listen, hon... look at me."

Brody raised his eyes to her, seeing the love, the tenderness there.

"None of this is your fault," she said.

"I know," he lied.

"Try again." She reached out, placing her hand on his arm. "Tyler's going through the same thing right now. The both of you feel responsible."

"It isn't Tyler's fault."

"Nor is it yours. It was an accident."

And accidental drowning is what they'd called it.

The little girl who was the best swimmer of all had drowned in a puddle of water after hitting the back of her head on a boulder on her tumble down that hill.

"A preventable accident," Brody said as he stood. "I really should go shower now."

"Okay," she said with a nod. "Okay."

Once showered and dressed, he stood in the doorway of Sammi's room, the place he'd slept every night since he'd lost her. He'd let Sheryl take his room, knowing that his camera equipment was safe with her.

He didn't know if he could ever handle the click of his camera again.

He didn't know if he could handle life again.

What was he supposed to do now? He'd moved back to take the children away from Frank, to ensure their safety. They were his prime focus, his reason for taking so many dangerous assignments to save up enough money to take care of them.

He'd proven to himself that he wasn't good enough for that task.

———————————

Catherine stomped around her apartment muttering to herself. "Stupid, ignorant people. Wanting to go to a funeral just to be seen, just to have something to gossip about. Gossip away, jerks. And have fun with those afternoon classes."

She sat down on her couch with a huff.

She didn't have a savings account; everything she made went towards her living expenses. Without a job and without having full access to her trust fund, she was at the mercy of her mother.

"Time to grovel," she said as she pulled out her phone. She sent a text first, asking if it was okay for her to call. It was hard to tell with her mother's position in her company if she would be free or not. Luckily, she texted back immediately, letting Catherine know she was there for her.

How times had changed.

She took a few deep breaths and called her mother.

"How are you?" Theresa asked, her voice full of genuine concern.

"I just did something stupid."

"Well, define stupid."

"I just quit my job. Before you say anything, they were refusing to let me have time off for Sammi's funeral. They did that so some other girls, people who didn't even know her, could go. And it isn't fair, and I need to be there."

"You never were happy at that place."

"Mom,"

"Relax, sweetheart. You've proven you're ready. I'm going to enact the clause that gives you full access to your trust fund. I know you enjoy Millerstown, or you said you did, but please know my door is always open."

Catherine was stunned silent, unable to reply at that moment.

Her mother... her mother just agreed to sign everything over?

"Catherine?"

"I don't want to move back there. My life is over..."

Well, it wasn't in Millerstown, or anywhere in the Easton metropolitan area.

But it wasn't in that house on the hill.

"You're a grown woman now, Catherine. You're free to make your own decisions. And now, you don't have to worry about those horrible people there. And they are horrible, trust me. I know horrible."

Catherine bit back a smile.

Her mother had been the Queen of Horrible once upon a time.

"I'm not going to comment on that," Catherine said, and she heard her mother laugh.

"Good call."

"I don't want to give up dancing, Mom." Catherine looked around her apartment, feeling its walls closing in on her. "I don't want to give up my dream."

"You don't have to."

"No," Catherine said with a sad smile, remembering Maxine, remembering Sammi's excitement over dancing with her troupe. "No, I don't." Maxine had worked with Frank, lowering Sammi's tuition, stating she was so talented, she deserved a shot to grow and learn.

And suddenly Catherine thought of a wonderful plan.

"Mom, I have to go. I need... I need to research something."

"Okay, love. We'll meet up after the funeral to get the papers signed. No worries, Catherine. You're well taken care of."

"Thank you."

"Thank your grandfather, rest his soul."

"Yes, thank you grandfather. Mom?"

"Yes?"

"I love you," Catherine said, meaning those words deep in her soul.

"I love you, too, sweetheart," her mother replied, saying those word for the first time in years.

And Catherine knew she meant it.

"So," Max said as he arrived with a tray full of homemade cookies, "have you talked to Catherine yet?"

"No," Brody replied softly. "Not really. And I can't right now."

"Got it, dude. Understood. Here." Max pulled out a cookie and handed it to him. "Have a cookie. Remember when we stole that whole plate off Nan's kitchen table?"

Brody smiled, and it felt foreign. "Yeah." He took a bite and nodded. "Oh, yeah. You nailed her recipe."

"Not nailed. Hi, Sheryl," Max said to Brody's aunt, who was curled up with her phone on the couch. "Those are from Nan. She said she'll see you tomorrow. Jase couldn't make it, though. Stupid fucking concert tours and obligations."

"The bastards," Sheryl quipped.

"Tell me about it," Max agreed. "I think I've gotten in touch with everyone. Catherine's mom will be there, too, and she's bringing Penny. Family visitation is an hour before, so... I'm going to be there with you. Deal with it."

"Dealt," Brody replied as he grabbed another cookie.

Dealt.

He was relieved that Max would be with him. As much as he wished it could be Catherine, he couldn't.

He just couldn't.

And he didn't know if he ever could again.

CHAPTER 27

Ready

Catherine had chosen a simple black skirt and jacket with a deep purple blouse. "Is this too much?" she asked Jen as she laid it out before her on her bed. "I mean, I could come up with a different blouse if the purple is too much."

"The purple's good," Jen replied reassuringly, then she continued straightening her teal hair. "And just for the record, I'm not the one to ask if something is 'too much,' in case you'd forgotten."

Catherine's smile wavered as she absentmindedly twirled the braid she had draped over her shoulder. She didn't have the hand coordination that she normally did as they'd decided to tremble the entire time she was getting ready. She'd kept her makeup light, but in the event that she cried—she knew she would—she put the products in her small bag for touch ups.

She wasn't ready for this.

She wasn't ready to say goodbye to the sweet little girl who had captured her heart.

She sat on the edge of her bed as she thought back to their time in her gym, where Catherine had begun to show Sammi how to do the perfect cartwheel and backflip, and how Sammi had taken to gymnastics the way that fish take to water. She'd shown so much promise and had been incredibly excited to learn.

And she loved her brothers.

She would bicker with Tyler frequently, but the love was unmistakable.

And Brody...he was her hero. He was the one who could do absolutely no wrong, who was always there for her whenever she needed him.

With as much hurt as Catherine was feeling, she couldn't begin to fathom how they must feel.

"Max was going with Brody," Jen began, "and said they'd be there around 6. I'm thinking even though regular visitation doesn't start until 7 that we should probably get there about 6:30."

"Thank you for driving," Catherine said. "Hell, thank you for everything. I couldn't have gotten through this week without you."

Jen walked into the bedroom, her hair freshly straightened, and gave Catherine a one-armed hug. "Anytime."

When Jen left the bedroom to make sure everything else was ready, Catherine let one tear fall down her cheek.

"It's almost six," Brody heard Max say as he stood before the mirror. Black suit, black shirt, purple tie, hair combed almost into place...heart a million miles away. He was as ready as he was going to be. With one last sigh, he turned from the mirror and walked out into the living room. Max and Em were also dressed in black, waiting for him.

"You look nice," Emily said softly.

"Thank you," Brody managed to say. "So do you."

The compliments seemed so out of place to him.

Getting dressed up seemed out of place.

All he wanted to do was retreat to Sammi's room, try to make some pact with a god he didn't know to trade places with her, let her live instead of him. But it was as pointless as this suit that he wore that wouldn't bring her back.

He felt like he was putting on a show.

"I talked to Delores, and our car will be second in line behind theirs tomorrow," Max was saying.

Second in line to take Sammi to the graveyard, the same one where their brother had been buried.

"Sounds good," Brody replied. His throat was tight, feeling closed off, and he loosened his tie a little. But it wasn't the tie having a stranglehold on him, it was grief, so profound that he'd lost track of the days and had to be reminded to get ready.

To get ready to go see her.

He couldn't get the image of her lifeless body out of his head.

"Okay, just got the text from Delores," Max said as he put his phone in his suit pocket. "They're already there. You ready?"

No... no, he would never be ready.

"Yes," he said instead and followed Max and Emily out to the car.

"There are so many cars here already," Jen commented as they pulled into the lot of the funeral home. Many people were lingering outside, talking to one another, smoking out in the back lot away from the door.

"How many of them are actually family?" Catherine asked, remembering that two people from her old job wanted to go even though they didn't know the family at all.

"Good point. Here." She pulled into the closest spot she could get. "You ready?"

"Hell no," Catherine breathed. "But we should go in anyway."

Catherine recognized a few of the faces as they made their way through the crowd that was assembling outside, waiting for the doors to open for regular visitation. When Max opened the door to Catherine and Jen, he let them in, asking everyone else to please wait and give the family some privacy.

It seemed like the whole community was coming.

Instead of somber church music, Catherine heard one of Sammi's favorite pop tunes playing over the sound system, catching her off guard.

"They wanted to make this as Sammi as possible," Max commented, his voice low. In the front lobby, there were poster boards, pictures galore, chronicling her life from start to...

Catherine couldn't think about the finish, not now, not when she was trying to hold herself together.

She and Jen made their way around the lobby, taking in each photo, each special occasion in her life. In one corner were awards and professional dance photos, each in a glittery costume, with one of said costumes on display.

"If you go through that hallway," Max pointed, "they have a video montage going of a lot of these pictures, plus some."

"This is beautiful," Catherine commented as she looked around. "She would have loved it."

"Oh, yeah. And the tapestry they have... in there... it's a dragonfly."

In there.

In the viewing room.

Where Sammi's body laid.

Catherine took in a shaky breath. "Thank you for letting us in early."

"Anytime, Queen C," he said, giving her a one-armed hug. "Anytime. Sheryl is in with Sammi now, and I know she wants to meet you."

Sheryl.

Their Aunt Sheryl, who would make them casseroles to heat up because she knew Brody wasn't the best cook.

Aunt Sheryl who had raised Tyler and Sammi for years.

"I... I don't think I'm ready to."

"Yeah, neither is Brody. He's back in where the video is playing."

Catherine nodded and took a deep breath before beginning her walk down that hall.

The pictures weren't in any particular chronological order, and Brody couldn't take his eyes off of them as he relived his sister's life. The latest one was Sammi on Brian's shoulders, smiling at the community pool.

"Is that you?" someone asked

"No," he replied softly, thinking of how Sammi was probably on Brian's shoulders now.

They were together.

It was double the hurt.

He took in a shaky breath as the picture changed again, this one taken at Sheryl's when she'd brought home straight As for the first time. The kids had blossomed with her. It pained his heart to think their own mother didn't want to take part in their lives.

Or their deaths.

Sandra was a no-show thus far at the funeral home.

His heart constricted as he caught the sight of Catherine out of the corner of his eye.

Catherine.

In his arms.

Loving him.

While Sammi lay dead at the bottom of a hill.

He kept his eyes on the screen, choking back a sob at the next picture of him, Tyler, and Sammi.

That's the way it should have been.

The three of them taking on the world together.

Catherine sat beside him on the couch, but he remained still. Focused. His eyes on the screen that brought up picture after picture.

"Have you been in to see her?" Catherine asked, and he shook his head.

The screen was blurring before him.

He couldn't hold it together much longer.

"It's almost time for the doors to open." He felt her hand on his arm, the touch burning him to the core. "You should go see her before everyone gets here."

He was the reason she was in that box.

He was the reason she wasn't alive anymore.

"Brody?" Tyler's voice broke through and he looked over at his little brother who was standing in the doorway. "Can we? Please?"

Tyler had been waiting for him.

He didn't want to go in alone.

He didn't want to go in with their father, whose sobs could be heard throughout the building.

He had said he wanted it to be Brody. Only Brody and him.

And the time had come.

He waited with Tyler at the door to the viewing room, his back turned away from it as the funeral director went in and asked the others to leave for a brief moment. With time drawing near the open visitation, they'd also been promised that the public would be kept out until they were ready. Brody could see out the front windows the throngs of people gathering out front, including a couple of news vans.

Sammi's death had been such a shock to the community, bringing it even closer together.

And yet, Brody felt miles apart.

"I'm ready," he heard Tyler's voice, imagining him a young boy calling out to him, telling him he was ready to catch the ball as Sammi played with her dolls inside.

One last exhale of breath, and Brody turned to walk into the viewing room, his arm around and supporting his little brother, who was almost as tall as he was.

And before them, in a white casket with a dragonfly tapestry draped across the bottom, lie their sister.

Brody could feel Tyler trembling as they neared, not from fear, but from the silent sobs as his grief spilled over, as suddenly this surreal nightmare became all too real for him. It was there, by the casket, holding his little brother, that Brody finally laid his eyes on Sammi.

She was all dressed up in the recital uniform down to the extra makeup and over-styled hair, all for the show she wouldn't get the chance to dance in. Inside her casket, she looked so frail, so thin. Gone were the mud and blood and wet leaves that had covered her body when he'd found her.

She looked peaceful.

Serene.

As if nothing in this world could ever hurt her again.

And Brody could feel his anger, the anger targeted at himself, creep in again.

"How do I tell her I'm sorry?" Tyler cried into his shoulder.

"You have nothing to be sorry for," Brody replied and held him a little tighter.

"But I was just playing video games and I told you she was fine, and she wasn't. What if we could have found her in time?"

But they couldn't have.

The coroner had placed her time of death before he'd even asked for Sammi's whereabouts.

"I can't do this, I can't do this again," Tyler cried.

Again.

He'd been so torn up over Brian.

And here they were again.

"And it was always 'Ty and Sammi.' Now it's just me, and I can't, I can't."

"It's not just you," Brody said soothingly. "It's not just you."

He felt every bit as alone as Tyler did right then, but Brody held himself together for his brother the way he always did.

He could do this... he could do this... he could do this...

But inside, his mind was screaming at him, telling him it was all his fault.

And that, in the end, Tyler would never forgive him, either.

CHAPTER 28

Why

"Some people are going over to Brody's," Jen said to Catherine as they got into her car. "Feel up to it?"

Catherine knew that Brody was avoiding her, but she also knew they needed to talk.

She knew he blamed her.

She knew that wasn't fair.

"Yes," she said through her tears which hadn't stopped since she'd seen Sammi in that white coffin. She thanked Jen for yet another tissue, discarding her used ones in the small bag that Jen kept in the front of her car for garbage.

"Okay." Jen started the car. "Max said there's plenty of food so we don't need to make any more."

"Now," Catherine added. "He may need continued support. Same for Frank and Delores. Seeing Tyler breakdown was just..." It had been the most heartbreaking scene she'd ever witnessed, and Brody, the way he held himself up and together for Tyler... she knew he had to be reaching his breaking point.

Hers had come seeing that sweet girl all ready for a dance recital that she'd never get to see. And she'd made it a point to mark Maxine's recital on her calendar.

That was the day she was going to decide her future.

And now... now it was going to be another reminder that Sammi was gone.

"It still doesn't seem real," Jen commented.

"Yes, it does," Catherine replied. "All too real."

"No scenes when we go to Brody's?"

Catherine shook her head. "We're not kids anymore."

The rest of the drive was in silence, up until Jen commented how many cars were already parked on the street. "We'll have to walk a little bit."

"I'm fine with that," Catherine answered.

She recognized Randall's car as well as a few others as cars that had been parked for Brody's homecoming party. How different this gathering was, with somber faces, tissues being passed around. These people had grown up with Brody, known Sammi or at least of her for her entire life. Catherine had only known her for almost half her life.

Half her life.

And the beginning... Catherine couldn't push the guilt away of how she'd treated both Sammi and Tyler in the beginning. Somehow she and Brody had put that behind them, but now...

Now she felt out of place.

"Can I get you anything?" Emily sounded cordial enough when she walked up to Jen and Catherine, who shook her head. "Brody isn't really socializing, but he's around here somewhere." She stepped closer to Catherine. "I know you need to talk, but I don't know if I should tell you now is not the time or see if you can get him to open up."

Catherine blinked in surprise. "I... I could try," she finally said with a nod. "Where is he?"

"Sammi's room."

Catherine excused herself and made her way through the crowd towards the hallway that led to the bedrooms. She paused outside of Sammi's room as a couple of people made their way out, but could tell that others were still in with him. She didn't know if her stepping in now would be good or not, but she decided to anyway, needing to see for herself that he was okay.

Brody was sitting on Sammi's bed, still holding himself together fairly well despite the redness of his eyes. He was nodding at something that Max had said to him when his eyes found hers and locked.

Was that love she saw there? Relief?

Regret?

"Queen C," Max said with a smile as he crossed the room to greet her, his arms opened wide. Catherine welcomed his embrace and quietly thanked him for staying with Brody, helping him as he needed.

"So this is Catherine," she heard a woman say, and judging that she looked like Sandra, she surmised this must be their Aunt Sheryl. She walked towards her, hand outstretched. "I'm their aunt, and it's so wonderful to finally meet you."

"Hello, Sheryl," Catherine replied with a soft smile. "It's nice to meet you, too."

"Oh, so you've heard about me."

"I could say the same."

"Could you give us a minute?" Brody spoke up, interrupting their greeting.

"I'm sorry," Catherine said, starting to walk out the door, but he stopped her.

"You, Cat. Us a minute. Please," he added, and she nodded as the others made their way out of the room. "Could you shut the door?"

"Closed doors," she commented, "this can't be good."

He was silent as he stood, his head down, his eyes on the carpeting. He took one heavy breath, then another, then another as his shoulders began to shake with the sobs he'd been holding in. As he dropped to his knees, Catherine walked over to him, her heart going out to him as he clung to her.

"Why?" His choked question as grief consumed him breaking her heart. "God, Cat, why? Why my Sammi? Why?"

He'd tried his best to hold everything in, to wait until those who'd come to lend their comfort were gone. He hadn't wanted anyone to see him like this, to see his world completely shatter. But the moment he'd laid eyes on Catherine, when his guilt reached a tipping point, he knew holding it back was pointless.

So he let it go.

He let the tears, the anguish, pour forth as Catherine held him, running her hands through his hair as she whispered words of comfort he was too far gone to hear.

Why his Sammi?

Why the beautiful girl with a bright future?

Why now?

How was he going to live without her?

How would he ever forgive himself?

"Brody, it's not your fault," he heard Catherine's voice as if it were a faraway dream.

"It is," he sobbed. "It is my fault. I was stupid and selfish and instead of being the man they needed, I..." He pulled away from her then and stood slowly, wiping his eyes. "I need you to understand this, Cat. I love you."

"I love you, too."

"But... but when I look at you, all I see is how that love destroyed everything. Everything."

"Brody, that's... it's not true."

"But it is, don't you see?" He reached out and touched her face gently before pulling back. "I couldn't even take my time, take time for us properly. I saw what I wanted, and I took it. And... stop. Don't interrupt me."

"Okay," Catherine said, her voice barely above a whisper.

"Sammi is dead because of it."

"That was an accident."

"An accident that was completely avoidable because I didn't want them to leave at all. I didn't want them to have friends over. It was our weekend, a time to... to get reacquainted, to find out if they wanted to live with me. And... and I did this to protect them! All I wanted was to protect them from Frank, and who they really needed protected from is me."

"That's not true."

"Isn't it?" He wiped his eyes again, unable to stop the onslaught of tears. "If I hadn't gone back to that room, she never would have taken the bike. She wouldn't have gone to the woods when it was too muddy to make it safely to that damn fort of hers. She wouldn't have fallen, she wouldn't have *died*." He covered his mouth, holding back a roar that would alert everyone that he was breaking, falling apart.

"Listen,"

"No, you… you need to hear me. You need to… you need to go."

He watched Catherine blink back tears. "You can't blame yourself, or me for that matter."

"I didn't say I blamed…" His voice trailed off and his eyes were on the carpet once more. "Catherine, I need you to leave."

"Brody,"

"Give me this time, this space that I'm asking for. Please."

"Look at me."

He met her gaze, his heart splintering at the hurt in her eyes. "Cat, please."

She nodded once and left the room, shutting the door behind her.

And he broke.

Dropping to his knees, his hands fisted in his hair, he muffled howls of agony as his entire world came crashing down.

CHAPTER 29

Chasing Dragonflies

The morning of the funeral was bright as if the world were celebrating Sammi's life. Catherine, however, cursed the sunlight through her slightly swollen eyes.

"Did you cut more cucumber," she said to Jen, who was also having the same problem.

"Yeah, I left some on the counter. Thank god for awesome concealer, too, otherwise…"

Neither one of them finished the sentence, each lost in their own silent contemplation.

It was a day for another black outfit, for being there for someone who'd told her in no uncertain terms that he didn't want to see her.

Still, she was going.

She was going for Sammi, for Tyler, for Brody even though he didn't want to see her. She'd keep her distance, but unless there was an outright ban of her coming to the service, he wasn't going to stop her.

"We can go a few minutes early," Jen suggested. "I know they asked for the service to be for friends and family, but we know how that goes."

"Yeah, it could be lined out the door even with just friends and family," Catherine agreed.

"Did you see all those school kids there last night?"

Catherine had.

It had broken her heart to see all of those young students crying, seeing them dealing with the death of one of their own far too soon.

"Nan was just beside herself, too. I'm glad she could come last night. She said she'd try to be there today."

"We'll save her a seat," Catherine said as she sat down on the couch, put her head back, and placed the cucumber slices over her eyes hoping they'd do the trick.

"Max is saving our seats," Jen reminded her as she also came out to the living room.

"Oh, right. Have him save one for her, too. Just in case."

"Catherine, are you okay?"

"Oh, I'm perfect," Catherine deadpanned as she removed the cucumbers so that she could see Jen. "We're mourning the loss of an amazing little girl, my... I don't know what he is to me... but he doesn't want to see me at all because he blames her death on being with me."

"He's going through a ton of shit right now," Jen said, a reminder that Catherine really didn't need. "And you're holding out on me if he's 'I don't know what' instead of 'my ex.'"

Catherine sighed as she closed her eyes, placing the cucumbers back in hopes of getting the swelling down. "There's obviously nothing to tell if he's going to look at me and say that all he sees is the reason his sister is dead."

"No, that asshole didn't."

"Nooooo," Catherine drew the word out and gestured with her hand to stop Jen's tirade that was sure to come. "He blames himself. He says he was being selfish and stupid."

"So what if he was? It was still an accident."

"A preventable one," Catherine reminded her. "I'm surprised I'm going to show my face at all at the funeral today, but I wouldn't miss it. There's no way that I would."

"Did you see Maxine yesterday? She was shook."

"We all are," Catherine said sadly.

"Yeah, that we are."

After getting ready, deciding that it was fine to have puffy eyes, they were getting ready to leave when Catherine received a call from Theresa. "Oh, this can't be good," she muttered.

"You can take it in the car," Jen said. "I'll only eavesdrop a little."

"Bitch."

"You love me, shut up."

"Yes, I do." She smiled at Jen, the first genuine smile of the day, as she got into the car. "Hello?"

"Honey, you'll never guess who is here at the funeral home."

Honey? Had her mother hit her head this morning? "I have no idea."

"Greta."

"Oh." Catherine drew the word out as she placed a hand on her heart. "We're heading over now."

"Good, good. I think I'm going to ask Greta if she'll come back."

"Mom, you were a total bitch to her."

"Yes, well I've seen the error of my ways. Besides, she did such a wonderful job with you, maybe I can steal her away to help with Penny some. That girl is a handful. She didn't quite understand what was going on. I sent her with Flo back to the house. Frank is a mess. I wanted to be here for him and Delores."

"Mom, you're all over the place."

"Yes, well, I'm trying to hold myself together, and what better way then by filling you in before you get here? I need to go, though. Catherine?"

"Yeah?"

"I love you."

Catherine drew in a shaky breath, her mother's words meaning more than she could possibly convey. "I love you, too," she replied before hanging up and reaching for the tissue that Jen was holding up. "Wow. I just..."

"Your mom sounds like she's done a bit of growing up herself."

Catherine nodded. "She has. She really has."

"When the service is over," the funeral director was saying, "we're going to have the family stand up by Samantha as everyone passes by."

Brody felt odd being included in this conversation, but he nodded when Delores looked in his direction. He could stand next to Tyler, help him the way he had been all morning.

"There are plenty of refreshments in the coffee area. Feel free to have whatever you like."

They'd said the same thing the day before, but Brody hadn't been able to eat a thing. He could make sure that Tyler did, though.

"Afterwards, we'll have you go to your cars, and... do you have pallbearers?"

Frank hesitated at the question, but Brody said a quick "Yes." He, Max, and other friends of his had decided the night before that they would carry Sammi's casket.

He could do this.

He could do this.

He could face everyone today, be there for Ty, hold it together as the throngs of people came through offering their condolences. He stayed close to his brother moving on autopilot, thanking people for coming to say goodbye to his little sister. He hugged Maxine who was beside herself with grief. He would motion to Max if it was okay to send someone over to greet him.

Catherine never did.

He saw her in the crowd, keeping her distance from him as he'd asked her to.

He was grateful for that small reprieve, knowing that being near her would only up his anxiety, remind him of what he'd done wrong.

Remind him that Sammi was in that white coffin because of him.

"Are you wanting to speak, dear?" Delores asked him at one point, and he shook his head. That was one thing he couldn't do. Tyler also declined, stating he'd never get through it. There was one request that Tyler did have, though.

"What's that?"

Tyler turned to Brody. "I want to help carry her, with you."

"Are you sure?" Brody asked him, and he nodded through his tears.

"We should be the ones to do it. And Max and... and Randall."

"Chris and David said they would, too," Brody said with a nod. "You're our sixth."

"And Dad... Dad wouldn't have to."

Brody looked over at Frank, who couldn't stop staring at his little girl lying there, gone. "Yeah," Brody said, feeling a twinge of... what was it? Remorse? Guilt?

Sympathy?

He couldn't tell as he watched the man who'd made his life a living hell try to say goodbye to his little girl.

When the time in the service came where others could stand up and speak, Frank was the first to.

He stood there for a moment, facing the crowd, a man consumed with grief. "Samantha Jayne brought so much light into my life, into all of our lives." A murmur of agreement went through the crowd. "She saw in me what I couldn't see in myself—a good man. A good father. I wish I could tell you what she was like growing up, but I can't. I can't because I was either working, or lost in the bottle, or lost dealing with..." He choked up, his lips quivering as he continued. "You're never supposed to bury your children. Now I'm burying my second. And I'm so sorry that..."

"Honey, it's okay," Delores said softly from the first row as Brody sat in shock, taking it all in.

"See, when we lost Brian, I lost myself. I became the worst version of me possible, worse than when I'd lose a job, or worse than when I was drunk all the time. I lost my kids because of it, and I'll never forgive myself for not being there for them. But I just got them back. I just got them back, and Samantha saw in me the man I've always wanted to be. That's what I'm going to do, for her, for Tyler, for Penny." His eyes met Brody's. "For Brody."

"Now, if you want to know how Samantha was growing up, they'd be the ones to tell you. Or their Aunt Sheryl, if she'd like to speak. I want to take a moment, though, to thank them all for loving Samantha the way they did, the way they do. And Delores, you, too. You loved her like she was your own."

"I still do," Delores said, so softly Brody barely heard her.

The crowd was still, hushed as they looked upon the man who'd put up appearances for years.

The man Brody remembered singing Sammi to sleep every night when she was a baby.

The man who'd taken them to the house on the hill.

The man who now admitted to him, to everyone, that he'd been a less-than-stellar father.

"She loved to dance, I know that." Frank smiled through his tears. "And tumble. Catherine, we have you to thank for introducing her to that. And Maxine, she loved working with you, learning the new routines. She was so ready for this upcoming recital. I wish I could see her dance in it, but I promise you I know the routine. I've watched her learn and practice until she had it perfect."

Frank licked his lips as he looked down at his hands. "And Samantha loved to wander. She loved to go for walks and bike rides, she loved exploring." His voice choked on the last word and it took him a moment to continue. "She loved to chase dragonflies, and now she can forever."

Slowly, methodically, he walked back to his chair, sinking down as sobs took over, and the trail of other speakers began.

Maxine.

Sheryl.

A girl from her school.

A boy who'd had a crush on her.

And as The Band Perry's *If I Die Young* played on a loop, one by one the visitors all walked by, offering condolences, promising to be there, telling them they'd see them at the gravesite.

When the time came, Brody and Tyler took the head of her casket, walking it with the others first to the hearse, and then to her gravesite, beside Brian.

Still, Brody couldn't wrap his head around Frank's words, and he had a feeling they would haunt him in the days and weeks to come.

CHAPTER 30

Not a Lie

"It was a beautiful service," Jen commented as they left the cemetery.

"Yeah," Catherine agreed, still in shock over Frank's speech. Had he really admitted the monster that he'd been?

Had he really changed?

"Are we going to Brody's?"

Catherine shook her head. "I think I just want to head home."

"Are you sure?"

"Yeah, but... could you do a favor for me?"

"What's that?"

"Go to Brody's," Catherine replied. "Make sure he's okay."

Jen was quiet for a moment. "I could do that. Are you sure you,"

"I'm positive," Catherine cut her off. "I promised him that I would give him space, and I'm going to."

"But what about you? Are you okay?"

Catherine contemplated her question. "No. Not really. But I will be, and he's the one that needs support right now."

"But I'm your best friend, not his."

"So let me know that he's doing well, reassure me that way."

"Catherine,"

"I insist."

Once back home, Catherine took off her heels and wiggled her toes in the carpet before heading back to her bedroom to change. Her dress clothes were the last thing she wanted on, and she decided on a pair of shorts and a light top. Her apartment was warm enough, being on the top floor and surrounded on both sides, and she wasn't up to going out or visiting anyone.

She just wanted silence.

Peace.

Not feeling the least bit hungry, she did the next best thing to being there with Brody by looking up his Facebook profile, seeing the outpouring of love and condolences there. She inhaled deeply, taking in the soft vanilla sent of her diffuser before typing a message of her own.

I'm always here for you

She was about to set her phone aside when it began to ring, and it was her mother's face she saw smiling up at her from her screen instead of Brody. She answered just before it would have gone to voicemail.

"How are you?" Theresa asked, and Catherine sighed.

"About as good as could be expected," she answered. She looked around her disheveled apartment knowing the first thing she was going to do once off the phone was give her home a good cleaning. "How are you holding up?"

"About the same. But we do have some good news. The lawyer is drawing up the papers, the first two million should be available to you within the week. You will need to sign, of course."

"The what?" Catherine couldn't hide her shock.

"Sweetheart, your grandfather was a shrewd business man, and I followed in his footsteps. Taking advice from your father, of course. He was always so good with numbers and the market."

But what Colin loved more than numbers was teaching.

He was happier in the Valley than he'd ever been in that house on the hill.

"I didn't know that you and Dad spoke. Like, ever."

"I opened up that line of communication as soon as you moved in with him," Theresa replied. "It was the least I could do. I... no, I don't wish you'd stayed. You have become such an incredible force all on your own, and I just don't think you would have if you'd remained here, surrounded with... well, with things that made you so unhappy."

First Frank's speech, and now her mother's.

Catherine couldn't wrap her head around any of it.

"I... I have plans for this, you know," she finally said. "I'm not going to squander it, but I have plans."

"You could always break your lease and move to wherever your heart desires."

But what did her heart desire?

She already knew that answer, but he was 20 minutes away in that house in Brentfield not wanting anything to do with her at the moment.

"I know," was all she said in return. "I know."

Brody stared at the email, its invitation to take an assignment overseas mocking the grief that surrounded his heart.

Could he leave now?

"You okay?" Emily asked as she entered Sammi's room, where Brody sat with his laptop while a few people lingered in the living room.

"Hmm? Oh, yeah. Yeah, I'm fine," he lied.

"Are you going to shut yourself in here the rest of the day?"

Yes, that was exactly what he had planned on.

"No," he lied.

"I'm surprised Catherine isn't here."

"I asked her not to come." Not a lie.

Emily sat on the bed next to him. "I don't know all the details, and I know I've gotten on your case about you using her as a crutch, but Brody... these are the times we need those we love."

"Well, I love you." He lifted one corner of his mouth in a half-smile. "And Max, I know he's still here."

"And Catherine."

He looked down at his laptop before setting it aside.

He needed out of this house, out of this town before he lost his mind.

"Hey, Em?"

"Yeah?"

"Could you watch the house while I go out on assignment?"

"So soon?"

"The world didn't stop, and I can't stop. Not now."

Not now.

But the camera, the clicking of the camera.

Over Sammi's body.

Could he handle it?

"Please," he added, and Emily sighed.

"Yeah, of course. If you come out here and talk to people, that is."

He glanced down at his phone, the notifications in the double digits, and he sighed. He wasn't up to reading them. He wasn't up to seeing how many people would tell him that they were sorry he'd lost his little sister.

His little sister who should have never left the house, never been in harm's way, but he'd been too busy, to selfish to stop her.

"Fine," he said with a sigh and stood.

He could talk to people. He could assure them that all was well, that they could leave.

So that he could grieve in solitude.

So that he could pack and go half way around the world and get away from the Valley for a little while.

Not many people remained. His Aunt Sheryl had just returned from Frank's house, this time with Tyler. "He's going to come visit me for a few days," she said discreetly, and Brody nodded.

That was best.

Best to be away from the man who'd just admitted what a horrible father he'd been.

At times.

At others, he'd been the man Brody'd always wanted him to be: kind, generous to a fault, funny, witty, playful.

Why couldn't he have been that way all the time?

"We have plenty of food," Brody said to his little brother.

"Are those Catherine's enchiladas?" Tyler asked, and Brody nodded. "Dude," was all he said before he stepped away to help himself to the feast his eyes were drinking in.

"What about you?" Sheryl asked. "Have you eaten?"

Brody looked over at the food, at the paper plates, at the plastic ware, at everything that Max and Emily—and even Catherine—had made possible. "I'm not hungry," he replied.

"Hey," Jen said as she stepped up to him, her teal hair in ringlets and in stark contrast to her black dress clothes.

Jen.

Was Catherine here?

"Let's face it, I'm here to spy on you, make sure you're doing well."

"I'm fine."

Lie.

What a lie it was.

He needed Sammi.

He needed Catherine... but he didn't deserve that kind of comfort.

He didn't deserve happiness.

"Hey, um, as you guys are leaving, take what food you would like," Brody announced to the room. "I don't need all of this."

"You could take it to Frank and Delores," Sheryl suggested. "They're both doing poorly right now."

"Or that," Brody said.

But he couldn't go over there.

He just... couldn't.

Two days had passed since the funeral, and Catherine had yet to hear from Brody. He was on her mind as she sat down with her mother to go over the papers, signing her trust fund over to her in chunks available every year for five years.

And her first year was a cool 2 million.

"You said you had plans," her mother said to her, striking up a conversation where Catherine seemed unable to still.

"I don't want to reveal them just yet, in case they fall through."

"Oh, an investment?"

Catherine smiled softly. "Something like that." She looked around the dining room of that house on the hill, smiling wider as Greta entered to remove the plates. "It's so good to see you here," she said. "Penny's a lucky girl. And Greta?"

"Si?"

"So was I."

"Oh, sweet girl." Greta, breaking from protocol, walked over to Catherine, who embraced her. "It was I who was lucky."

"Oh, you two," Theresa said, dabbing at her eyes with a tissue. "I think I've cried enough this year. And thank you again, Greta."

"Si, Ms. Garner. Thank you."

"I'm over the moon that she agreed to come back," Theresa commented as Greta left the room. "Penny absolutely adores her."

"I did, too. I mean I do, but I did before I became such a bitch."

"Catherine Denise!"

"Well, it's true." Catherine shrugged. "I was a horrible person."

"Don't talk about my daughter that way," Theresa scolded, reaching out to cradle Catherine's cheek. "Ever. Got it?"

Who was this woman and what had she done with the person who'd raised her to be the bitchmonster that she'd been?

Catherine pushed the question away as she took her mother's hand in hers. "Penny's the best thing that's ever happened to you,

Mom. And I'm lucky to have her for a sister, and… and to have you."

"What did I tell you about making me cry?" Theresa asked with a laugh and dabbed her eyes again. "I don't feel like touching up my makeup, so let's get back to business."

"I signed."

"Good, then our business is done. Play time?"

Play time.

Her mother scheduled play time with Penny, often taking her to Catherine's gym to do so.

"I'd love to," Catherine replied, ready to make new, happy memories in that house on the hill.

Brody sat with his camera in hand, shaking, the clicks bringing him back to the bottom of that hill.

Back to Sammi.

Covered in mud, in leaves, in blood.

Lifeless.

"Shit," he muttered, then shook his head.

He had wanted this assignment, needed it to get away.

"Is it okay if I take your picture?" Brody asked a young man who was sitting on a crumbled concrete wall, staring at where his house had been, where his family had been before the mudslide. His interpreter repeated his question, then nodded after the young man had given his consent.

Click, click, click

All the mud.

All the lives gone.

Click, click, click

Sammi, gone.

Click, click, click

"I need to take a break," Brody said again, stepping back as emotions overwhelmed him. Anger, sadness, grief continued to plague him every waking moment and in the few fitful hours of sleep he would get.

But he'd wanted this.

He'd wanted away from the Valley.

But no matter how far he ran, her lifeless eyes followed him.

Click, click, click

He could reach out to Catherine, make everything okay, make life worth living again.

Click, click, click

But he wasn't worthy of her, not now.

Not anymore.

CHAPTER 31

Princess

It had been just over two weeks since Sammi's funeral, since Catherine had walked off her job, when her bank account officially showed that she had access to her trust fund. Despite her lethargy, she joyfully put a call into her dad, asking him if he would like some company.

His response was immediate, telling her that he would love to see her.

Checkbook in her wallet and wallet in hand, she left her small apartment in Millerstown and made the 20 minute drive to Groves Point and the small house she'd shared with him. He greeted her with a smile and a warm embrace that she'd needed.

She was feeling better already.

"To what do I owe this surprise?" he asked, and she grinned sheepishly.

"I need you to call your landlord."

"Oh? And why's that? Would you like some coffee?"

She crinkled up her nose and shook her head. She hadn't been able to stomach her coffee that morning. "Just some water would be great." She followed him to the dining room and sat down at the table, the seat right next to his where he'd been working on lesson plans.

"One bottle of water," Colin said as he handed it to her.

"If you're too busy,"

"For my little girl? Never."

"I'm hardly a little girl now, Dad."

"You'll always be my little girl, Catherine."

Catherine blushed and smiled, so grateful for the wonderful memories she'd made with him in her short stay in that house in the Valley. "I know," she replied, and her smile wavered.

"I imagine it's been a rough few weeks for you."

"Yeah, well, not working does not sit well with me. I need something to do."

"That wasn't what I was referring to."

He was referring to Sammi.

To finding her body.

To the funeral.

"Yeah," she finally said, her eyes downcast.

"How's Brody doing?"

"I'm not sure. I mean, I'm told he's thrown himself back into work, but it's all from other people. He says he's not ready to talk to me just yet."

"I don't understand."

"We were together when she left the house," she replied. "And he feels guilty. I think he's pushing some of that guilt my way."

"Or he's unwilling to be comforted just yet. Give him time."

"I am." Her smile returned. "But that's not why I came over."

"Oh, do tell."

She looked around the small house that her father had put so much love into. "Do you like it here?"

"I love it here. I've never been happier."

"This house, I mean."

"It's home, Catherine. I've done the repairs, I've fixed it up how I want it. And there's even a spare bedroom for guests, if that's what you're asking."

"No, no, actually." She shifted in her chair and placed her hand over his. "I talked to Mom, and she said you helped out with my trust fund."

"I never wanted you to be without."

"And I don't want you working two or three jobs to make ends meet, especially when they take time away from what you really love. You're a wonderful teacher. You know that, right?"

"You don't get your trust fund until you're 25. Or you're not supposed to. I could talk to your mother if you need some help."

"No, no, I already did, and she signed part of it over to me. I want to buy you a house, Daddy."

"Baby girl,"

"And if this is the house you want, I want to buy it for you, and don't tell me 'no' like I know you're trying to."

"That's not what your trust fund is for, sweetheart."

"It's for me to do as I please, and nothing would please me more."

Colin blinked back tears as he looked down at his lesson plans he'd fallen far behind on. "I... I would love to stay here, Princess. Right here, in this house close enough to my work that I could walk to it. And I'd love to retire here, play with any potential grandchildren in that backyard."

"Now you're getting ahead of yourself," Catherine laughed. "But I want you to call your landlord, okay? And I want you to quit both of your other jobs today. Today, not two weeks from now."

"I can't do that to them, sweetheart."

"Fine, fine, in two weeks, or one week, or whatever. But you, sir, are a one-job man who gets to save for his own retirement now. You earned this, Daddy. Trust me."

It took four hours for everything to be done, for the check to be written to his former landlord, for Colin to give his notice to his other jobs, and the time wore on Catherine. So unused to having nothing pressing to do, she'd taken a nap curled up on her father's couch, and had woke up to her favorite fuzzy blanket of his draped over her.

"You're looking a little pale. Let me get you something to eat, raise your blood sugar."

"Can we have tacos?" she asked with a grin.

"Anything for you, baby girl."

He would have said it without her paying for his house.

He would have said it if she'd shown up in her worst mood ever.

He would do anything for her.

She'd never been more grateful to be blessed with him as a father.

"I do have one more stop I need to make. What time is it?"

"Almost 4."

"Wow, I slept that long? Okay, you start tacos. I'll be right back."

"Where are you going?"

She smiled. "To see an old friend."

And when she walked into Maxine's studio that afternoon, she knew her life's purpose was just beginning.

Brody put the finished edits of his photos together and sent them in, knowing this payday was going to be a big one.

But he didn't care.

It was pointless, useless.

Everything he'd done was to get his brother and sister back with him, and now his sister was gone.

He finished the last of his coffee and slowly walked the cup out to his kitchen, where dishes sat undone despite having a dishwasher. He turned and left the kitchen, pausing at his dining room table which seemed overrun with mail and other various papers he'd left there.

Fuck it.

It could wait until another day.

He needed a shower.

That could wait until later.

As he stumbled over a pair of his boots he'd left in the middle of a floor, a small, hesitant knock sounded at the front door.

Catherine?

He was surprised to instead see his little brother at the door, hands in his pockets, waiting for him. "Hey," Tyler said as Brody stepped back and let him in.

"Hey yourself, kid. How you holding up?"

Tyler sighed as he looked around Brody's unkempt house. "Kinda like you, I guess."

Brody nodded and gestured for Tyler to sit down. Tyler took a seat on the couch instead of the gaming chair and turned slightly to face him. "I have a ton of homework, and that's what I should be doing, but I..." He looked down at his hands, then back up at Brody. "It doesn't make much sense, her being gone. I had some fun at Aunt Sheryl's, but there's not much she can do right now, not with chemo and everything."

"She's going to be okay," Brody said, catching onto Tyler's morose mood. "She's a fighter."

"Yeah, she's really doing better. They say she's going to beat it."

"That's good to hear."

"But that's not... Dad's different, Brody. He really is. And he's so lost, and he needs me. I know he does."

"I understand."

"No, I don't think you do," Tyler disagreed. "Dad needs me, but I need you. I need my big brother right now for so much. And... and I don't know if someday Dad's going to snap again. You know?"

Brody nodded once.

He knew all too well how Frank's mood could change on a dime.

"And don't take this the wrong way, but he always took it out on you. But you're not there, and I'm glad... I'm glad you don't deal with that anymore. I can't be that person, Brody. I can't. He's okay now, but he's slipping, hanging on by a thread. We all are."

Because their glue was no longer with them.

"I need you, Brody."

"I'm here, kid," Brody said as he took Tyler into his arms where the young boy broke, sobbing.

"I can't do this without you."

"And you don't need to."

"Are you sure?" Tyler pulled back and gestured around the house. "This... you... man, you need a shower."

Brody let out a laugh that seemed foreign to him. "Yeah, I do."

"I can help, you know. With house stuff."

Brody ruffled his brother's hair. "The first thing you need to do is your homework."

"I have time. They're giving me time."

"I know, but don't put it all off until the last minute."

"Can I just be a kid today?" Tyler begged through his tears. "Just today, and I promise I'll do my homework tomorrow."

"You know where the controller is," Brody joked, and Tyler smiled.

"I guess I should tell them I snuck out."

"Kid." Brody drew the word out and reached for his phone. "I'll tell them, and I'll tell them you're staying for dinner."

"You're gonna,"

"Pizza," Brody cut him off as he sent a text to Delores.

"And maybe Catherine can be here, too."

"Not today," Brody replied, his voice soft. "Today it's just us."

After showering and ordering pizza, he returned the phone call he'd missed, the first one he'd returned other than work since losing Sammi. When Delores answered, he went straight to the point.

"Tyler's staying with me."

"Oh, Brody, I don't think,"

"You didn't know Frank before, not the way we did. And if Tyler says he sees him slipping, it's my job to step in."

"He's just testy because,"

"Because he lost his daughter, I get it. We lost a sister. Tyler needs someone who's there for him, not someone who needs him to be the grownup. He's just a kid."

"He has me."

"He has *me*," Brody replied, his voice stern. "I have everything he needs here, and he'll be in the same district. And before you ask, yes we are going to take this through the legal channels, even if it's only temporary. I will not let Frank do to him what he did to me."

Delores was silent for a moment before she said a simple, "Okay."

"I'll be there to get his school things and some clothes in about an hour. Make sure they're ready."

When he set his phone down on his dresser, he noticed Tyler standing in the doorway. "Are they pissed?"

Brody shrugged. "Let them be. I'm going to get your things on my own. You stay here. I want to gauge the situation before I have him near you."

He was unprepared for Tyler's quick rush into his arms, but once recovered, he returned the bear hug his brother gave him.

And for the first time since losing Sammi, he felt a sense of purpose.

He kept this with him that Monday, after sending Tyler off to school, when he kept his appointment with his lawyer to draw up the custody papers.

He kept it with him as he made his way to a small, rundown office building he'd frequented many times in his youth.

He needed help.

Tyler needed help.

And as he made the appointments at the desk, Laura came out of her office and smiled.

"Welcome back."

CHAPTER 32

Responsible

It was a grey and rainy morning, and Catherine found that it matched her mood. She'd finally managed a doctor's appointment as she hadn't been feeling better at all, and had been told then that a stomach bug was running rampant in the community. She managed a few bites of toast before heading out the door, bottle of water in hand.

"This sucks," she muttered. She wished she could stomach coffee, it might curtail her nagging headaches. Or maybe even a decent meal would, but her appetite was sorely lacking, hiding behind her nausea the way the sun hid behind the clouds that morning.

At least the weather was warmer. A large warmup had spread across the entire region reaching down into the Deep South, where hundreds of miles from them was facing severe weather. A tropical storm had even begun to form, super late for the season.

Catherine wondered briefly if Brody would go to photograph it should it hit the coast.

"Shit," she managed to say, slamming on her brakes in time to keep from hitting a car that pulled out in front of her. Her wandering mind was going to get her into trouble if she didn't stop letting it take her to faraway places, faraway times.

Brody.

The parking lot at her doctor's office was packed full, as she'd been warned it probably would be. The only spaces remaining were in the far back, leaving a trek to the front door in the slow drizzle that began to fall.

"And of course," she said as she exited her car, "I forgot my umbrella."

Maybe she should start carrying one, the way she still carried an emergency bag of clothes in her car.

Maybe she didn't need either and simply needed to plan better.

Maybe...

"Catherine?"

Hearing Brad's voice pulled her out of her mental battle, and she squinted her eyes in his direction as he began to walk closer.

"I thought that was you. How are you?"

She'd forgotten they had the same primary care physician.

It was one of the many things she'd forgotten about him.

"Well," she said, and she gestured towards the doctor's office.

"Yeah, me too," he replied, stopping short. "Damn stomach bug. I was told it's a virus and I need to wait it out."

"They'll probably tell me the same thing."

"Yeah, my girlfriend said..." His voice trailed off and he grinned sheepishly. "I guess I shouldn't have sprung that on you."

"Sprung what? Oh!" Catherine gently tapped her forehead with her palm. "Girlfriend. Right. Um, don't worry about it."

And she meant that.

She knew then, when she felt happiness for him, relief that he'd moved on, that she'd made the right decision.

And that decision had nothing to do with Brody.

Brody... there her mind went again.

"Catherine?"

"I'm sorry, I'm just so... scattered," she said, finally coming up with a word. "I haven't been eating right, I have a nagging headache, and I can't concentrate for shit."

"Wow. You rarely curse, so you must feel terrible."

She nodded, which only hurt her head worse. "I really should get in there."

"Oh, of course, of course."

"And Brad?"

"Yeah?"

She smiled at him. "I'm happy for you. Not about the stomach bug, of course, but the girlfriend. I'm happy for you."

Brad smiled in return. "And maybe someday you'll tell me all about your fabulous boyfriend."

She doubted that, but remained smiling anyway. "You never know. I'll see you."

The waiting room was packed, several people in masks flipping through magazines, a few others with their eyes closed. Some were watching whatever health information was on the television that played at a soft tone. Catherine wondered how many of them felt as poorly as she did, if this really was some random virus, or perhaps the flu as she signed in at the front desk.

"When you're ready," the receptionist was saying, "let us know. We can collect a urine sample."

A urine sample? Well, that was odd. "Okay," Catherine said with a shrug. "I can do that now."

It took nearly an hour before she was finally seen by her doctor, who seemed nonplussed that so many had made their way to the office that day. "Catherine, how good to see you," he said with a grin.

"You just want my money," she mumbled, and his laughter hurt her head all the more. "Aren't you going to do a nasal swab for the flu?"

"Hmm? Oh, yes, as a precaution, of course. Your symptoms should subside in a couple of months."

"Months?" Catherine narrowed her eyes. "What stomach bug lasts that long?"

"The kind that lasts about 40 weeks. You, my dear, are pregnant."

Catherine laughed at his statement. Her? Pregnant? She hadn't...

Brody.

Brody...

"I'm sure you have a lot to think about," her doctor said as he pulled out a few brochures. "You can see your gynecologist for a follow up soon, check to see how things are progressing, how far along you are."

"Wait, don't people... like, don't they not have symptoms for a while? How did I have symptoms this early?"

"Every pregnancy is different, Catherine. You could have both a virus and be pregnant, and just got lucky enough to find out early."

Early.

Earlier than she'd found out in high school, with the baby she'd lost.

"What... I mean, I had a miscarriage years ago."

"Early miscarriages are common."

Common.

She didn't think she could go through that kind of pain again.

And she'd used birth control religiously, taking her pills the same time every day. So this baby was in that .01 or so percentile.

This baby had been conceived the same day they lost Sammi.

Brody needed to know.

"I'm sure you have a lot to think about. Be sure to follow up with Dr. Petersen as soon as possible, okay? She'll put your mind at ease."

Somehow Catherine doubted that Dr. Petersen was the one who could help her racing mind.

A baby.

Brody's baby.

And she knew before she ever left that office that she had chosen to become a mother.

"Are you sure this is what you want?" Delores was asking Tyler when she dropped off a few more of his things. Brody noticed that she'd come alone, Frank wasn't even in the car waiting.

"Yeah, I'm sure," Tyler said as he reached for his bag. He left the room after thanking her, and yet she stood there, staring off into the distance.

"Is there something I can help you with?" Brody asked her, and she shook her head.

"I'd like if he'd come stay with us when you go off on your excursions."

"They're jobs, and if he's comfortable with it, that's what we'll do."

"All the alcohol is out of the house. Frank's really... he's wonderful now."

Brody nodded, not quite sure what to say. He'd seen Frank throw out the alcohol before, witnessed the change in him when he was clear-minded. Calm.

Wonderful.

"Are you sure you're ready for this? To be a father, I mean. Because essentially, that's what you're going to be doing."

No, he wasn't sure.

He didn't think he'd be cut out to be a father at any time, not after the way he'd been raised.

Still, his brother needed him, and he'd made a promise to take care of him, keep him out of harm's way.

Even when he'd failed so miserably with Sammi.

After Tyler left for school, Brody busied himself around the house, continuing to clean up the mess he'd let accumulate since losing his sister. So many thoughts were floating around in his head, the most prominent of which had come from Delores earlier.

By early that afternoon, the paperwork for Tyler's guardianship was in place, with a notice that child services would most likely be following up. He hadn't thought it would be this easy. When he'd moved to Brentfield, he'd been prepared for a drawn-out legal battle, one that would take months, one that would put the kids through far too much.

But it was worth it.

Everything he did to prepare himself for this was worth it.

Still, he found himself walking around Groves Point, the town he'd grown up in, wondering how he would proceed with his future plans. What was he going to do about work? Would he turn down jobs to stay with Tyler, or would he pick a few choice ones to ensure their wellbeing?

What did it take to actually be a father?

He wandered around the park, finally settling at the bench which still bore Brian's artwork. With a heavy sigh, he placed his head in his hands, and he let his tears begin to fall. Here he and Tyler were, the last remaining of Sandra Harris's children, a mother who couldn't be bothered with her only daughter's funeral.

And Brody was now completely responsible for Tyler.

He was relieved.

He was anxious.

He was grateful.

He was terrified.

Luckily, he was stepping in to parent a teenager who was already a great kid with a promising future ahead of him. He knew he couldn't have taken them back when they were younger, when he was fresh out of the mental health facility his mother had sent him to. Did he see himself as Tyler's father? No, not in any way. He was his big brother.

He was going to keep him safe.

He'd let himself dream of being a father once, way back when life was fresh and new and the possibilities endless. He'd always sworn he'd be nothing like Frank, ever.

And then that was who he'd begun to become.

Now he couldn't see himself ever having children of his own, far too fearful of what kind of monster he could potentially be. He'd seen his dark side, and yes, he'd made it out the other side.

But how would he be able to promise he'd stay there when long hours behind the camera blended into longer nights with a crying baby, or a precocious toddler, or worse yet, a teenager who acted the way Brody had after their mother had picked him up from the house on the hill?

He huffed out a sigh and ran his fingers through his hair. It didn't matter that he never saw himself becoming a father. The only woman he'd even think about sharing a child with was Catherine, and he couldn't even bring himself to call her, to reach out, to let her in.

He wished he deserved her.

"Get it together, Harris," he said, noting the time and that Tyler would be home from school soon. He patted the tabletop, as if he were saying goodbye to Brian, and made his way back home.

"You're what?"

"Jen, I just told you. I'm pregnant."

"You're *what*?"

"I'm not going to repeat it a million times, bitch." Catherine curled up with her phone on the couch, feeling guilty that the first person she told was her best friend.

It should have been Brody.

"I'm bringing ice cream. See you in a few."

"Lord," Catherine said with a groan after she hung up the phone. Jen sounded far too excited about this. Truth was, Catherine was terrified to feel excited.

But she was too alone, and refused to be any longer.

When she opened the door to Jen's knock, she was met with the biggest hug she'd ever gotten. "Oof, easy. I may vomit on you."

"I brought chocolate chocolate chip ice cream."

"No, thank you."

"No? You're turning down chocolatey goodness? This sounds serious. C'mere, get comfy. On the couch, you."

"Stop bossing me around in my own home," Catherine said with a laugh.

"What can I get for you?"

"Nothing, just come sit with me."

"Let me put this in the freezer then."

"After you get me one tiny scoop of it, please." Catherine batted her eyelashes and laughed as Jen bounded into the kitchen.

"I'm am so fucking excited over this, you don't even know."

"I'm gathering that now."

"So, what did Brody say?"

"He doesn't know."

Jen stopped mid-scoop and looked over her shoulder. "What do you mean he doesn't know?"

"Like I just said, he doesn't know."

"You know what?" Jen walked back into the living room with two bowls of ice cream. "I'm tired of you two being stupid."

"Excuse me?"

"You heard me. You're being stupid. What you choose to do with your body, got it."

"I'm having this baby."

"Which I gathered, but half that DNA belongs to the boy you've been obsessed with ever since I met you, even when you were with Mr. Snooty."

"Brad is not... okay, maybe he is a little, but you're supposed to be on my side of this. Calling me stupid is,"

"Harsh, but kinda true. The Catherine I've always known would still be checking in on him every damn day."

"I have been, sort of, through other people."

"He really needs you right now, and you need him."

Catherine took a small bite of her ice cream in lieu of answering, both angered and annoyed.

Because Jen was right.

CHAPTER 33

Opening Line

"Just an opening line," Catherine said to herself as she drove towards Brody's house, as she'd promised Jen she would. "That's all I need, just an opening line. One line that gets me in the door before..." Her voice trailed off as she pulled over, feeling nauseated. "Not now, kiddo. Bean, that's what I'm going to call you for now. But not now, okay?"

With one pat to her lower abdomen, already loving the contents within, she continued on her trek, talking to herself the entire way.

"He's a great guy. Yeah, he's taking Sammi's death hard, but I expected him to. He's just... well, he's either going to accept that a baby is on the way, or he's not. He wouldn't just... would he? Fuck, I don't know."

She growled in frustration as traffic on the freeway slowed to a crawl. This wasn't helping her nerves in the least, let alone her stomach which was protesting her breakfast of scrambled eggs and toast. "I should have skipped the eggs," she said, knowing she would eat them again tomorrow anyway because the protein was good for her and her growing baby.

She could do this.

It was a simple five-minute chat, if that, to let Brody know he was going to become a father.

She rehearsed it in her car over and over to the point where she knew she could say it, get all of the words out. But when she finally pulled up in front of his home, she noticed he was just coming out of his door and locking it behind him.

"Well, shit," she muttered as she parked strategically behind his car, keeping him from leaving before she had said what she needed to.

What she should have said to him the moment she had left her doctor's office, but it had taken Jen and nearly a pint of ice cream to get up the nerve.

"I'm kinda in a hurry," he said as she exited her car.

"This won't take long."

He sighed, and Catherine took that as a bad sign. Maybe he was having a bad day.

Maybe she was about to make it that much worse.

"Catherine, I really don't have the time,"

"Make the time." She crossed her arms, standing her ground, and he sighed again, this time in resignation.

"Make it quick, please. I have to pick Tyler up and take him to an appointment."

"They have you doing that?"

"He's staying with me now."

"Oh." Catherine blinked in surprise, taken off guard. "So… you kinda are playing Dad now, huh?" she asked, keeping her tone light.

"No, I'm playing big brother. I'm definitely not ready to bring a child into this world."

Catherine inhaled and crossed her arms. "Well, this conversation just got awkward."

Brody shook his head, "I'm just saying,"

"I'm pregnant."

Brody stood there for a moment, his mouth opened as if he had something to say, but hadn't wrapped his head around it yet.

"Yeah, I know," she said quickly. "I didn't miss a single pill and we used protection. Except in the shower, but, yeah. I know. It surprised me, too."

"Catherine," he said softly, his eyes still wide.

"You need to go, I know. Here's the deal: I'm having this baby. That's my decision, and I made it way back when I lost my first baby. And I know you're having trouble dealing with Sammi's death, and not just the where you've refused to talk to me. I've asked. Do you honestly think Sammi would want you to wallow around in misery? No, you know she wouldn't. So I'm glad that Tyler's with you, especially after Frank's speech and what I've seen. When you've gotten your shit together and figured out what you want, you know how to reach me."

"It's not that simple."

"Like fuck it isn't," she snapped. "I've always been here for you. Always. I don't know why you continuously push me away unless all of that 'I love you' business was just bullshit."

"You know it isn't."

She threw up her hands in exasperation. "Then get your shit together before you lose me forever. Yeah, I know you have a lot to think about, especially now. Think about it. I'll see you in a week."

"Cat,"

"If I give you that long," she called over her shoulder as she hurried back to her car and drove away as quickly as she could.

She couldn't bear to let him see her cry.

Not now.

He wasn't ready to be a father. He'd already said it.

All that was left now was for her to wait.

Brody was quiet that evening over dinner, one that Brody had somehow managed to not ruin by simply following the directions. Tyler was looking over his phone at the table, despite Brody asking him not to, but he'd had a rough day.

Brody knew that all too well.

On top of Catherine's announcement, he'd also received an offer to go to the Carolina coast, cover the hurricane that would be barreling down in a few days' time. How could he take the job, having just gotten Tyler?

How could he turn it down with a baby on the way?

He exhaled as he sat back, his mind too full to concentrate on much of anything.

"Dinner's good," Tyler commented.

"I got a job offer. An assignment, I mean."

"I'm not going back," Tyler said quickly. "I can stay here; I can take care of myself."

"No way," Brody said with a half laugh. "I can get someone to come stay with you."

"Like Catherine?"

Brody frowned. That was the last thing Catherine needed right now. "No, probably Emily."

"Doesn't she have school, too? Never mind, forget I said anything. Emily's cool. I like Emily. Your job's not dangerous, is it?"

"It's taking pictures."

"But a lot of your pictures are in places that are practically destroyed."

Tyler had a point.

"I'll be going to one of the Carolinas," Brody replied. "Whichever one they think will get the worst of the storm coming."

Tyler was silent for a moment. "But what if something happens to you?"

"Nothing is going to happen to me."

"I'm not going back with Frank, Brody. I'm it. I'm it. If he loses his shit, it comes down on *me*."

"Right now, until you're old enough, you're my responsibility."

"And what if something happens to you?"

Brody hadn't thought that far. "Let's not,"

"I want to go with Catherine if something does."

Brody was quiet, stopping himself from telling Tyler to not worry about it. How could he not? Look how quickly, how easily they'd lost their sister. "I'll talk to her about it," he promised.

But not right at that moment.

Not when she had enough on her plate, not when he needed to wrap his head around how to promise Catherine he'd be there for their child even though he'd said he wasn't ready.

He wanted more than that.

So much more.

But he didn't deserve her, or her kindness, or the happiness she could bring.

What was it that Laura had told him? Oh, right. He was punishing himself. And incorrectly, also according to Laura, not that he agreed with her.

After dinner, he closed himself back in his bedroom and began to pack for his upcoming trip, ensuring his equipment was secured. When he was certain Tyler wasn't listening in, he picked up his phone, calling Catherine's number.

Straight to voicemail.

Which was just as well, he didn't have a speech or anything prepared. What he had to say to her shouldn't be in a voicemail anyway, so he decided he'd call her when he got back.

"Maybe I shouldn't have my phone off," Catherine said to Jen through her sniffles.

"Yes, you should," Jen argued. "Make him suffer."

"For what, saying he wasn't ready to be a father before I'd even told him about the baby?"

"No, for telling you before that he couldn't talk to you. I'd still like to give him a black eye over that."

Catherine shook her head. "No, it was what was best at the time. I know how he gets."

"Don't be stupid." Jen took Catherine's phone and placed it out of her reach. "Now, when is your first OB appointment?"

"Monday," Catherine replied. "I guess they're doing a blood test to check levels. I don't need a calculator to figure it out;

Brody's been it for a while, even long before Brad and I broke up. Did I tell you he's seeing someone else?"

"No, and I don't really care about him."

"Turns out I'm happy for him."

"Well, good for you." Jen smiled. "Want more ice cream?"

"Ugh, no."

"Well, I do. How did you find out Brad's dating someone else?"

"I saw him when I was going to my doctor's."

"He doesn't know, does he?"

Catherine shook her head. "I thought I had that stomach bug that was going around."

"Some kind of bug you have," Jen laughed.

"Bean. That's what I'm calling the baby right now. Stupid, I know."

"Not stupid. Adorable. I'm calling myself Aunt Jen, by the way."

"You haven't told anyone, have you?" When Jen didn't answer right away, Catherine sat up straighter. "Have you?"

"I may have let it slip to Sarah. She says congratulations, by the way."

Catherine groaned. "Oh, great. Sarah knows, which means Max knows."

"Not necessarily."

Catherine raised an eyebrow.

"Okay, maybe."

"Brody, dude, have you talked to Catherine?" was the question Brody was asked by Max when he'd called to see if he or Emily could stay with Tyler.

"Briefly, why? Is something wrong?" Brody asked, instantly concerned.

"I don't... I mean, we discuss, so did she say anything important to you today?"

"It's time for us to man up and admit we gossip."

"Not even close. Did she?"

"Yeah," Brody said as he sat down. "Yeah, I know. And her phone is going to voicemail, so no, I haven't talked to her since."

"Why don't you go over there and talk to her?"

"Because I need to get on a plane to Charlotte before they start closing the airports down. Can you or Em stay with Tyler?"

"We can both make sure he's good. Em is best for mornings, though. I'm up and out the door before 4."

Brody sighed in relief. "I owe you both, huge."

"What kind of party do they have for dudes that are becoming fathers?"

"I'm not having a party, Max. And how many people know?"

"Not many. Jen told Sarah, who told me thinking that you already had."

"No offense, but that's a conversation I need to have with Catherine. It's just going to have to wait. How soon can you get here?"

"I can be there within an hour."

"Good. I gotta finish packing. I'll have to leave pretty much as soon as you get here."

"And then what?"

"Then I go face down a hurricane. I'll talk to Catherine when I get back."

"You sure that waiting's such a,"

"No time, Max."

He was already running behind schedule, and as he scrambled to pack, he almost forgot his essentials from the bathroom. He checked in on Tyler, telling him to finish his homework before resuming his killing of zombies online, and tried Catherine's phone one last time.

Still straight to voicemail.

"Hey," he said, finally leaving her a message. "It's me. Let's talk, okay? Really talk. I'll call you when I get back."

He hated leaving it, but he had no other choice.

This hurricane wasn't going to wait.

He had one short stop to make on the way.

A slight mist was falling as Brody stepped out of his car. The cemetery was fairly deserted, only a few people visiting graves that afternoon. When Brody rounded the corner, he stopped short.

Frank Harris was at Brian and Sammi's graves.

He was knelt between them, seemingly in silent prayer as Brody approached. Not wanting to startle Frank, but also not knowing what to say, Brody cleared his throat causing Frank to look over his shoulder. The dark circles around his eyes matched Brody's, and in that instant Brody could also see that Frank was crying.

Something he was so close to doing at that moment.

"Isn't the stone beautiful?" Frank asked through his tears, and Brody glanced at the stone beside Brian's, carved with a dragonfly, *Beloved Daughter, Sister, Dancer, Friend* engraved below those dates with the dashes, the ones even closer than Brian's had been.

It took all of Brody's will to not weep at the sight of it.

"I'd like to think that she's with Brian, that they're up there looking down, telling us everything is okay, but I'm not so sure they'd say that to me," Frank continued, his eyes shifting between the two stones. "I fucked up, Brody. I was such an asshole, especially to you."

One lone tear escaped down Brody's cheek.

Frank turned towards Brody, his eyes showing the vastness of his pain. "I saw so much of myself in you and I didn't want you to make the same mistakes I did. And there I was, acting just like my father, thinking beating it out of you was the only solution. But it doesn't work, it only teaches you..." Frank sniffled, his voice choked with emotion as he continued. "It only teaches you that violence is the answer. And it's not. And for every time I laid my hand on you that way, I'm sorry."

Brody inhaled sharply, his vision blurring with tears from hearing the words he'd longed for.

"And look at you! My son, a great man, putting his... his brother before himself, taking responsibility, taking your talents and using them for good in this world. You turned into a fine young man in spite of... in spite of me."

Two large tears escaped Brody's eyes despite his efforts to stop them.

"Regret, it's... it's a horrible thing to live with, Brody. Please... when the time comes, when you bring your own children into this world, and you should. You'd make a wonderful father, so long as you aren't like me. Promise me that you aren't like me."

"I'm not," Brody finally managed to say.

Frank nodded. "Good. Good. I know that Tyler's in the best hands with you, because I failed him. He's afraid of me. He shouldn't grow up in fear. That's why I agreed for him to be with you. Break the cycle. Promise me you'll break the cycle."

"I promise," Brody choked out, standing stiff and still as Frank put his arms around him, holding him tightly. Slowly, so slowly he could feel each minuscule movement, he wrapped his arms around the man who'd raised him, needing that closure, that acceptance.

That love.

"I don't have the right to ask for forgiveness," Frank sobbed, "but I'm going to. Can you forgive me? Please?"

Brody was silent for a moment, and he finally said. "Someday."

"That's more than I'd hoped for." Frank stepped back, smiling even with his tears still falling. "I'm proud of you, son." Frank patted his arm once before he walked away, leaving Brody alone at Brian and Sammi's graves.

So full of emotions, the tide swirling and spilling over, he dropped to his knees and wept.

CHAPTER 34

Perfect

Catherine was greeted with a warm hug and a kiss on the cheek when she met Maxine for their appointment the following day. "Hello, love," Maxine said, cupping Catherine's cheek in the palm of her hand. "How are you?"

Catherine was nauseated and exhausted, but smiled anyway. "Well," she replied.

"Good, good. Sit. We have much to discuss."

"I've missed this place so much," Catherine commented as she wrapped her arms around herself. "Even being in here when I needed reprimanded."

"Coached, love. You were being coached."

Catherine's smile widened. "Coached, then. I love the feeling this place gives me."

"You don't get that at your new job?"

"I don't work there anymore. I quit when they weren't going to give me time off for Sammi's funeral."

"Oh, how heartless."

"That's what it lacked," Catherine said as it finally hit her. "I'd been trying to pinpoint what it was, but.. yeah. It was missing heart. Or at least mine, since it was here."

"You flatter me so."

"I'm telling the truth."

"I know, love," Maxine said, still smiling. "So I put together a list and a contract, or agreement, whichever you'd like to call it. I'd like for you to look it over."

Catherine took the papers from Maxine's outstretched hand and began to read. "Did you reach out to,"

"Oh, yes," Maxine cut her off. "Full agreement, and gratitude as well. This does help the studio, too. I take on so many who have hardships."

Catherine knew all too well. She'd been one of those students, although she paid her way by working for Maxine, learning the business, helping with form. She'd never been able to take any of the advanced classes, such as the one that Audrey was in, because of her work schedule.

Oh, but Catherine had learned.

And she'd learned from the best.

"I like it," Catherine commented with a smile. "I especially like how soft the wording is, how it doesn't come across... am I making any sense today?"

"Plenty." Maxine took the papers from her hand and placed them in her "to copy" pile that Catherine knew all too well. "I have no assistant to help me."

"Is there anything I can do?"

"Oh, you are so kind. I can get them copied as soon as I finish up this financial report."

"Let me do it for you," Catherine offered. "For old time's sake."

There was a spark of humor in Maxine's eyes. "Oh, so I'm old now?"

"No," Catherine laughed as she stood and took the papers from the bin. "How many copies?"

"Let's go with three, if that's alright."

"It's perfect."

Catherine busied herself at the old copier, knowing exactly how to get it to comply with her wishes despite the fact that it barely wanted to work. A new copier, that's what this office needed, and Catherine would make sure that there would be one by the end of the week. She even knew which office supply store to use, as she'd done many of the orders all those years ago.

"You seem different," Maxine said as she passed by her with more files to go into the cabinet.

"I've grown up."

"No… no, this is more."

Catherine bit the inside of her lip before answering in her most casual tone. "Oh, I'm just pregnant is all."

"Oh my word!" Maxine's arms were suddenly around her, holding her in a tight embrace. "Oh, this is just wonderful news!"

Catherine returned the embrace, fighting back tears. Was it wonderful news? She really couldn't tell. "Thank you," she finally managed to say as she stepped back.

"Why tears? Is it not wonderful?"

"Oh no, it is. It is."

Maxine crossed her arms. "Where is the father?"

Not 'who' but 'where' as if Maxine already knew.

"On assignment, I suppose."

"You suppose?"

Catherine sighed as she handed the papers back to Maxine. "It's a long story."

"So shorten it."

"I told him after he'd already said he wasn't ready to become a father." Catherine could feel her tears threatening once more, and Maxine ushered her back to her seat and handed her a tissue. "Thank you."

"No thanks needed, love. Does this mean you're doing it on your own?"

Catherine shrugged. "I don't know." The tears finally began to fall as her heightened emotions took over. "He left me a voicemail saying we needed to talk, but that it would have to be when he got back."

Maxine let out a short huff of air. "Men."

"Right?"

"No tears, Catherine. You have what it takes, no matter what. And you're going to be a wonderful mother."

"Am I? I can't stop crying at, like, everything."

"It's the hormones." Maxine patted Catherine's shoulder. "It will pass. But this love that you feel? Because I can see it in your eyes. That will not pass, only grow. Trust me, I have three boys of my own." She gestured to a family photo that Catherine had seen many times. "They've moved away, but they still keep in touch. You think a baby is wonderful? Have your adult child tell you that they love you. That's wonderful."

Catherine's tears began to subside as it hit her.

She had to tell her parents.

Maybe she should wait. She'd had a miscarriage before, after all.

"I see you thinking."

"So much to think about." Catherine looked through the opened office doors into a classroom, this one with mirrors on the wall much like her own gym in that house on the hill. "I miss dancing, Maxine. I miss teaching it."

"You could always do that."

"I'm not sure that I could."

"What, you think being pregnant will stop you? Don't let it. You'll be around here enough anyway, there's no need for you to give up something you love so much."

"Are you sure?"

Maxine smiled. "I'm positive."

This time it was Catherine's turn to initiate the hug. "You're the best, you know that?"

"Of course I do," Maxine said with a teasing laugh.

"So... what do we do now?"

"Well, everything is in place." Maxine smiled at Catherine, cupping her cheek once more. "You don't know how much this means to me."

"I think I have an idea." Catherine stood with a smile. "Go ahead and have them sign up. The Samantha Jayne Harris scholarship will help all of you."

Cell reception had been spotty at best all day, so Brody had called Emily with the hotel information and phone number from the phone in his room on the fifth floor. It was still sunny outside, not much wind, but the storm was coming. It would be there within a few hours, and he had to be ready.

Ready.

He'd told Catherine he wasn't ready to become a father.

He'd said that before knowing she was pregnant, before knowing that life was throwing another curveball in his direction.

He hadn't even swung at it.

He'd just let her drive away without knowing that he'd be there for her every step of the way.

He couldn't live with that regret.

"Soon," he said aloud as he pulled the covers back on the bed, set his phone to silent with the exception of an alarm that would have him up in time to prepare to take photos. He was one of a few in this hotel who had shown up with equipment, so he knew that the competition for the best photos would be fierce.

He could do this.

Except sleep was eluding him once more, his thoughts taunting him over losing Sammi, over letting Catherine drive away before he even took the chance to speak with her. What was it Frank had said? Regret... it was a...

Frank.

His apology.

"Fuck, head, shut up," Brody muttered as he ran his fingers through his hair and tugged lightly. But his head wouldn't listen, so he turned on the radio to try and drown out his thoughts. The first song he heard was Two by Ryan Adams, and he cursed under his breath.

Catherine.

He missed her immensely.

He longed to hold her in his arms, tell her everything was going to be okay.

And there went his head, reminding him he wasn't good enough for her. He wasn't good enough to be a father, especially not to an infant. He wasn't worthy of calm and serenity and hope.

"Fuck this," he said as he pushed himself upwards and out of the bed. Sleep was not going to be his friend. Instead, he changed into his workout clothes and went down to the gym with his iPod. Maybe a good workout would do.

And there on the nightstand he left his phone, missing the flashing screen with Catherine's smile, and not realizing she'd called him until he returned two hours later.

CHAPTER 35

Hurricane Catherine

Catherine sat in her car outside her father's house, the churning in her stomach telling her that maybe now wasn't the time for her to tell Colin Garner that he was going to be a grandfather. Instead, she was just going to say hello, tell him she'd been in the area and wanted to stop by.

The smell of dinner cooking hitting her the moment her father opened the door derailed those plans immediately, leaving her dashing for the hall bathroom where the contents of her stomach came up violently.

"Are you okay?"

"Yeah," she lied, calling over her shoulder before another wave hit.

Or was she lying?

With every symptom that popped up or remained, it calmed her nerves, the ones that wondered if everything was okay. She was smiling slightly as she rinsed out her mouth and washed her hands before emerging from the bathroom to her father's inquisitive gaze.

"How far along?" Colin asked, and Catherine blinked a couple of times.

"What do you... oh, fuck it," she said in defeat, a blush touching her cheeks. "Not very."

She waited for the onslaught of questions, the berating of asking her how she could let something like this happen. Instead, she was met with a warm hug as her father exclaimed how excited he was for her.

Excited.

Not ashamed, not afraid.

Excited.

"I know you're young," he continued as he stepped back, urging her to sit on the couch. "But I also know you're going to make an amazing mother."

Catherine blinked back tears. "You think so?"

He sat in his chair, still beaming. "I know so. Is it,"

"Brody," Catherine cut her father off. "And he knows. He had to go off somewhere on assignment, but we're going to talk afterwards."

Colin chuckled. "Like you're going to let him wait."

Catherine gasped even as she began to blush again, remembering her earlier call that had gone to voicemail. "Yes I... well, maybe, but... why are you laughing?"

"Ah, sweetheart, I know you. You're probably chomping at the bit to find out where he is. And if you knew, you'd probably drive straight there and demand he talk to you right then and there."

"Nooooooo I wouldn't," she disagreed.

But that was a lie.

Because the moment she left her father's home, she headed straight for Brody's house, knowing someone might be there, and that if they were, they would know exactly where Brody was.

Brody's cell service was practically nonexistent, so he decided to wait to call Catherine back. All he needed was to be in mid-sentence and have the call drop. He knew her, anyway. He knew she'd demand to know where he was, and then she'd probably throw one of her major tantrums knowing that he was in North Carolina, waiting for a hurricane to hit at Category 3, or possibly 4.

She wouldn't be wrong.

He knew he was in harm's way; it was part of the job. He could have declined, he could have said he'd come in after the storm, knowing that his expertise was capturing the human side of tragedy.

It had all started with the tornado that hit Brentfield.

Brody had a hard time remembering that day, remembering how he'd calmed Sammi's fears as best he could.

How she'd wished she had her dad.

And now…

"Ah, fuck," he muttered as sleep eluded him again. He stood and stretched, deciding on finding some food before the storm was sure to hit approximately 12 hours away.

He took his phone with him this time, cursing the WiFi calling that wasn't working and the cell service that was all but nonexistent.

With determination in every step, Catherine marched up to Brody's front door, knocking twice before she crossed her arms, waiting. She knew someone was there; the lights were on and she'd seen movement and shadows through the curtains. It wasn't long before the door opened and Emily stood before her.

"Brody isn't here," were Emily's first words.

"Why are *you* here then?"

"Because he asked me to be."

"Catherine?" Tyler's voice came from inside the home, and Emily stepped aside to let Catherine walk in, where she hugged the tall teenage boy.

"How are you?" Catherine asked him and Tyler shrugged as he stepped back.

"It sucks," was all he said.

"Is your homework done?" Emily asked him, and he sighed.

"Almost. Man, you're worse than Brody about that."

"I have my own to do, too, so no whining. And Catherine, you're looking at the reason why I'm here. No ideas need to sprout about anything and... Tyler, could you give us a moment, please?"

When Tyler begrudgingly went to his room and shut the door, Catherine stood with her arms crossed, staring down one girl she just couldn't seem to get along with. "There's no need for you to be rude, you know."

"No, but I know what's going through your head. Don't let it, okay?" Emily sighed in frustration. "I don't know what else to say other than that."

"Of course you do. Where is he?"

"On assignment."

Catherine shifted her weight from one leg to the other. "I already know that, but I can't reach him and I need to."

"Is something wrong? Yes, I know about..." Emily's voice trailed off and she made a motion with her hand towards Catherine, who was equal parts grateful that she didn't blurt out her pregnancy with Tyler able to hear and annoyed that she, of all people, knew.

"The only thing that's wrong is we keep playing phone tag, and I need a better way of getting in touch with him."

"Look," Emily said with an exasperated sigh, "I don't know why he didn't tell you where, but,"

"There's no buts to it. He wouldn't have left here without telling you where he was going, especially with Tyler here. Stop the game, Emily."

"There's no game, Catherine."

"Just give me a better phone number. Please," Catherine added as nicely as she could.

"What are you going to do with this, give him ten kinds of hell for being in North Carolina?" Emily asked as she turned and picked a pen and paper up off the table.

"North Carolina?" Catherine took a quick picture of the slip of paper that Emily held out rather than write everything down. "I have to go."

"What, go down there? Are you insane? There's a hurricane coming."

"Yeah, there is. And her name is Catherine."

The storm was getting closer. The skies were a dark grey and the winds had begun to pick up as Brody took a few shots off of the hotel roof, sure to not get any of the other photographers in his frame. How many people were down here doing the same as he was? He figured he'd get a few good ones in as the storm approached before being forced indoors, only getting what shots he could through the windows.

The gusts of wind had only reached the 40 miles per hour mark, a far cry from what they were about to be, and Brody felt the familiar rush of adrenaline kick in. Soon he'd be at nature's mercy, hoping that no tornadoes rolled through taking out the hotel he and several other news agencies occupied. One lone car was driving into the parking lot as he took another shot of the trees beginning to bend.

And he stopped.

From all those stories above, he could see the small woman, so full of either fury or determination that she pushed that car door closed and began marching her way towards the front of the hotel.

It couldn't be.

It couldn't be.

Brody rushed to the door and down the stairs that led to a hallway where employees only could access. He wouldn't bother anyone to get him back up to that roof, not if that small woman was the same woman whose arms he longed for even through his conflicting emotions. He ran to the elevator, pushing the down button several times before the doors finally opened. He made his way to the first floor and pushed the elevator doors as if he could open them quicker himself. The lobby was just down the hall, but by the time he reached the front desk, no one aside from frightened employees, was there.

With a sigh, determining that he must be losing his mind, he went back to the elevator, taking it to the fifth floor. As he stepped out he could hear persistent knocking, and a voice that sounded like heaven.

"I know you're in there, I know this is your room. Just open the damn door."

"I'd have to be in there to do that, and what the ever loving hell are you doing here, Catherine?" Brody asked, surprised and angered by her presence.

"What am I doing here? What the hell are *you* doing here, putting yourself in harm's way like this? No, we don't have time to talk about it. Just get your things and get in the rental car. We can get out of here before it gets too bad."

"It's too late to get out of here," he said as he reached around her and used his key card to unlock the door, ushering her inside to take their conversation a place more private. "I'm on assignment, Catherine."

"You have the ways and means to take care of Tyler without this damned assignment."

"Not after paying for Sammi's funeral costs."

An uneasy silence stretched between them as he looked at Catherine.

Truly looked at her.

"You," she continued, "are just… you can ask for help, you know that, right? But noooo, Brody would never dream of asking anyone for help. He'll just bottle everything up all on his own and walk around like he has a death wish or something."

Her face was red, her eyelashes showing the remnants of tears that she had been crying.

"And why? Why this assignment?"

"Because I could take time off afterwards," he replied, his voice soft as his eyes drank in her presence.

"You are an idiot, you know that, Brody? You don't need this damned assignment. I can help you. My mother released part of the trust fund to me."

"I don't want your charity."

"Well, what the hell *do* you want, aside from playing the 'do as I say not as I do' card?"

Another silence as he contemplated her question, feeling the answer deep within his soul.

"Damn it, Brody, answer me!"

"You don't get to be angry with me, Catherine, not after pulling a stunt like this."

"A stunt?"

"What's in the bag, things for you to get all dolled up in? Because newsflash for you, doll,"

"Doll?"

"…there's a hurricane that's reaching us right about," Brody looked at his watch, "now, and you are pregnant, for fuck's sake, why would you do something so stupid?"

"Oh no, you don't get to call me names."

"I'm not calling you names."

"You just said I was stupid!"

"I said you *did* something stupid, goddammit, Catherine, what has gotten into you?"

His reflexes had him catching her hands before she could push him and they stood there, his hands wrapped around her wrists, a warring of wills between them.

"How dare you take this fucking assignment without thinking about what could happen to you and the ramifications of it," she said through clenched teeth. "And you call me stupid?"

"I didn't."

"What is it that you see when you look at me, Brody? Huh? What do you see?"

His grip softened.

"Tell me," she said through her tears. "Just fucking tell me."

He rested his forehead on hers, their eyes locked, when he finally answered.

"I see the mother of my child."

CHAPTER 36

I See You

"You have a lot of nerve, you know?" Catherine said, her voice barely above a whisper even as the sound of the howling winds began to increase. "Trying to use the whole sexy-eyes thing to get out of me being mad at you."

Brody threw his head back in laughter even as Catherine pulled away from him.

"This is not funny."

"Sexy-eyes thing?" Brody's laughter began to die down. "Look, this is my job. This is what I do. The pictures, not the sexy-eyes thing, and I was just looking at you, Cat, that's all."

"And good save, Mr. Brownie Points, with your 'mother of my child' line."

Again, Brody was laughing. "Ah, Cat, I've missed you."

"Really? You sure don't act like it. Where's my hug, huh? And a kiss, you should have at least kissed me after you said that. And now the moment is gone."

Brody sat on the edge of the bed, his shoulders shaking from laughter even as he held his face in his hands.

"And you're laughing at me. Brownie points gone, mister. Now you're just being a..."

"Jerk?" He smirked as he looked over at her, using the word she'd once called him by numerous times.

"Yeah. A real jerk."

"Cat?"

"What?"

He held out his arms. "C'mere."

"Don't wanna," she said, arms crossed in front of her, despite the fact that she was moving towards him.

"Yeah, you do."

"Don't be,"

"A jerk?"

"Rude. Stop laughing at me."

He stood then, his smile reaching his blue eyes for the first time that she could remember since they'd lost Sammi. "What do you want me to do, Cat?"

She leapt into his waiting arms and circled her legs around his waist, and he barely budged. "Shut up and kiss me," she said.

And he did.

He kissed her with love that she could feel from the top of her head to the tips of her toes which curled when their tongues touched with an immense tenderness, one that made her love him all the more.

He kissed her as she slid down his body and he deftly removed her shirt along the way, their lips only parting as the fabric passed between them.

He kissed her as she moved his shirt up his body, the muscles in his stomach tightening as she grazed her fingernails across them.

He kissed her as she felt the softness of the bed beneath her while he laid her down and stretched out beside her, his hands free to roam the length of her at leisure as the storm raged on outside.

He kissed her before she left his lips to explore his body with lips, with hands, with teeth, with tongue.

He kissed her lower abdomen where their child was growing, whispering words of love as he did so.

He kissed the top of her head as she left her own kiss on his chest where his heart hammered beneath.

He kissed her neck, her collarbones, her chest, her breasts, on down as he nibbled on her hip bones and between her thighs and back up again.

He kissed her as he entered her, capturing her gasp as they moved together as one.

He kissed her as their passion grew, as their movements quickened, as their release hit one after the other, tumbling into bliss together.

He kissed her as the winds rattled the windows, thunder crashing as her fingernails dug into his back, as she arched beneath him.

He kissed her and she felt the love emoting from him with every breath he took.

And with their bodies sated, her heart overflowing, he kissed her as she drifted into a light slumber.

She'd never been loved more completely.

Brody kissed the tip of Catherine's nose as a siren began to sound. "Let's go."

"Go?" Catherine mumbled sleepily.

"Tornado siren."

She sat up abruptly, holding the sheet to her. "Oh, shit."

"Yeah, oh shit. Here." He tossed his t-shirt in her direction and she slipped it on. It hung low enough to be a short dress on her. Still, as he pulled his pants on and grabbed shoes, she slid her own pants on. "Grab your shoes," he commanded before they went into the bathroom, away from windows.

"Why did I grab my shoes?"

"Frank always told us to, in case of glass."

"Oh," she breathed. "Something he said that I actually believe."

"I have much to tell you," Brody said, kissing her forehead. "So much."

"Me, too."

They huddled together in the bathtub, holding one another, their lips touching as the building began to shake.

"We're together, by the way," she announced amidst it all.

"We are."

"No, I mean," Catherine turned his face to hers. "We're together. This, us. If you had other plans, get over them. And don't give me the you need to think about it,"

"Are you really telling me this now?" Brody chuckled and kissed the tip of her nose. "Relax, Cat. I wouldn't have it any other way."

"Except without hurricanes."

"You ever put yourself in harm's way again,"

"Look who's talking!"

"Just promise me you won't, Cat."

She snuggled in and kissed his bare chest. "I love you, Brody."

"I love you, too."

The electricity flickered and failed, followed up with dimmer lights.

"What,"

"Generator," he replied as the siren ceased.

"Are we safe?"

He pulled back and looked down at her, one eyebrow raised. "We're in a hurricane, Cat. No, we're not safe."

"And you take pictures of this?"

"When I'm not otherwise occupied." One corner of his mouth lifted in a grin. "I could take some pictures now."

"You're not going out there."

He kissed the tip of her nose. "Of you."

"Oh," she breathed as he kissed her softly.

"I can't wait to watch as this baby grows inside of you," he said, his hand protectively over her lower abdomen.

"You mean watch me get fat."

"No, I mean watch you glow. You're glowing now, you know that? I've never seen you look more beautiful."

"I have JBF hair."

"No, JBL," he corrected her. "Just been *loved*."

"You're so slick," she giggled before she kissed him. "That's one of the things I love about you."

"And you, little spitfire, I should have known you'd pull something like this."

"Like what, get us back together? I wasn't the one being stupid."

"I wasn't being stupid."

"Well, according to Jen, we both were."

Brody groaned as he stood and helped Catherine out of the tub. "You tell her everything, don't you?"

"Like you telling Emily?"

"No, Jen told Max, who is the biggest discusser when it comes to stuff like that."

"Discusser?"

"We don't gossip," Brody reminded her as he cautiously opened the door. Their room was unscathed, aside from the mess of the bed and clothes strewn about. "Okay, we can go back out here. Just be ready to go..."

The sirens began again.

"Back to the tub, I know."

"I'd feel better if we were on a lower floor."

"We're not the absolute top."

"Not the point."

"I know, I know." She reentered the tub and he ensured she was in the proper position before covering her. "Why are you doing that?"

"I'm protecting you," he said softly, knowing he would do so for the rest of his life if she would let him.

"Where's my rental car?" Catherine peered out the curtains, then opened them wide, revealing the destruction outside.

"That way," Brody replied, pointing in the direction of a line of trees. There was the rental car, wrapped around one of them. "I think that's it. It may just be gone."

"Remind me to thank the person who convinced me to take the insurance on it."

"Yeah, no shit." He kissed the top of Catherine's head. "Start making your phone calls if you can get a signal."

"I may need to use their phone."

"I think it's out, too."

"Then we wait." He pulled her close and she snuggled into his chest.

"Can we wait with a cheeseburger?"

His laughter was genuine, boisterous. "That's my girl. Let me go down and see if anyone is here for the kitchen."

"You love me, so be nice about it."

"I do, and I will."

Once alone, Catherine looked out the window again, at the mangled cars, the trees uprooted, leaves stripped bare, some missing their bark. Stragglers of people began to wade out into the still slightly flooded lot, cameras in hand, shooting.

What Brody would be doing, had she not shown up.

She wondered briefly if he was upset with her of everything he'd missed out, then she smiled softly.

She knew better.

He'd told her how happy he was to have her there, in his arms, despite the fact that she'd put herself in harm's way.

He'd made her promise to never do so again.

She'd made him promise to think about never doing so.

She jolted with shock as her phone began to ring, and when she answered it, the reception was horrid, but still she heard Jen on the other end, "Are you fucking crazy?"

"Yes," she replied with a grin as she flopped backwards on the bed, her arms outstretched. "And I've never been happier in my entire life."

It was another 24 hours before Catherine and Brody were able to leave, helped out of the area by rescue workers, his pictures long forgotten. He'd held Catherine's hand the entire way instead of pulling out his equipment, capturing the images.

His focus was firmly elsewhere.

"Brody," Catherine said with wonder as she stared out the window. "Is that... a dragonfly?"

Brody turned his gaze outside the window where one lone dragonfly buzzed beside the vehicle, as if it were peering inside at them.

As if Sammi was visiting them from above.

"I see you," he whispered, and smiled as the dragonfly flew away.

CHAPTER 37

Family

Home life was calm, invigorating, joyful as they entwined their lives together piece by piece. Catherine spent much of her time at the house, even staying for Tyler when Brody went on assignment—non-dangerous, of course, as he had promised. The morning of her first sonogram, they drove back to that house in silent wonder, Catherine staring at the images of their child that was growing, thriving within her.

"You know," Brody broke the silence, "it's time."

"I agree," she replied, smiling in wonder.

"Your lease is coming up for renewal, and it's just pointless with you staying there."

"Wait, what?" Catherine turned in her seat to face him. "I thought you meant it was time to tell Tyler."

"Yeah," Brody smiled, "that, too."

"No, not 'that too.' Did you just demand that I move in with you?"

"Merely suggesting."

"Well, you could try asking first."

"Catherine, will you,"

"Let's ask Tyler," she interrupted him. "It's his home, too."

Brody reached over and took her hand in his. "Fair enough."

The rest of the drive back to the house in Brentfield was silent, and Catherine continued to stare in wonder at the pictures in her hand.

This was really happening.

She was going to be a mother.

They were going to be parents.

And they had yet to tell Theresa.

Once back at the house, with Catherine on the couch ready for a nap already, she said to him, "You know you're going with me when we tell my mother."

Brody's laugh could be heard from the kitchen. "Fine, I think I can handle it."

"I don't know how she's going to react."

"Well... something I forgot to tell you." Brody walked in with her decaffeinated tea and handed it to her. "I talked to Frank yesterday, while I was out. He caught me looking at baby stuff and I tried to play it off, but I guess I was smiling too much."

Catherine sat up straighter and took a sip of her tea, wishing she could have the caffeine to get rid of her headache. "So how did Frank take it?"

Brody sat in the chair and turned it more to face her. "That's why I was late. We had a long talk about parenting and how to deal with stress, and I had to promise him a million times that I would break the cycle. He's really working on that shit."

Catherine crinkled up her nose. "Language, Brody."

"Yeah, I know, I need to break cursing all the time."

"The last thing we need is for this baby's first word to be 'shit' or something worse."

"Nah. The first word will be 'mom.' I bet you one date night of your choice."

"Oh, we're going that route?" Catherine smiled at him. "I bet the first word will be 'dada' because the baby books say it is statistically the first word. And I bet you..." She thought for a moment. "A night out at your favorite dive bar, where I am designated driver. And Max is with us, of course, so the two of you will keep me entertained."

"You're on."

Catherine knew she would win, and wasn't the least bit bothered by it. Having Brody and Max in the same place was always entertaining, and he'd been coming over more and more with various treats, and to check on Brody, make sure he was okay.

Losing Sammi had been hard on all of them.

"There was something else I talked to Frank about," Brody continued, back on the original subject. He leaned forward, his elbows on his knees and his hands clasped. "That idea that I had? The one that I pitched to you? He gave his blessing."

Catherine's mouth dropped open. "You're kidding."

"I'm not worried about Mom because she's off doing who knows what, but Frank said yes."

"So it's a go?"

"The Samantha Jayne Harris Foundation, offering assistance to domestic violence victims. Yes, Cat, it's a go."

Catherine squeaked in delight as she bounded across the living room and onto Brody's lap. "This is going to be amazing, you realize that, right?"

His kiss was soft against her lips, just enough for her to feel it before he pulled away. "You're the one who put this ball in motion, and I'm so fucking grateful for that."

She crinkled up her nose. "Language, Harris."

"That's her last name, you know," he said, placing his hand over her slightly swollen belly.

"We still don't know."

"I know." He rubbed her belly as he smiled. "Bet me."

"I bet you that you can't stop that language coming out of your mouth, I'm not betting on the sex of our baby."

"Our baby," he whispered against her lips before he kissed her once more.

Brody was a bundle of nerves when Tyler arrived home from school. What if he had a problem with Catherine moving in? What if he had a problem with a baby arriving? There was no way he would send him back to Frank, even with Frank's progress.

Tyler belonged with him.

"Dude, what's up with the pacing?" Tyler asked as he walked towards the hallway.

"Can you come out here for a minute?" Brody asked. "After you put your things in your room."

"Yeah, sure," Tyler replied with a shrug, and Brody turned to Catherine.

"Relax," she said as she stood and took his hands in hers.

"Trying to."

"You look like you're about to ask him to jump off the Empire State Building, which you're not."

"What's up?" Tyler's tone was casual as he walked into the living room, and Brody gestured towards the chair.

"Have a seat."

"Oh shit, am I in trouble for something?"

"See?" Catherine looked up at Brody. "Language."

"He hears it all the time at school."

"I really do," Tyler agreed.

"Great," Catherine muttered, throwing up her hands, and Brody stifled a laugh. Her little tantrums had always amused him.

"No, you're not in trouble," Brody began, returning his attention to Tyler. "But we have a few things to talk to you about."

Tyler inhaled sharply and Brody watched as his face paled a little before turning a bright red. "I already know about the birds and bees stuff, if that's what this is."

"No. Well, kind of, but no." Brody sat on the ottoman, facing his little brother. "You know Catherine has been spending a lot of time here lately."

"She kinda lives here, doesn't she?"

Brody opened his mouth to correct him, then he smiled. "Kind of, but we'd like for it to be full time."

"Oh."

"And one more thing." He pulled Catherine closer, his eyes still on Tyler. "Catherine and I are having a baby."

Tyler looked at Catherine, then down at the carpet. "You want to send me back."

"No! No, no, no, nothing like that," Brody reassured him.

"We would like your blessing," Catherine said.

"What do you need my blessing for?" Tyler asked as he looked up at her.

"For her to move in," Brody answered.

"You live here, too," Catherine added.

Tyler's smile was wistful. "Sammi would have loved this, you know?"

Brody's heart constricted in his chest. "You think so?"

"Are you kidding? You should have heard her go off about Catherine marrying someone else. You'd think that the whole world was coming to an end."

Brody was unable to speak with his threatening tears, but Catherine laughed.

Oh, that laugh.

He loved this girl.

"That's the best news I've heard in... well, since this." She handed the strip of sonogram pictures to Tyler who frowned as he glanced at them.

"I don't see it."

"See? Here's the eyes. And this is a profile picture."

"Oh, I see it now." Tyler smiled. "I'm going to be an uncle, holy shit, this is amazing!"

"Language," Brody said.

"Hypocrite," Catherine scolded him.

"We're really going to do this, aren't we?" Tyler asked with a smile. "Live together, as a family. What... will you change... you know, Sammi's room?"

"All it needs is a crib. It's perfect," Catherine replied, and Brody smiled up at her through his tears.

"So you agree it's a girl, and her room should be purple with dragonflies?"

"I'm not agreeing to anything other than you better stick to those cooking classes that Max offered you."

"Finally," Tyler piped up. "But no making Aunt Sheryl's casserole. We had enough of that."

"I'm supposed to learn how to cook steak and shit like that," Brody said as he stood.

"Language!"

"I think that's going to be the baby's first word," Tyler said with a mischievous grin. "Language."

"You want in on the bet?" Brody asked as Catherine laughed.

"No way, I'm not going to be on dishes duty for a month. I know better. It will be 'mama' or something like that. I'm just being... Where's Sammi's dictionary?"

"What word are you wanting to look up?"

"Facetious. A girl in my class used it today, and she's hot, so,"

Brody refrained from telling him that he could always look it up on his phone. Instead, he led his brother into Sammi's room and over to her bookshelf, where her well-worn dictionary sat with a thin layer of dust on it.

"Maybe we should clean this room up, before the baby comes," Tyler suggested. "I kinda suspected, but didn't want to say anything."

"What gave it away?"

"Besides her heaving every morning?" Tyler grinned. "She's changing, Brody. She's being... mom-like, more mom-like than I remember our mom being. Who woulda thought?"

"I would," Brody replied softly.

"But not at first."

Brody laughed. "No, not at first. No way."

"I gotta get this assignment done," Tyler said as he picked up the dictionary. "And see if I can come up with something to impress that girl."

"Text Jase," Brody suggested. "He's always using words like that."

Tyler smiled before throwing his arms around his brother. "I love you, Brody. And I know that Sammi and Brian are happy for you, for us."

Brody felt it, too.

And later that evening, when the three of them visited Brian and Sammi's graves, he sat on the ground between them and said, "I can feel you, you know? I can feel you all around me, every day. Sometimes it makes me sad, sometimes angry, but most of the time... most of the time I feel at peace. I know that Catherine's presence helps with that, but you two..." He reached out and touched their stones. "You two, watching over us, making sure all the pieces fall into place, it's like having our own guardian angels looking out for us. Thank you both for your love, and for all the lessons you've taught me. Penny's in good hands, and Tyler...I'm going to make sure that he has everything he needs, and that he's safe. I promise you."

Catherine wiped a tear away as Brody stood, and Tyler had turned and begun his walk back to the car, hiding his expression, his emotion.

"That was beautiful, you know?" She reached out and he took her hand in his, and he felt her love.

He felt her love.

"What are we going to tell our baby?" Brody asked Catherine. "How are we going to tell her we met?"

"We met in a stairway and I thought you worked for Frank."

"No, I mean the history?"

"When we didn't like one another?"

"Yeah."

"We'll tell her the truth."

"Yes," Brody agreed quickly. He'd been lied to so much in his youth. He didn't ever want to do that with his child.

"But we'll skip your horrid language."

"I've heard you say 'fuck' a few times."

"What I say when we're having sex is none of our child's business."

Brody's head threw back in laughter as they walked towards his Jeep. "I wasn't talking about that. You've slipped."

"Have not. Maybe a little, but it's a slip, not intentional like you."

"I love you, Cat."

"Well it's a good thing you do," she teased as she moved closer to him. "Our lives are entangled, Harris. Forever. Admit it."

"Forever?"

"Yeah," she said with a contented sigh. "Forever."

Brody smiled as he let go of her hand and put his arm around her. "I'm good with that."

EPILOGUE

Apple

"Hello?" Max peeked his head through the door into the hospital room and smiled. "I brought goodies!"

"No fair," Catherine whined from the bed. "I can't eat them yet."

"Fear not, Queen C," he said as he walked in, "these are just for you. Apple pie cupcakes, apple fritters, and a couple of apple dumplings. You know, since you two are about to meet the apple of your eye."

"Oh, that's a good one," Brody said as he approached the baked goods that Max was laying out.

"No way, dude. These are hers. There are more in the waiting room. And the nurses lounge." Max grinned. "Got a hottie to give me her number, too."

"Maximillian, are you seriously using my pain to get into a girl's pants?" Catherine asked, and Brody shrugged in Max's direction.

"They haven't done the epidural yet."

"And they better fucking hurry," Catherine snapped through clenched teeth. "Get over here and let me break every bone in your hand."

"Language," Brody teased, then quickly apologized after the look Catherine shot him. He placed his hand in hers and waited for the next contraction to start. His girl could definitely squeeze, and he was sure his hand would be bruised at the very least before this was all over.

"Where's my Jen?" Catherine pouted. "I need my Jen."

"She'll be right back, I promise," Max replied. "She's,"

"If you say she's eating, I'm coming up out of this bed."

"On the phone," Max said slowly before he grinned at Brody.

"Max," Jen said as she walked into the room, "those cupcakes are to die for." She washed her hands and fluffed her hair, which was both blue and pink. Catherine and Brody had opted to be surprised that day, and the bets were going strong.

"Jen, you betrayed me," Catherine said with a pout, then reached for her hand. "Remember what I said?"

"Film from your head and don't get your lady parts in the picture. Got it." Jen leaned down and kissed Catherine's sweaty forehead. "You're doing wonderful, girl, and I'm so proud of you."

"Where's my candy man?" Catherine cried as the next contraction hit. The anesthesiologist, or as Catherine called him, the 'candy man,' had yet to appear with the epidural to ease the pain.

"Do you want me to check?" Jen asked, and Catherine shook her head.

"Max, would you?" Catherine asked. "Please? And thank you for the goodies. I'm sorry I'm being such a bitch."

"Language," Brody said softly with a smile.

"Yeah, I know. It's my rule, and oh... oh, fucking *hell*." Another contraction had hit, this one bringing tears to Catherine's eyes. "I don't ever want to do this again, okay? Promise me I'll never have to do this again."

Brody leaned down and kissed her forehead before grabbing a cool cloth to wipe away the sweat. "I promise, baby," he whispered in her ear. He hated seeing her in so much pain, his eyes conveying to Max to get whomever would come and to do so immediately. After Max exited the room, Brody pulled a chair close to the bed so that he could sit while she held his hand.

"They keep getting closer together, and stronger," Jen commented as she looked at the monitor and watched the number begin to rise again. "Here comes another one, sweetie. Just breathe. Just breathe. You're doing amazing."

"I want my mom," Catherine cried, her bottom lip quivering.

"You want me to get her for you?" Jen asked, and Catherine nodded. "Okay, I'll be right back."

The chaos and hustle in the room silenced as Jen left in search of Theresa, leaving Catherine and Brody alone for the first time since they'd arrived at the hospital.

"I ruined the baby shower," Catherine pouted as Brody pushed her hair back.

"Are you kidding? Babe, what better shower gift than having our baby arrive."

"Yeah, but... Ow."

He helped her breathe through her next contraction, promising her that it would all be over soon.

"I shouldn't have waited so long, you know?" Catherine sniffled. "I should have told Jen that last month was okay, but I really wanted everyone there."

"And now everyone is here." Brody kissed her forehead once more as Theresa and Jen entered the room, both smiling.

"Hi, sweetheart," Theresa greeted her daughter as she walked to the other side of the bed and took her hand.

"Mom, I don't think I can do this."

"Of course you can."

"I need drugs."

Theresa's smile only grew warmer. "He's coming. It seems there are quite a few deliveries today."

"None with as big of an entourage as ours, of course," Jen added as she snapped a couple of pictures.

"If my face is in those,"

"You look beautiful," Jen cut her off.

Catherine looked tearfully up at her mother. "I changed my mind."

"You can't change your mind, sweetheart. And you're doing so much better than I did. Remember what a mess I was when I had Penny?"

"Yeah, well, they cut her out of you. I think I want that instead."

"Baby, trust me, you don't unless it's absolutely necessary."

Catherine whimpered as another contraction hit, then followed Brody's breathing instructions as he gently pushed her sweat-dampened hair back. "What if it's too late for an epidural? Mom, I've had broken bones and competed with sprained ankles and all kinds of injuries. It's nothing like this. Nothing."

"But you're Catherine Denise Garner," her mother said softly. "You can handle anything."

"Good afternoon," a young man said as he and a nurse entered.

"Tell me you're my candy man," Catherine said quickly, and he chuckled.

"Yes, I'm the anesthesiologist. Let's see about getting you some pain relief."

"Oh, hallelujah."

It wasn't too late for her epidural, and once in place, Catherine lay in her bed, relaxed, happy.

Excited.

"I can't believe he's coming!" Catherine exclaimed with a bright grin as Brody reentered the room.

"I'm telling you, *she's* going to be worth every ounce of pain." He leaned down and kissed her lips softly.

"Could you do me a huge favor? Let me see how bad I look."

Brody threw his head back in laughter. "You're as beautiful as ever," he promised as he handed her bag to her. She pulled out a mirror which showed her messy hair and total lack of makeup.

"Do I look like a mom?"

"I've watched you with Tyler, Cat. You absolutely look like a mom."

As Catherine regathered her hair up into a perfect messy bun, she smiled. "I should have opted for drugs from the beginning. This shit's great."

"Language," he teased.

"I'm getting all the bad words out before he gets here."

"She."

"Is our bet still on?"

Brody kissed her forehead. "Of course."

"Okay. And people can come back in now that I won't go all bitch-monster on them. I need to apologize to my dad. And Brody?"

"Yeah, baby?"

"I decided I want my mom in here, too. You on one side, her on the other. And Jen filming from up there," she added as she pointed to the head of her bed.

Brody smiled. Catherine and Theresa were finally growing close.

Finally.

"Absolutely," he agreed.

"Can you ask my dad to come in?"

"Of course."

When Colin Garner walked in the room, his eyes welled up with tears. "Hi, princess," he said as he walked over to his daughter and kissed her cheek.

"I'm so sorry, Daddy."

"Don't apologize. Trust me, you're handling this much better than your mother did."

"Heard that," Theresa said as she reentered the room, her tone light and teasing.

"So Mom was telling me." Catherine smiled up at her parents as they stood over her. "I know I was a hellbeast growing up,"

"Oh, shush."

"Don't talk about yourself that way," Colin added.

"And I know the three of us weren't always close, but I'm glad we are now," Catherine said with a smile. "Thank you both for growing up along with me and being able to be in the same room again."

Colin took his daughter's hand. "Anything for you."

"Yeah, he's not so bad to be around now that he's happy with what he does," Theresa teased. "Charlotte is an absolute doll, by the way."

"Thanks. Richard is pretty stellar, a great guy."

Theresa lifted one shoulder. "Eh, he's alright," she said with a laugh that they shared.

The afternoon seemed to slow after Catherine's epidural, and her visitors one by one brought in their gifts that had been meant for the baby shower. Emily's collection of poems for young children was among Catherine's favorites, and she teared up as she turned through the pages.

"This is beautiful, thank you."

Emily blinked a couple of times before recovering. "You're welcome," she finally said, and after she left the room, Catherine looked over at Jen.

"She's okay."

"Just okay?"

"It's not my fault you keep dating people I loathe."

"She's no Bethany."

"Which is a great thing," Catherine added. "I suppose I can kinda like her now."

When Tyler shyly approached her, he held out a small bag.

A teddy bear.

Sammi's teddy bear.

"She'd want your baby to have it."

"Oh my goodness," Catherine said with a rush of tears as she held out her arms to Tyler, who hugged her as tightly as he could. "It's perfect, thank you."

"Thank you," Brody also said as he hugged his brother tight. "Life's about to become a lot noisier. You ready?"

"Oh, yeah," Tyler replied. "You?"

"So ready," Brody answered, a beaming smile on his face. He was certain his heart was as full of love as it was ever going to get.

But he was wrong.

So wrong.

Two hours later when they placed his daughter into his arms, his capacity for love increased exponentially. Through his tears he counted ten fingers and ten toes, kissed the tip of her nose which resembled her mother, and marveled at her dark hair, the way her eyes were shaped like Sammi's, like Brian's.

Like his.

He couldn't stop kissing her tiny face as he made promise after promise to keep her safe from harm.

And when he finally placed their daughter in Catherine's arms, he knelt beside her bed, watching as the baby's eyes opened, squinting beneath the bright lights of the room.

"She's perfect," Catherine breathed.

"Yes, she is," Theresa beamed as she kissed her daughter's forehead. "Those were the same words I said about you."

"Really?" Catherine asked in wonder.

"This is so beautiful, all of it," Jen spoke up as she continued filming. "I can't wait to watch this over and over. Hi, sweetheart. I'm your Auntie Jen."

"What's her name?" Theresa asked, and Catherine looked up at Brody, smiling knowingly.

"Give us a minute?" he asked Theresa and Jen, who quickly agreed and left the room to announce that Baby Harris had arrived.

"We're so taking her to Hawaii when we get married," Catherine said, her eyes back on their daughter.

"Deal."

"You know what we should name her."

Brody kissed the top of Catherine's head. "Yes."

And when their friends and family gathered into the room, much to the nurses' chagrin, Brody and Catherine introduced their daughter.

Brianna Jayne Harris.

Frank stifled a sob as he hugged Brody tightly. "It's perfect."

"Glad you think so, Grandpa," Brody said softly, squeezing just a little bit harder before letting go.

That summer evening, as Catherine and Brody watched their child sleeping in Brody's arms, their lives began another twist on their journey, the one that had started on a summer day not unlike this one.

The moment their lives collided.

Entangled.

"She's perfect," Catherine whispered.

"You're perfect."

She let out a huff of a laugh. "Hardly."

"You're my perfect, how's that?"

She was his perfect, his better half, the yin to his yang, or as Max called it, the potato to his chip. She'd helped him overcome the worst of himself, loved him when he was his most unlovable. Made him see the world through much brighter eyes.

And he was forever grateful that the rest of his life would be lived by her side.

Authors (especially indie!) rely on your reviews. Please take a moment to review this novel on the platform that it was purchased from. It is appreciated more than you will ever know!

ABOUT THE AUTHOR

Carlie Yates (That One Writer Chick) has been writing stories since she was in the fifth grade, convinced that if she didn't get her thoughts and characters down on paper, her head would 'plode; it could be ex- or im-, but either way, it wouldn't be pretty. Inspired by S.E. Hinton, she always said when she grew up that she would be a published author. She is currently renouncing her pledge to grow up. This Midwest mom of boys has addictions to reading, road trips, hair dye, and the Oxford comma, and is thoroughly convinced at any given time the theme track to *My Three Sons* will start playing in the background of her home.

STALK ME

Actually, just follow me, but hey… that was catchy

www.thatonewriterchick.com
www.facebook.com/thatonewriterchickakacarlie
www.instagram.com/thatonewriterchickakacarlie
www.goodreads.com/thatonewriterchickakacarlie

ALSO BY THE AUTHOR

Entitled (Entangled Book 1)
Entrapped (Entangled Book 2)

COMING SOON
Wrong Number (Time Stands Still Book 1)

RESOURCES

This book is a work of fiction. In no way do I condone any of the acts within. They are, however, important issues that many people face, no matter their age, gender, or social status. If you or someone you love has dealt or are dealing with any of them, please reach out. Help is available. You can look for local resources or contact one of the national centers below.

National Suicide Hotline
1-800-273-8255
https://suicidepreventionlife.org/
https://www.crisistextline.org
Text HOME to 741741

National Sexual Assault Hotline
1-800-656-4673
https://www.rainn.org/get-help

National Domestic Violence Hotline
1-800-799-7233
https://www.thehotline.org

The Trevor Project (for LGBTQ)
1-866-488-7386
https://www.thetrevorproject.org

Grief Resource Network
https://www.griefresourcenetwork.com

THANK YOUS AND LOVE BOMBS

Rose for knowing Brody so well that all I had to do was ask. And for knowing me even better.

Tami for being my preview bitch. You're the T to my J always.

Stephanie my editor extraordinaire! I love you for everything.

Cody Bailey for the amazing covers, for undertaking the production of the audiobooks, for talking me out of doing stupid things.

Amber Haehnel You are such a rockstar! You're giving Catherine the perfect voice to tell her and Brody's story.

Crissy Connor my graphics and website guru, I love you beyond the telling of it.

Nellie Corriveau for your loving nudges in the right direction. Always forward. Always.

Christa for believing in me when I didn't believe in myself, and I'm not just talking about the books.

Anna Bitters for keeping me indistractable.

My beta readers for taking the time and giving amazing feedback.

The Authors' Table authors and readers, for giving me an internet home and making me feel loved and accepted.

Food FOOD food...and BOOKS for your love and support, and your recommendations for amazing reads.

Marianne and everyone New & Olde Pages Book Shoppe for giving this indie girl a chance and putting my books in an actual store! Each employee gives their all, and I'm so appreciative of all of you!

My tribe for loving me unconditionally. I love all of you!

My readers yes, YOU. Thank you for embarking on Catherine and Brody's journey. I hope you love it and them as much as I loved writing them.

Typos if you made it this far, kudos to you for hiding in plain sight.